UNDELIVERED

A Post Office Romance

Love always finds its way home

Book One of The Willow Creek Series

Wren Calloway

TABLE OF CONTENTS

Author's Note 5

Dedication..6

Chapter One 7

Chapter Two 20

Chapter Three 33

Chapter Four..47

Chapter Five..63

Chapter Six 79

Chapter Seven 93

Chapter Eight..107

Chapter Nine 119

Chapter Ten 133

Chapter Eleven 145

Chapter Twelve 158

Chapter Thirteen 173

Chapter Fourteen 186

Chapter Fifteen..199

Chapter Sixteen...211

Chapter Seventeen 223

Chapter Eighteen...234

Chapter Nineteen 247

Chapter Twenty..261

Chapter Twenty-One 269

Chapter Twenty-Two..281

Chapter Twenty-Three..293

Chapter Twenty-Four 305

Chapter Twenty-Five 323

One Year Later..323

About The Author...336

A Note From The Author 337

Acknowledgments 341

Coming Soon From Wren Calloway..343

    Overdue..344

    Rerouted...346

    Todd's Story...348

    The Last Letter...350

    The Keeper's Light 352

    The Recipe Box..354

Sneak Peek Overdue Chapter One 358

About The Publisher..361

AUTHOR'S NOTE

Dear Reader,

Welcome to Willow Creek, a small town where the past and present collide in the most unexpected ways. UNDELIVERED is a story about inheritance—not just of buildings and belongings, but of love stories that refuse to be forgotten.

When I first imagined Harper standing in her grandmother's old post office, surrounded by decades of letters, I knew this was a story about connection. About the distances we travel to find home, and the people who've been waiting there all along.

Thank you for choosing to spend your time in Willow Creek. I hope Harper and Colby's story finds its way into your heart.

With love,

Wren Calloway

DEDICATION

For everyone who believes in second chances, and for the letters that never stop waiting to be read.

CHAPTER ONE

The fluorescent lights of the conference room hummed their usual headache-inducing frequency as Harper Delaney stared at the PowerPoint slide projected on the wall. **Q4 Performance Metrics: Exceeding Expectations.** Her metrics. Her campaign. Her eighty-hour work weeks distilled into bullet points and bar graphs that her boss, Richard Hoffman, was currently presenting to the executives as if he'd conjured them from thin air.

"And as you can see," Richard said, laser pointer dancing across numbers Harper had triple-checked at two in the morning, "our social media engagement increased by forty-seven percent quarter over quarter."

Our. The word stuck in Harper's throat like a fish bone.

She'd pitched this campaign six months ago. Fought for the budget. Negotiated with influencers. Monitored analytics until her eyes blurred. And now Richard stood at the head of the table in his designer suit, accepting congratulations with practiced humility while Harper sat in the back corner with cold coffee and a tension headache that had taken up permanent residence behind her left eye.

Her phone vibrated against her thigh. Harper glanced down, expecting another email that could wait. Instead, her brother Todd's name flashed across the screen.

Call me. It's about Grandma Stella.

The conference room tilted slightly. Harper read the message again, her pulse suddenly loud in her ears. Todd never called during business hours unless…

She stood abruptly, chair scraping against the floor. Eight pairs of eyes swiveled toward her.

"Excuse me," Harper murmured, already moving toward the door. Richard's expression flickered with annoyance, but she was past caring. Past pretending this job was anything more than a gilded cage with excellent health insurance.

The hallway was mercifully empty. Harper's heels clicked against the polished floor as she hurried to the nearest empty office, a vacant space where fired employees' desks went to gather dust. She closed the door and called Todd.

He answered on the first ring. "Harp."

That single syllable carried more weight than it should. Todd only called her "Harp" when things were bad.

"What happened?" Harper's free hand pressed against her stomach, bracing for impact.

"Grandma Stella died this morning." Todd's voice was gentle, the way it used to be when they were kids and he'd explain why Mom was crying again. "Peacefully, in her sleep. Mrs. Chen from the café found her."

Harper sank into the dusty office chair, the leather cracking beneath her. Estelle Delaney, Stella to anyone who'd ever mailed a letter in Willow Creek, was gone. The woman who'd taught Harper how to tie her shoes, how to sort mail by zip code, how to make the perfect cup of coffee with a splash of vanilla. The grandmother who'd called every Sunday without fail, even after Harper stopped visiting. Even after Harper got too busy, too important, too *Chicago* to come home for the holidays.

"Harper? You there?"

"Yeah." Her voice came out rough. "I'm here."

"There's something else." Todd paused, and Harper could picture him running his hand through his hair, the way he did when he had to deliver news he knew she wouldn't like. "She left you the post office."

Harper blinked. "What?"

"The building, the business, everything. Her lawyer called me this morning. Apparently, she updated her will six months ago." Another pause. "I got the house in Seattle and some money. But the post office...that's all you, Harp."

The post office. That tiny brick building with the crooked sign and the front step that creaked. The place where Harper had spent every summer of her childhood, sorting letters and listening to Stella's stories about the people in town. The place Harper hadn't set foot in for eleven years.

"I don't..." Harper started, then stopped. Didn't what? Didn't understand? Didn't want it? Didn't deserve it after abandoning her grandmother to chase a career that left her hollow and exhausted? "I can't just leave. I have a job; I have a lease..."

Harper stared at her desk, at the legal pad covered in campaign notes that suddenly seemed meaningless. She should probably call her mother, tell her about Stella's death, about the building, about the mess she'd inherited. But she could already hear the carefully neutral tone, the unspoken "I told you small towns were traps," the relief that she herself had escaped Willow Creek thirty years ago and never looked back.

Harper put that thought away. This conversation could wait.

"You have three weeks of PTO you've never used," Todd interrupted, his tone shifting to the practical big-brother mode she knew well. "Take it. Go to Willow Creek. Handle the estate. You can figure out what to do with the building later."

Through the office window, Harper could see back into the conference room. Richard was shaking hands with the CEO, basking in praise for work he hadn't done. Her work.

Something snapped.

Not dramatically—there was no shouting or throwing of objects. Just a quiet, fundamental shift, like the first crack in ice before it breaks. Harper had spent five years at Morrison & Klein Marketing. Five years climbing a ladder that led nowhere she actually wanted to go. Five years of sacrificing sleep and sanity and, apparently, the last remaining connection to someone who'd actually loved her unconditionally.

"I need to go," Harper said.

"To Willow Creek?"

"To quit."

Todd laughed, short and surprised. "Seriously?"

"Seriously." Harper stood, brushing dust off her pencil skirt. "Call me with the funeral details?"

"Will do. And Harp?" Todd's voice softened. "I'm sorry. I know you two were close."

Were. Past tense. Because Harper had made it past tense, choosing client meetings over Sunday calls, choosing bonuses over Christmas visits.

"Thanks, Todd."

She ended the call and stood there for a moment, staring at her reflection in the dark computer screen. Auburn hair pulled into a ruthless bun. Hazel eyes shadowed by concealer that couldn't quite hide the sleepless nights. A designer blouse that cost more than her first month's rent. She looked successful. She looked polished. She looked like a stranger.

Harper walked back to the conference room, knocked once, and entered without waiting for permission.

"Harper," Richard said, clearly irritated by the interruption. "We're in the middle of..."

"I quit."

The room went silent. Even the projector seemed to hum more quietly.

Richard's eyebrows rose. "Excuse me?"

"I quit." Harper's voice was steady now, gaining strength from repetition. "Effective immediately. Those metrics you're presenting? I did that. The entire campaign was mine, and you know it." She turned to the CEO, a silver-haired woman named Patricia who'd once told Harper she had "real potential." "I've documented everything. You'll find my work files completely organized and ready for transition. My two weeks' notice is waived, I'll pack my desk today."

Patricia leaned back in her chair, studying Harper with sharp eyes. "This is rather sudden."

"Yes." Harper felt a smile tugging at her lips, unfamiliar after months of practiced corporate neutrality. "It really is."

She didn't wait for a response. Didn't wait to see Richard's face or collect her final paycheck or do any of the things a reasonable person would do when throwing away a six-figure salary. She simply walked out, pulling the conference room door shut behind her with a satisfying click.

Her desk took twenty minutes to pack. Five years distilled into a single cardboard box: a photo of her and Todd at his wedding, a desk plant that had somehow survived her neglect, a coffee mug that said *But First, Caffeine* in gold script. Everything else belonged to Morrison & Klein, the laptop, the company phone, the carefully curated professional persona she'd worn like armor.

Harper dropped her keycard on Richard's desk with a note that said simply: *Good luck explaining the actual metrics.*

Then she walked out of the building and into the unseasonably warm November afternoon, feeling simultaneously terrified and more alive than she had in years.

The drive from Chicago to Willow Creek, Wisconsin took four and a half hours in good traffic. Harper made it in five, stopping twice for gas station coffee and once to sit in a parking lot and wonder if she'd lost her mind.

The landscape shifted gradually from urban sprawl to suburban sameness to the rolling hills and farmland of rural Wisconsin. Trees lined the highway, their branches mostly bare, creating a stark silhouette against the gray November sky. The GPS cheerfully announced each turn, counting down miles until she reached the town she'd fled at eighteen, desperate for something bigger and brighter.

Turn right onto Main Street. Your destination will be on

the left.

Willow Creek looked exactly the same. The same weathered welcome sign, the same hardware store with Parker's painted in fading red letters, the same stoplight that only turned red if you waited long enough. The Copper Kettle café still had its striped awning and window boxes, though the flowers were gone for winter.

Harper's chest tightened. Eleven years, and nothing had changed. Or maybe everything had changed, and she just couldn't see it yet.

She drove slowly down Main Street, past the library with its stone steps and brass fixtures, past the Hayes Family Bakery with its painted wooden sign. A few people walked the sidewalks, bundled in coats, carrying shopping bags, moving with the unhurried pace of those who had nowhere urgent to be. An elderly man waved as Harper passed, though he couldn't possibly recognize her through the windshield.

Small towns were like that, Stella used to say. Everyone waved, just in case.

The post office sat at the corner of Main and Oak, a small brick building with tall windows and a blue door that Stella had repainted every spring. The sign above the entrance read *Willow Creek Post Office* in simple block letters, with *Est. 1923* beneath in smaller font.

Harper pulled into the gravel parking lot, really just a widened patch of dirt and stones, and turned off the ignition.

The engine ticked in the sudden silence.

She'd expected...what? Some surge of emotion? A flood of memories? Instead, she felt numb, staring at the building through the windshield like it might disappear if she blinked.

The last time she'd been here, she'd been eighteen and insufferable, rolling her eyes at Stella's small-town stories and counting the days until college. She'd promised to visit during breaks, had meant it sincerely at the time. But breaks became internships, internships became jobs, and somehow eleven years had evaporated while Harper focused on becoming someone important.

Mission accomplished. She was important. And miserable. And now the only person who'd loved her without condition was gone.

Harper grabbed her purse and got out of the car. The November wind cut through her thin city coat, carrying the scent of woodsmoke and fallen leaves. She'd forgotten how quiet small towns could be, no car horns or construction or the constant white noise of too many people in too small a space. Just wind, and the distant sound of someone's dog barking, and her own footsteps crunching across gravel.

The front door was locked, which made sense. Stella wasn't there to open it anymore.

Harper dug through her purse for the keys Todd had sent via overnight express. Her hands shook slightly as she tried three different keys before finding the right one. The lock stuck, resisting, before finally turning with a grudging click.

The door swung inward, hinges creaking their familiar protest.

The smell hit Harper first, old paper, wood polish, and the faint vanilla scent of Stella's signature coffee. Everything else was shadows and shapes in the dim interior until Harper found the light switch.

Fluorescent bulbs flickered to life overhead, revealing the post office in all its vintage glory. The main counter ran along the back wall, dark wood polished smooth by decades of elbows and envelopes. Behind it, rows of brass mailboxes lined the wall, each with its own combination lock and small glass window. The sorting table sat to the left, covered in neat stacks of what looked like undelivered mail. A corkboard hung near the entrance, cluttered with community announcements and faded Polaroids of town events.

And everywhere, absolutely everywhere, there was dust.

Harper stepped inside, letting the door close behind her with a soft thud. Dust motes swirled in the fluorescent light. The hardwood floor was scuffed but solid. The air tasted stale, like the building had been holding its breath.

On the corner of the main counter sat Stella's coffee mug, the one with the chipped handle and *World's Best Grandma* in peeling letters. A pen lay beside it, cap off, as if Stella had just set it down and would be back any moment.

The numbness cracked. Harper pressed her hand to her

mouth, trying to hold back the sob that wanted to escape. Stella was really gone. Had been gone for hours while Harper sat in that stupid conference room, worried about PowerPoint presentations and whether Richard would steal credit for her work.

What a waste. What a monumental, selfish waste of time.

Harper walked to the counter and picked up the mug, cradling it carefully. The ceramic was cool against her palms. She closed her eyes and could almost hear Stella's voice: *Well, sweet pea, what are you going to do now?*

Good question.

Harper opened her eyes and surveyed her unexpected inheritance. The post office needed work, that much was obvious. Deep cleaning, repairs, probably a complete inventory of what was what. She had three weeks of PTO, assuming Morrison & Klein didn't contest her abrupt exit. Three weeks to figure out if she was keeping this place or selling it to some developer who'd turn it into a boutique hotel or artisan coffee shop.

Three weeks to decide what her life looked like on the other side of the best worst decision she'd ever made.

Harper set down the mug and pulled out her phone, taking photos of the interior for reference. The logical part of her brain, the part that had built marketing campaigns and negotiated contracts, was already making lists. Clean, organize, assess, decide.

But another part, quieter and easily ignored, whispered something different: *Stay.*

Which was ridiculous. Harper Delaney wasn't a small-town girl anymore. She was a career woman, a professional, someone who wore Louboutin heels and knew how to expense client dinners. She didn't belong in Willow Creek, where everyone waved at strangers and the most exciting event was probably the annual Harvest Festival.

Harper looked at the post office, at the dust and the memories and the massive question mark of her future. Stella's coffee mug still sat on the counter, patient and waiting.

What are you going to do now, sweet pea?

Harper picked up the mug, carried it to the small kitchenette in the back, and began looking for coffee.

If she was staying for three weeks, she might as well start with caffeine.

Behind her, through the front windows, Willow Creek went about its evening, lights flickering on in shops, people heading home for dinner, mail carriers finishing their routes. The whole town, moving in rhythms Harper had forgotten but that her bones still somehow recognized.

She poured water into Stella's ancient coffee maker and hit the start button.

The machine gurgled to life, and Harper Delaney took her first real breath since walking into that conference room.

Whatever came next, at least she'd be awake for it.

CHAPTER TWO

Colby Hayes had been delivering mail in Willow Creek for twelve years, and he could navigate his route blindfolded. Not that he would, the postal service frowned on that sort of thing, but he knew every mailbox, every porch step, every dog that barked warnings from behind chain-link fences. He knew who checked their mail at exactly 10 a.m. and who let it pile up for days. He knew which houses smelled like fresh bread and which ones always had their Christmas lights up, even in July.

This morning, his route felt different. Wrong, somehow, though the streets looked the same as always.

Colby parked his mail truck, a white LLV with the familiar blue and red stripes, outside the Hayes Family Bakery on Main Street. His mother, Rosie, would have coffee ready and probably an "extra" cinnamon roll that just happened to appear whenever he stopped by. She'd been doing that since he took over the route from his father, as if Colby couldn't feed himself at thirty-two.

The bakery's door chimed as he entered, bringing with it the scent of vanilla, butter, and yeast. The morning rush had cleared, leaving only old Pete Armstrong at the corner table with his newspaper and coffee. Pete raised a hand in greeting without looking up, his usual acknowledgment of the world around him.

"Morning, sweetheart," Rosie called from behind the counter, already reaching for the coffee pot. His mother was a whirlwind of efficient movement, even at sixty-two, her brown-and-gray hair pulled back in a practical bun. Flour dusted her apron in a pattern that suggested she'd been elbow-deep in dough since dawn.

"Morning, Ma." Colby leaned against the counter, accepting the mug she handed him. Black, no sugar, exactly how he'd drunk it since he was sixteen and trying to impress his father with his toughness. The coffee was perfect, as always. "Smells good in here."

"Maple scones. New recipe." Rosie studied him with the particular intensity only mothers possessed, the kind that could detect a bad day from across a room. "You heard about Stella?"

There it was. The wrongness he'd felt all morning crystallized into a single name.

Colby set down his mug carefully. "What about her?"

"Oh, honey." Rosie's expression shifted to sympathy, which told Colby everything before she said the words. "She passed away yesterday. Maggie found her this morning when she brought over breakfast. Peaceful, in her sleep."

Stella Delaney. The woman who'd run the Willow Creek Post Office for forty years, who knew every resident by name and remembered their birthdays without checking a calendar. The woman who'd given Colby his first real job at sixteen, sorting mail after school while his father delivered it. The woman who'd told him, after his engagement fell apart, that heartbreak was just love with nowhere to go, and that someday he'd find the right place for it.

"When?" The word came out rough.

"Yesterday afternoon, they think. Maggie's organizing the funeral arrangements." Rosie reached across the counter to squeeze his hand. "I know you two were close."

Close didn't quite cover it. Stella had been...a constant. A fixture of Willow Creek as permanent as the buildings themselves. The idea of the post office without her felt fundamentally wrong, like showing up to work and finding the streets renamed and the houses rearranged.

"Her granddaughter's coming," Pete announced from his corner, not looking up from his newspaper. "Todd's sister. The one who left for the city."

Colby remembered Harper Delaney vaguely, a girl with red hair and an attitude, always in the post office during summers, counting down days until she could leave. That had been years ago, though. More than a decade, actually. She'd left for college and never come back, as far as Colby knew.

"Harper," Rosie confirmed, releasing Colby's hand to wrap a cinnamon roll in wax paper. "Stella left her the post office. The whole thing, building, business, everything."

Pete snorted into his coffee. "City girl like that won't keep it. Probably sell it to some developer. Turn it into condos or one of those fancy coffee places."

"Now, Pete, we don't know that," Rosie chided, but her tone suggested she'd had the same thought. She handed Colby the wrapped roll. "Eat. You've got a long route ahead."

Colby accepted the roll automatically, his mind already churning through implications. The post office was more than just a building to Willow Creek. It was the town's hub, the place where people gathered to collect more than mail, gossip, advice, the occasional shoulder to cry on. Stella had understood that. She'd made the post office into a community center disguised as a federal building.

Would Harper understand? Or would she see it as Colby suspected she might, as real estate to be liquidated, converted, monetized?

"When's she getting here?" he asked.

"Could be here now, for all we know." Rosie wiped down the counter with practiced efficiency. "Maggie said the lawyer called the family yesterday."

Colby drained his coffee and set the mug on the counter. "I should get going. Thanks for breakfast."

"Colby." His mother's voice stopped him at the door. When he turned back, she was watching him with that knowing expression he'd never quite learned to evade. "Be nice to her. Harper. She just lost her grandmother."

"I'm always nice."

"You're always polite," Rosie corrected. "There's a difference."

Colby didn't have an answer for that, so he just nodded and headed back to his truck.

The morning route took him through the residential streets first, the Sullivans' house where the youngest kid, Emma, always waved from the window; the Rodriguez place with its garden even in November; the Mitchell home where Sheriff Sawyer probably hadn't checked his mailbox in three days. Colby knew this not because he kept track specifically, but because noticing was part of the job. You noticed when someone stopped picking up their mail, or when packages accumulated, or when the usual patterns shifted.

It was how he'd noticed Mrs. Patterson had fallen and couldn't get to her door. How he'd realized the Greenfield kid was home from college when he wasn't supposed to be. How he'd figured out that something was wrong at the old Brenner farmhouse before the sheriff got the call.

People thought being a mail carrier was simple, pick up mail, deliver mail, repeat. But Colby had learned from his father that it was really about bearing witness. About being the thread that connected houses into neighborhoods, and neighborhoods into communities.

The route took him past The Copper Kettle, where Maggie Chen was visible through the window, setting up for the lunch rush. She caught sight of his truck and waved, her expression sad. The news had spread, then. By tonight, everyone in Willow Creek would know about Stella, and by tomorrow, they'd all have opinions about what should happen to the post office.

Small towns were like that. Everyone's business became everyone else's concern.

Colby made his way through downtown, past the hardware store where Dylan Parker was opening up, past the library with its morning book drop collection. He saved the post office for last, the way he always did. Something about ending his route where it logically concluded felt right, dropping off mail at the place designed to handle it.

Except this time, when Colby pulled up to the curb outside the familiar brick building, something was different.

The parking lot, if you could call the gravel patch a parking lot, held a car. A sensible gray sedan with Illinois plates, covered in a light film of road dust. Someone was here. Not just someone, Harper. Had to be.

Colby grabbed his delivery satchel and approached the post office, noticing details with the attention his job had trained into him. The front door was closed but looked recently opened, scratch marks around the keyhole suggesting someone had struggled with an unfamiliar lock. Through the windows, he could see lights on inside, bright after weeks of the building standing dark.

He tried the door handle. Locked, but he could see movement inside, a figure moving between the counter and the back room. Auburn hair caught the fluorescent light. Definitely Harper.

Colby knocked, two sharp raps that he knew would carry through the building.

The figure froze, then turned. Even through the window, Colby could see her eyes, hazel, wide, startled. She looked...different from his memories. Older, obviously, but also more put-together and simultaneously more frazzled. She wore city clothes, a dark coat over what looked like business attire, and her hair was pulled back in a way that seemed both severe and elegant.

She stared at him for a beat, clearly debating whether to answer the door. Then she moved forward, heels clicking on the hardwood floor, and unlocked the deadbolt.

The door swung open, and Colby found himself looking at Harper Delaney for the first time in more than a decade.

"Sorry," Colby said, taking an instinctive half-step back. He'd clearly startled her. "I didn't realize anyone was here. The sign said closed."

"It is closed. I'm just..." She gestured vaguely at the interior, and Colby caught a glimpse of dust motes swirling in the light behind her. "I'm Harper Delaney. Stella's granddaughter."

He knew, of course. But the introduction gave him a chance to look at her properly, to reconcile the irritated teenager from his memories with the woman standing in front of him. She had freckles across her nose that her makeup didn't quite hide. Shadows under her eyes suggested she hadn't slept well. Her hands were shaking slightly, though she tried to hide it by crossing her arms.

"Colby Hayes," he said, offering his hand. "I'm sorry about Stella. She was...everyone loved her."

Harper's expression flickered, something raw and painful before the professional mask slid back into place. Her handshake was firm but brief, her fingers cold despite the warm office behind her.

"Thank you." Her voice was steady, controlled. Colby recognized the tone of someone holding themselves together through sheer will. He'd used it himself, once. "I appreciate that."

An awkward silence settled between them, filled only by the distant sound of traffic on Main Street and a dog barking somewhere blocks away. Harper looked like she wanted to close the door. Colby knew he should leave, he had mail to deliver, and she clearly wanted to be alone with her grief.

But something made him hesitate.

"I have the route mail," he said, gesturing to his satchel. "Wasn't sure if you'd want me to just leave it, or..."

Harper blinked, as if the concept of ongoing postal operations hadn't occurred to her. "Oh. Right. Yes. Come in."

She stepped back, pulling the door wider, and Colby entered the post office for the first time since Stella's passing.

The familiar scent hit him immediately, paper, wood polish, and that faint vanilla undertone that had always meant Stella was brewing her signature coffee. But now the smell was overlaid with dust and staleness, the scent of a building that had been abandoned even if only for a day.

Everything looked the same and completely different. The brass mailboxes still lined the wall, the sorting table still sat to the left, Stella's counter still dominated the back of the room. But without Stella herself, without her red lipstick smile and the sound of her humming while she sorted mail, the building felt hollow. A shell of itself.

Colby made his way to the sorting table with practiced familiarity, hyperaware of Harper watching him. He could feel her gaze tracking his movements as he set down his satchel and began unloading the day's delivery.

"I can leave it here for now," he said, stacking envelopes with automatic precision. "When the office reopens, whoever takes over can integrate it with the rest."

"When it reopens." Harper's voice came from behind him, tinged with something Colby couldn't quite identify. Doubt, maybe. Or resignation. "You think it will?"

Colby turned to face her, studying the woman who held the future of his town's post office in her elegant, city-polished hands. She looked completely out of place here, too refined for the worn floorboards, too sophisticated for the vintage brass fixtures. She looked like she belonged in a corner office with a view, not a small-town post office with creaky hinges.

"I hope so," he said honestly. "Town needs a post office."

Harper's eyebrows rose slightly. "Can't you just deliver mail to people's houses?"

There was no hostility in the question, just genuine confusion. She really didn't understand. How could she, when she'd spent the last decade in a city where everything was transactional, where buildings were just buildings and neighbors were just people who happened to live nearby?

"That's not how community works," Colby said.

The words came out gentler than he'd intended, without the edge of judgment he'd been holding. Because looking at Harper now, at the grief she was trying to hide, at the exhaustion written in every line of her posture, Colby realized she wasn't here to destroy anything. She was just lost, standing in the ruins of a relationship she'd let slip away, trying to figure out what she was supposed to do next.

His mother's voice echoed in his head: *Be nice to her. She just lost her grandmother.*

Harper's expression shifted, something defensive flickering across her features before she controlled it. "I'll figure it out," she said, lifting her chin slightly. "I have three weeks."

Three weeks. To decide the fate of a building that had been part of Willow Creek since 1923. To determine whether the town would keep its heart or lose it to whatever Harper decided was more practical.

Colby nodded, shouldering his empty satchel. "If you need anything, information about routes, or how Stella organized things, I'm around. The whole town is, actually. Stella helped a lot of people over the years."

"I know."

The words came out sharp, almost defensive, and Colby saw Harper's jaw tighten immediately after. She knew she'd snapped at him. He could see the awareness in her eyes, the brief flash of regret before she looked away.

Colby recognized emotional armor when he saw it. He'd

worn his own for years after Amanda left, that careful distance, that refusal to let anyone close enough to hurt him again. Harper was doing the same thing, using sharpness to keep the world at arm's length while she dealt with grief she probably wasn't ready to face.

"Right." Colby moved toward the door, giving her the space she clearly needed. "Well. Good luck with everything."

He left before she could respond, pulling the door closed behind him with its familiar creak. Through the window, he could see Harper standing in the middle of the post office, arms wrapped around herself, staring at nothing.

She looked small in that big empty building. Alone. Lost.

Colby climbed back into his mail truck and sat there for a moment, hands on the steering wheel, not starting the engine. He should finish his route. He had mail to deliver, people waiting for packages and letters and the connection to the world beyond Willow Creek's borders.

But he kept seeing Harper's expression, that careful blankness that hid so much pain.

Be nice to her.

Colby started the truck and pulled away from the curb, watching the post office shrink in his rearview mirror. Harper was still visible through the window, a solitary figure in a building that was meant to be filled with people.

Three weeks, she'd said. Three weeks to decide what mattered more, the past or the future, tradition or practicality, community or whatever waited for her back in Chicago.

Colby hoped she'd choose to stay. For the town's sake, obviously. For the post office and the people who depended on it and the way Stella had made that brick building into something more than just a place to buy stamps.

Not because Harper Delaney had looked at him with those haunted hazel eyes and made him feel something he'd spent three years carefully not feeling.

Definitely not that.

Colby finished his route on autopilot, his mind replaying the brief interaction. The way Harper's hand had felt in his, cold, trembling slightly. The shadows under her eyes. The defensive lift of her chin when she'd said she'd figure it out.

She reminded him of a bird with a broken wing, trying to convince everyone, including herself, that she could still fly.

By the time Colby returned to the post office depot to clock out, he'd made a decision. Harper needed help, whether she wanted to admit it or not. She needed someone to show her what Stella had built, to explain why the post office mattered beyond federal regulations and zip codes.

And Colby knew this town, knew its people and its rhythms and its history, better than almost anyone.

He'd help her understand. Not because he was attracted to her, that would be stupid, getting involved with someone who'd made it clear she was only staying three weeks. Not because he felt protective of a stranger who'd hurt his feelings with a single sharp response.

He'd help her because it was the right thing to do. Because

Stella would have wanted someone to look out for her granddaughter. Because the post office deserved a chance, and so did Harper, even if she didn't know it yet.

Colby pulled out his phone and texted Dylan: *Breakfast Friday morning? Need to talk.*

The response came almost immediately: *The Copper Kettle. See you there. You buying?*

Yeah. I'm buying.

Colby pocketed his phone and headed home, already planning what he'd say to convince Harper Delaney that Willow Creek was worth staying for.

Or at least worth three weeks of her time.

CHAPTER THREE

Harper stood in the middle of the post office, listening to the silence settle around her like dust. The coffee maker gurgled in the back room, filling the air with the scent of dark roast and a hint of vanilla, Stella's signature blend. For a moment, Harper could almost pretend her grandmother was just in the next room, sorting mail or humming along to the ancient radio that probably still sat on the shelf above the sorting table.

But the coffee maker clicked off, and the illusion shattered.

Harper wrapped her hands around the warm mug she'd found, not Stella's "World's Best Grandma" cup, which felt too sacred to use, but a plain white one with a small chip on the rim. The coffee tasted like memory and regret, bitter despite the vanilla.

Outside, Main Street went about its Thursday afternoon business. Through the tall windows, Harper could see people walking past, a woman with a stroller, an elderly man with a newspaper tucked under his arm, a teenager on a skateboard who probably should have been in school. Small-town life, slow and steady, the way it had always been.

The way Harper had spent eleven years trying to escape.

She set down her coffee and surveyed the post office with what she hoped was a practical eye. If she was staying for three weeks, and apparently she was, unless she wanted to slink back to Chicago as a jobless failure, she needed to organize this place. Make an inventory. Figure out what was valuable, what was trash, what belonged to the federal government and what had belonged to Stella.

The sorting table seemed like a logical place to start. Harper approached it carefully, as if the stacks of mail might bite. Some of the envelopes looked recent, yesterday's delivery, probably, what Colby Hayes had left. Others were clearly older, marked with dates from weeks ago, maybe months. Had Stella been falling behind? Or had she been saving these for some reason?

Harper picked up an envelope at random. *Mr. and Mrs. Sullivan, 247 Oak Street.* The handwriting was shaky but determined, probably an older person, maybe someone with arthritis. She set it back down gently, feeling like an intruder in her own inheritance.

The brass mailboxes along the wall gleamed dully in the fluorescent light, each one numbered and labeled. Harper walked along the row, reading names she half-remembered from childhood summers: Patterson, Rodriguez, Armstrong, Mitchell. Some boxes were stuffed full, mail visible through the small glass windows. Others were empty, waiting.

How many of these people had known Stella for forty years? How many had grown up coming to this post office, bringing their children and eventually their grandchildren? How many stories lived in this building, stories Harper had never bothered to learn because she'd been too busy planning her escape to care about the place she was leaving behind?

The guilt sat heavy in Harper's chest, making the coffee taste even more bitter.

She turned away from the mailboxes and focused on the main counter, Stella's domain. The surface was cluttered but organized in that way that suggested a system only its owner understood. Stamps in one corner, receipt pads in another, a jar of pens with most of the caps missing. A desktop calendar still showed October, the date circled where Stella had written *Harper's birthday* in her distinctive looping script.

Harper's 29th birthday had been six weeks ago. She'd spent it working late on a campaign proposal, eating takeout sushi at her desk, ignoring Todd's texts asking if she wanted to video chat. She'd meant to call Stella, had even picked up her phone twice, but something always interrupted. A meeting, an email, a deadline that seemed more important than a five-minute conversation with the woman who'd raised her every summer.

The woman who'd still remembered her birthday and marked it on a calendar she'd never live to finish.

Harper pressed her hand to her mouth, fighting back the sob that wanted to escape. She would not cry. Not yet. Not when there was work to do and decisions to make and a future to figure out.

She moved behind the counter, into Stella's space, and immediately felt like a trespasser. This was where her grandmother had stood for forty years, sorting mail, selling stamps, listening to the endless stream of small-town gossip and genuine concerns that flowed through a post office like water through a riverbed. This was where Stella had built a life that mattered, while Harper had spent a decade chasing a career that left her empty.

The desk behind the counter was old, older than the building itself, probably. Dark wood with ornate carved details along the edges, the kind of antique that belonged in a museum or an estate sale catalog. Harper ran her fingers along the smooth surface, feeling the grain of the wood, the slight depression where decades of paperwork had worn a hollow.

Three drawers on each side, all unlocked and surprisingly organized. The top drawers held office supplies, paper clips, rubber bands, sticky notes in colors Stella had probably thought were cheerful. The middle drawers contained forms, receipts, and what looked like forty years of postal regulations that no one had bothered to throw away.

The bottom drawer on the right side was locked.

Harper tugged the handle experimentally. Definitely locked, the mechanism holding firm. She tried the bottom left drawer, unlocked, filled with ancient magazines and what appeared to be every greeting card Stella had ever received. But the right bottom drawer wouldn't budge.

Curiosity sparked, cutting through the grief and guilt. Why would Stella lock one drawer? What was inside that needed protecting in a post office in a town where nobody locked their doors?

Harper searched the desktop, looking for a key. Nothing. She checked the middle drawers again, more carefully this time, shuffling through papers and folders. Still nothing.

Where would Stella keep a key?

The answer came immediately: *The same place she kept everything precious.*

Harper left the counter and walked to the back room, a small space that served as break room, storage closet, and Stella's private retreat. The coffee maker sat on a card table, still warm. Next to it was the ancient radio, its dial frozen on the local station that played golden oldies and farm reports. A folding chair. A small bookshelf crammed with paperbacks, their spines cracked from multiple readings.

And on the top shelf, tucked between a potted plant that had somehow survived and a framed photo of Harper and Todd as children, was Stella's jewelry box.

Harper reached for it with careful hands. The box was wooden, painted with faded flowers, the kind of thing that had probably been beautiful fifty years ago. She'd seen Stella wear jewelry exactly three times, her wedding ring, which she'd never removed even after Grandpa Joe died; small pearl earrings for church; and a cameo brooch for special occasions.

The jewelry box opened with a soft creak.

Inside was a modest collection: the pearl earrings, nestled in worn velvet. The cameo brooch, its profile elegant and old-fashioned. A tarnished silver bracelet. And underneath everything, wrapped in a faded handkerchief, a small brass key.

Harper's heart beat faster as she lifted the key. It was old, ornate, the kind that belonged to antique furniture. The kind that might fit a locked desk drawer.

She carried the key back to the front, feeling like a detective in some cozy mystery novel. This was ridiculous, it was just a drawer in a desk she owned, filled with probably nothing more interesting than old tax returns or personal correspondence. But Harper's hands shook slightly as she crouched beside the desk and inserted the key into the lock.

It turned smoothly, the mechanism well-oiled despite its age.

The drawer slid open.

Inside, resting on the bottom as if they'd been waiting patiently for decades, was a bundle of letters tied with a faded blue ribbon.

Harper lifted them carefully. The envelopes were yellowed with age, their corners soft from handling. The top envelope bore a address written in masculine handwriting, strong, confident strokes despite the obvious care taken with each letter:

Miss Nora Whitfield

412 Maple Street

Willow Creek, Wisconsin

And stamped across the front in red ink, as official as a verdict: **RETURN TO SENDER.**

Harper's breath caught. She checked the postmark: *May 15, 1973.*

Fifty-two years ago.

Her hands trembling now, Harper flipped through the stack. Twenty, maybe twenty-five letters, all addressed to Nora Whitfield in the same handwriting. All postmarked between May 1973 and December 1974. All stamped with that brutal red declaration: **RETURN TO SENDER**.

Why did Stella have these? Why had she kept them locked away, hidden in a drawer that only she could access?

Harper carried the bundle to the counter and sat on Stella's stool, the letters resting in her lap like something sacred. She should probably leave them alone, they were obviously private, meant for someone named Nora Whitfield who for some reason had rejected them.

But Harper's fingers were already working at the ribbon, pulling it loose with a whisper of fabric. The bow came undone, and the letters shifted in her hands, eager to be read after decades of darkness.

She selected the first one, the oldest, dated May 1973 and carefully opened the envelope. The paper inside was thin, the kind used for aerogrammes, covered in the same careful handwriting as the address.

Harper unfolded it and began to read.

May 12, 1973

My dearest Nora,

I'm writing this from a motel room in Indiana, somewhere between everything I've ever known and a future I'm not sure I want. The room smells like cigarettes and regret, and the neon sign outside keeps flickering, painting the walls in alternating shades of red and shadow. I should be sleeping. I've been driving for eight hours and have another six ahead of me tomorrow but all I can think about is you.

Is that pathetic? Probably. My father would say so. He'd tell me to be practical, to focus on the opportunity ahead instead of mourning what I'm leaving behind. But he doesn't understand that leaving Willow Creek means leaving you, and that feels less like opportunity and more like amputation.

I know you said we had to be realistic. That your parents would never approve of us, that my father's plans for veterinary school in California were already set, that long distance never works for people as young as us. I know you said it would be better to end things cleanly, to remember what we had as something beautiful instead of watching it fade over miles and months and missed phone calls.

But Nora…God, Nora…how am I supposed to forget you? How am I supposed to walk away from someone who makes me believe in words like "soulmate" and "destiny"? You're not just some girl I dated. You're the person who knows me better than I know myself. You're the one I want to tell when something good happens, and the one I need when everything falls apart. You're…

I'm sorry. I'm rambling. It's late, and I'm tired, and I'm heartsick in a way I didn't know was possible.

I love you. I know I'm not supposed to say that anymore,

that we agreed to move on, but I need you to know: I love you with everything I am. And maybe in six months or a year, maybe I'll meet someone else and my father will be right about me getting over this. But right now, in this terrible motel room with the flickering neon and the cigarette smell, I can't imagine a future where you're not the first thing I think about when I wake up and the last thing I wish for before I fall asleep.

I don't know if you'll even read this. I don't know if you'll throw it away unopened, or read it and hate me for making this harder than it needs to be. But I had to try. I had to at least tell you that leaving you is the hardest thing I've ever done, and that no amount of career success or paternal approval could possibly be worth this feeling in my chest, like something vital has been torn away and I'm expected to just keep breathing as if it doesn't matter.

If you change your mind, if any part of you feels even a fraction of what I'm feeling, please write to me. I'll be at the address I gave you, at least through the end of the month. After that, I'll be at school, and I know that's farther away, but Nora, I would cross the entire country if I knew you wanted me to.

I would do anything for you. I always will.

Yours, whether you want me or not,
Jamie

Harper finished reading and realized she was crying.

Not the controlled, dignified tears of someone processing grief appropriately. Real, messy crying, the kind that came with hiccuping breaths and a running nose and the kind of ache in her chest that felt like her heart was physically breaking for two people she'd never met.

Jamie, whoever he was, had loved Nora Whitfield with the kind of love that poets wrote about and movies tried to capture but never quite managed. Raw, desperate, consuming love that made every word feel like it was bleeding onto the page.

And Nora had sent the letter back.

No...not Nora. The envelope was stamped *Return to Sender*, which meant the letter had never reached her. Which meant...what? That the address was wrong? That Nora had moved? That someone...parents, maybe, who wouldn't approve...had intervened?

Harper wiped her eyes and picked up the second letter, dated three weeks later. Then the third. The fourth. Each one more desperate than the last, Jamie writing from veterinary school in California, asking why Nora wasn't responding, begging for just one word to let him know she still thought about him.

Did I do something wrong? Please, Nora, just tell me what I did.

I saw a girl today who looked like you from behind, and for a moment I thought maybe you'd changed your mind, maybe you'd come to find me. But when she turned around, she was a stranger, and I felt like an idiot for hoping.

My father asked if I'm seeing anyone. I told him no. How could I, when you're still the only person I want?

The letters continued through summer, into fall, each one

a little more resigned, a little less hopeful. By December 1974, Jamie's tone had changed:

I don't know why I keep writing to you. You've made it clear you don't want to hear from me. I should respect that. I should move on.

But I can't seem to stop. It's like these letters are the only thing keeping me connected to the person I was when I loved you...before I learned to be practical, before I accepted that some love stories don't get happy endings.

This is the last one. I promise. I'll stop haunting your mailbox and your memory. I'll finish school, I'll build a career, I'll probably even get married someday to someone practical and appropriate.

But I'll never love anyone the way I loved you. I don't think I'm capable of it anymore. You took that part of me with you when you let me go.

Goodbye, Nora.

Jamie

Harper set down the last letter with shaking hands. The entire story was there, preserved in fading ink and yellowed paper, a love affair destroyed by distance and circumstance and letters that never reached their intended recipient.

Why did Stella have these? How did they end up in her desk, tied with ribbon and locked away like treasure?

And most importantly: Did Nora Whitfield know that Jamie had written to her? Did she know he'd loved her so desperately, had grieved their relationship for over a year, had thought she'd chosen to ignore him?

Harper looked at the envelopes again, studying them more carefully. The addresses were correct, 412 Maple Street, Willow Creek. The postage was paid. There was no reason these letters shouldn't have been delivered.

Unless someone had intentionally marked them *Return to Sender.*

Unless someone had decided that Nora Whitfield and Jamie, whatever his last name was, weren't meant to be together, and had taken it upon themselves to ensure the letters never reached their destination.

Harper's stomach turned. Stella? Had Stella done this?

No. That didn't make sense. Stella believed in love, in second chances, in the kind of happily-ever-afters that only existed in romance novels. She wouldn't have sabotaged someone's relationship.

Would she?

Harper gathered the letters carefully, retying the ribbon with unsteady fingers. She needed to know more. Needed to understand why these letters had ended up here, locked away in Stella's desk. Needed to know if Nora Whitfield was still alive, still in Willow Creek, still unaware that a man named Jamie had loved her enough to write twenty-five letters to someone who'd never answered.

The post office suddenly felt different, not just a building full of dust and memories, but a place where stories lived.

Where connections were made and sometimes broken. Where the distance between two people could be measured in stamps and envelopes and the cruel finality of a red stamp.

Harper stood, still holding the letters, and walked to the window. Outside, Willow Creek continued its evening routine. Lights were coming on in shops as afternoon shifted toward dusk. People were heading home for dinner, for family time, for all the small rituals that made life feel stable and real.

Somewhere out there, maybe, was a woman named Nora Whitfield who'd spent fifty years wondering why the boy she loved had never written.

And somewhere, maybe California, maybe anywhere, was a man named Jamie who'd spent fifty years believing she'd chosen silence over him.

Harper looked down at the letters in her hands and made a decision.

She had three weeks in Willow Creek. Three weeks to figure out what to do with the post office, with her life, with the unexpected inheritance that had somehow become both a burden and a gift.

Three weeks to find Nora Whitfield and deliver the letters that had been waiting for over fifty years to reach their destination.

Because if Harper had learned anything from five years in marketing and a lifetime of running from her past, it was this: some messages were worth waiting for. Some stories deserved endings, even if those endings came decades late.

Harper thought about her mother, who'd fled Willow Creek to avoid exactly this, the weight of other people's stories, the obligation of small-town connection, the way everyone knew everyone's business. Her mother had chosen distance, professional boundaries, a life where other people's mail was just mail. Harper had always thought that was wisdom. Now, holding these letters, feeling their weight, she wondered if it might have been loss.

And maybe, just maybe, if she could help reunite a love story that had been undelivered for half a century, she could figure out what real love was supposed to look like.

Harper set the letters gently on the counter, next to Stella's "World's Best Grandma" mug. The coffee had gone cold, but she took a sip anyway, letting the bitterness ground her.

Tomorrow, she'd start looking for Nora Whitfield.

Tonight, she'd read the rest of Jamie's letters and remember what it felt like to believe in love so complete, so consuming, that it could survive being returned unread.

Outside the window, the November darkness settled over Willow Creek like a blanket. And inside the post office, Harper Delaney sat surrounded by other people's stories and began to wonder if maybe, just maybe, she was exactly where she was supposed to be.

CHAPTER FOUR

Friday morning dawned cold and clear, the kind of November day that reminded Colby why he loved living in Wisconsin. Frost painted the windows of his truck in delicate patterns, and his breath clouded in the air as he scraped ice off the windshield. The sun was just cresting the horizon, painting Main Street in shades of gold and amber.

Colby had woken up thinking about Harper Delaney, which was both inconvenient and unwelcome. He'd spent most of yesterday's route trying not to think about the way her hazel eyes had gone sharp with defensiveness, or how her hands had trembled when she'd taken his delivery, or the shadows under her eyes that suggested she'd been crying.

He'd failed spectacularly at the not-thinking-about-her part.

Now, driving toward The Copper Kettle for his breakfast meeting with Dylan, Colby caught himself glancing at the post office as he passed. The lights were off, the building dark and silent. Harper was probably still asleep, or maybe already awake and staring at the ceiling, trying to figure out what she was supposed to do with an inheritance she clearly hadn't wanted.

Colby parked in front of the café and checked his phone. A text from Dylan: *Already here. Maggie's making your usual.*

The Copper Kettle was Willow Creek's unofficial town hall, the place where everyone gathered for coffee, gossip, and Maggie Chen's famous cinnamon rolls. The café occupied a corner building with large windows and a striped awning, and walking through its door felt like stepping into someone's well-loved kitchen. Mismatched tables and chairs, walls covered in local art and faded photographs, the constant smell of coffee and baking bread.

The morning rush was in full swing. Colby recognized most of the faces, Pete Armstrong in his usual corner with a newspaper, Lucy Rodriguez and her husband sharing breakfast before opening the flower shop, a handful of teachers from the elementary school grabbing coffee before first bell. Everyone looked up when Colby entered, offering waves and nods and the casual acknowledgment of people who'd known each other for decades.

Dylan Parker sat at their usual table by the window, already working on what looked like his second cup of coffee. Colby's best friend since elementary school was everything Colby wasn't, blonde where Colby was dark, outgoing where Colby was reserved, perpetually optimistic where Colby tended toward caution. Dylan ran Parker's Hardware Store, the business his father had started forty years ago, and seemed to genuinely love every minute of it.

"You look tired," Dylan said by way of greeting, pushing a mug of black coffee across the table.

"Good morning to you too." Colby slid into the chair opposite and wrapped his hands around the warm ceramic. The coffee was perfect, as always, Maggie knew how everyone took their drinks and never had to ask.

"Long night?" Dylan's green eyes glinted with curiosity. "Or were you too busy thinking about a certain redheaded city girl to sleep?"

Colby nearly choked on his coffee. "What?"

"Come on, man. This is Willow Creek. You were seen at the post office yesterday afternoon. With Stella's granddaughter." Dylan grinned. "Maggie says she's beautiful. Mrs. Patterson says she's stuck up. Lucy Rodriguez says she drives a sensible sedan, which apparently means something significant, though I'm not sure what."

"She's grieving her grandmother," Colby said, more sharply than he'd intended. "And she's trying to figure out what to do with a building she just inherited. Maybe everyone could give her five minutes before deciding who she is?"

Dylan's eyebrows rose. "Wow. Defensive much?"

Before Colby could respond, Maggie Chen appeared at their table with two plates. She was in her late sixties, with short gray hair and warm brown eyes that missed absolutely nothing. She'd owned The Copper Kettle for thirty years and had perfected the art of knowing everything about everyone while making it feel like friendly concern rather than gossip.

"Morning, boys," she said, setting down plates loaded with scrambled eggs, bacon, and toast. A cinnamon roll sat on each plate, still warm from the oven. "Dylan, I added extra bacon. Colby, you look like you need it."

"Thanks, Maggie." Colby accepted the plate gratefully. He'd skipped dinner last night, too preoccupied with thoughts he didn't want to examine.

Maggie didn't leave. Instead, she pulled out a chair and sat down, which in The Copper Kettle meant serious conversation was about to happen.

"So," she said, folding her hands on the table. "Harper Delaney's back in town."

Here it comes, Colby thought.

"I saw her yesterday," Maggie continued. "Drove past the post office around closing time. Lights were still on. Girl was sitting at Stella's desk, looking like the weight of the world was on her shoulders." Her expression softened. "Poor thing. Losing Stella, having to deal with all this while she's grieving. Can't be easy."

Dylan shot Colby a look that clearly said *See? I told you everyone knows everything.*

"Have you talked to her?" Maggie asked Colby. "Beyond the mail delivery?"

"Briefly." Colby focused on his eggs. "She

seems...overwhelmed."

"She's scared," Maggie said with the confidence of someone who'd spent decades reading people. "Stella called me about three months ago, told me she'd updated her will. Said she was leaving the post office to Harper, wanted to make sure the girl had support when the time came." Her voice caught slightly. "I told Stella she'd be around to explain it herself. Guess we were both wrong."

The table fell silent for a moment, the bustle of the café continuing around them.

"Do you think she'll keep it?" Dylan asked quietly. "The post office?"

Maggie shook her head slowly. "I don't know. She's been gone a long time. Made a life in the city. And that building needs work, new roof, updated heating system, probably a dozen other things Stella was putting off." She paused. "Victor Brennan stopped by yesterday, asking questions about the property."

Colby's head snapped up. "Victor Brennan?"

"Don't know him?" Maggie's expression turned sour. "Real estate developer from Madison. Bought the old Brenner farmhouse last year, gutted it, turned it into some kind of luxury vacation rental. Now he's looking for more properties to 'develop.'" She made air quotes around the word, her tone making it clear what she thought of development.

"And he's interested in the post office?" Colby felt something tighten in his chest.

"Prime location," Maggie said. "Corner lot, Main Street visibility, historic building that could be 'renovated.'" More air quotes. "He asked if I knew whether Stella's heir would be open to selling. Told him I had no idea, which is true. But I don't trust him, Colby. He doesn't understand what places like this mean to a town. To him, everything's just potential profit."

Colby set down his fork, appetite suddenly gone. The post office was more than real estate. It was the heart of Willow Creek, the place where everyone gathered, where news was shared and comfort was offered. It was where Stella had spent forty years building connections that held the town together.

If Victor Brennan got his hands on it, he'd turn it into condos or a boutique hotel or some sterile, expensive thing that served tourists instead of the community that had sustained it for nearly a century.

"Someone needs to talk to Harper," Dylan said, reading Colby's expression. "Explain what's at stake."

"She knows," Colby said, though he wasn't sure that was true. Harper had said she'd figure it out, but did she understand what the post office meant? Or did she just see it the way Victor Brennan probably did, as an asset to be liquidated, a problem to be solved?

"Does she?" Maggie asked gently. "She left when she was eighteen, Colby. She's been gone eleven years. She might not remember what this place means to people. Might not understand that some things are worth more than their market value."

"Then someone should remind her," Colby said.

"You offering?" Dylan's grin was back, infuriating and knowing.

Before Colby could answer, the café door opened with a cheerful chime, and a man in an expensive suit walked in. He looked wildly out of place in The Copper Kettle, too polished, too urban, checking his phone before he'd even finished scanning the room. His salt-and-pepper hair was perfectly styled, his watch probably cost more than Colby's truck, and his gray eyes swept the café with the assessing gaze of someone calculating property values.

Victor Brennan. Had to be.

Maggie's expression confirmed it, her mouth tightening as she stood. "Excuse me, boys. Looks like I have a customer who needs educating about how we do things around here."

She walked back to the counter, her posture radiating polite hostility. Colby watched as Victor approached, his smile professionally friendly, his phone still in one hand.

"Good morning," Victor said, his voice smooth and confident. "I'm looking for information about a property on Main Street. The post office? I understand the owner recently passed, and I'd like to..."

"The post office isn't for sale," Maggie interrupted, arms crossed.

Victor's smile never wavered. "I haven't even made an offer yet. I simply want to speak with the new owner about possibilities. Development opportunities that could benefit everyone in town."

"Harper Delaney," Maggie said coolly. "Stella's granddaughter. And I'm sure she'll let you know if she's interested in selling. Until then, might I suggest you enjoy some coffee and mind your own business?"

Victor's smile tightened slightly, the first crack in his professional veneer. "I'm simply being proactive. In my experience, out-of-town heirs are often eager to liquidate inherited properties, especially ones requiring significant investment to maintain."

Colby felt his hands clench into fists under the table. Dylan kicked him gently, a warning to stay calm.

"Harper's from Willow Creek," Maggie said, though technically that wasn't entirely true anymore. "And the post office is a historic landmark. Federal property. Not exactly easy to liquidate, even if she wanted to."

"Everything's for sale at the right price," Victor said, finally looking away from his phone to meet Maggie's gaze. "I've found that most people are quite reasonable once they understand the financial realities."

"And I've found that most developers don't understand that some things matter more than money," Maggie shot back. "Now, are you ordering coffee, or are you just here to insult our town?"

Victor's professional mask slipped back into place. "Coffee. Black. To go."

As Maggie went to pour the coffee with obvious reluctance, Victor's gaze swept the café again, landing on Colby. Their eyes met for a brief moment, and Colby saw the calculation there, sizing him up, dismissing him as irrelevant, moving on.

Colby had seen that look before, mostly from Amanda's friends when she'd announced she was leaving Willow Creek. The look that said small-town people were quaint and simple, easily managed or ignored as needed.

It made his blood boil.

Victor collected his coffee, left cash on the counter without waiting for change, and walked out with the same phone-checking, hurried efficiency he'd entered with.

The café erupted in low conversation the moment the door closed.

"Who does he think he is?" Lucy Rodriguez said from her table.

"City people," Pete Armstrong muttered into his newspaper. "No respect."

Maggie returned to Colby and Dylan's table, shaking her head. "That man is going to be trouble."

"He can't force Harper to sell," Dylan said reasonably. "She owns the building outright, right? Stella's will was clear?"

"Legally, yes," Maggie agreed. "But that doesn't mean he can't make things difficult. Or appealing. If he offers enough money, and Harper's struggling to keep the place running..." She didn't finish the sentence, but she didn't need to.

Colby pushed away from the table, appetite completely gone despite barely touching his breakfast. "I need to go."

"Where?" Dylan asked, though his knowing grin suggested he already knew.

"The post office." Colby pulled out his wallet, but Maggie waved him off.

"On the house. And Colby?" She waited until he looked at her. "Be nice. That girl's been through enough without everyone in town pressuring her before she's even had time to grieve."

"I'm always nice," Colby said, echoing what he'd told his mother yesterday.

"You're always polite," Maggie corrected, just like his mother had. "There's a difference. Harper needs a friend right now, not a lecture about civic duty."

Colby nodded, grabbed his jacket, and headed for the door.

Behind him, he heard Dylan say to Maggie, "Twenty bucks says they're dating by Christmas."

"I'll take that bet," Maggie replied. "I give it two weeks."

Colby pretended he hadn't heard them and stepped out into the cold November morning.

The walk from The Copper Kettle to the post office took less than five minutes, but Colby used the time to organize his thoughts. He needed to explain to Harper about Victor Brennan, about what was at stake, about why the post office mattered. He needed to be helpful without being pushy, informative without being condescending.

He needed to stop thinking about how her hazel eyes had looked in the fluorescent light, or how her voice had gone sharp when she'd said *I know*, or how she'd looked so completely lost standing in that big empty building.

The post office lights were on now, visible through the tall windows. As Colby approached, he could see Harper inside, standing at the sorting table with what looked like stacks of mail surrounding her. She wore jeans today, a change from yesterday's business attire, and a sweater that looked too thin for Wisconsin in November. Her auburn hair was pulled back in a ponytail, and even from outside, Colby could see the determination in her posture.

She was trying. That counted for something.

Colby knocked on the door, two sharp raps.

Harper looked up, startled, then walked to the door. Through the glass, Colby saw her expression shift, recognition, then wariness, then something that might have been resignation as she unlocked the door and pulled it open.

"Mr. Hayes," she said, her tone carefully neutral. "I wasn't expecting another delivery this early."

"It's just Colby," he said. "And I'm not here for work. Can I come in? There's something you should know."

Harper hesitated, and for a moment Colby thought she might say no. Then she stepped back, holding the door open.

"Sure. Though I should warn you, I have no idea what I'm doing with any of this." She gestured at the chaos behind her, mail sorted into haphazard piles, boxes stacked precariously, papers covering every surface.

Colby stepped inside, and the familiar scent of the post office washed over him, paper and wood polish and that faint vanilla undertone. But today there was something else, something floral and light that he realized must be Harper's shampoo or perfume.

He forced himself to focus. "There's a developer in town. Victor Brennan. He's asking questions about this property."

Harper's expression didn't change. "Okay."

"He wants to buy it," Colby continued. "Turn it into condos or a hotel or something that serves tourists instead of the community. Maggie Chen said he stopped by The Copper Kettle this morning, asking about you."

"I see." Harper crossed her arms, her posture going defensive again. "And you're here to tell me not to sell to him?"

"I'm here to make sure you understand what you'd be selling," Colby said carefully. "This isn't just a building, Harper. It's been the heart of this town for almost a century. People come here for more than stamps. They come for connection, for community, for the knowledge that someone cares about more than just processing their mail efficiently."

Harper's jaw tightened. "I spent every summer here as a kid. I know what this place meant to my grandmother."

"But do you know what it means to everyone else?" Colby kept his voice gentle, trying not to sound accusatory. "Do you know that Mrs. Patterson comes in every Tuesday to check her mail even though she could have it delivered, because Stella always asked about her arthritis? Or that the Sullivan kids learned to write addresses here, and that Stella gave them stamps to start their own collections? Or that when the Rodriguez family's house flooded last spring, Stella organized the relief effort from this building, because everyone checks their mail and everyone passes through here eventually?"

Harper looked away, her arms tightening around herself. "I get it. It's important. But I also know it needs a new roof, new heating, probably electrical work. I know it's barely breaking even. And I know that I have three weeks to figure out what to do before I have to go back to..." She stopped, seeming to catch herself. "Before I have to make a decision."

"Go back to what?" Colby asked quietly.

Harper's expression closed off completely. "Nothing. Forget it."

They stood in awkward silence, surrounded by decades of accumulated mail and memories. Outside, Main Street was waking up, shops opening, people starting their day. Normal Friday morning in Willow Creek, the routine continuing even as the future of one of its most important institutions hung in the balance.

"I found letters," Harper said suddenly. "In Stella's desk. From 1973. Someone named Jamie writing to someone named Nora Whitfield. Except the letters were marked 'Return to Sender.' Twenty-five of them, all sent back."

Colby blinked at the sudden change of subject. "Nora Whitfield?"

"You know her?"

"Everyone knows her. She was my English teacher in high school. Lives on Maple Street, still teaches Sunday school at the Methodist church." Colby tried to process this information. "She was getting love letters in the seventies?"

"She was supposed to be getting them," Harper corrected. "But someone sent them all back. And I think..." She hesitated, then seemed to make a decision. "I think Jamie never knew she didn't receive them. I think he spent fifty years believing she rejected him, and she probably spent fifty years wondering why he stopped writing."

Colby felt something shift in his chest. "That's..."

"Tragic," Harper finished. "It's tragic. And I'm going to find out what happened, and I'm going to fix it if I can. Because someone deserves to get the letters that were meant for them, even if it's fifty years too late."

She looked at Colby directly for the first time since he'd entered, and he saw something in her hazel eyes that hadn't been there yesterday, purpose. Determination. A glimpse of the person she might be underneath the defensive armor and the exhaustion.

"So," Harper continued, her chin lifting slightly. "If you want to help with that instead of lecturing me about civic responsibility, you're welcome to stay. Otherwise, I have a lot of mail to sort and a mystery to solve, and I'd appreciate being able to do it without half the town telling me what I should or shouldn't do with a building I inherited twenty-four hours ago."

Colby felt a smile tugging at his lips despite himself.

"You've got a lot of fire for someone who looks like they haven't slept in two days."

"I'll sleep when I'm dead," Harper shot back. Then her expression crumpled slightly. "Sorry. That was, given the circumstances, that was inappropriate."

"It's fine." Colby made a decision. "I'll help. With the letters, I mean. Nora Whitfield is a good person. If there's a way to give her closure after fifty years, she deserves it."

Harper's expression softened, just a fraction. "Thank you."

"But," Colby added, "you should know that Victor Brennan isn't going to give up easily. He's going to make you an offer, and it's probably going to be substantial. And if you're planning to sell, you should at least consider what happens to this town when its post office becomes a vacation rental."

Harper's defenses snapped back into place. "I'm aware of the situation, Colby. I'm not an idiot."

"I never said you were." Colby held her gaze. "I said you've been gone a long time. Things change when you're not looking."

"Yeah," Harper said quietly, looking around the post office with an expression Colby couldn't quite read. "They do."

The moment stretched between them, loaded with things neither of them knew how to say. Then Harper broke eye contact and turned back to the sorting table.

"So," she said, her voice deliberately lighter. "Want to

help me figure out this disaster of a mail system? Because I have no idea what half these codes mean, and I'm pretty sure Stella had a filing system that made sense only to her."

Colby moved to the table, standing close enough to see what Harper was working with but far enough to maintain appropriate distance. Professional distance. Helper distance.

Distance that felt simultaneously too close and not nearly close enough.

"Okay," he said, forcing his mind back to the task at hand. "Let's start with the basics."

And as Colby began explaining the intricacies of small-town mail delivery, he tried very hard not to notice how Harper's ponytail caught the morning light, or how she bit her bottom lip when she was concentrating, or how the vanilla scent seemed to surround her like an aura.

He tried very hard, and failed completely.

This was going to be a problem.

CHAPTER FIVE

Harper was knee-deep in the sorting system Colby had tried to explain, something about zones and routes and priority versus standard that all blurred together in her exhausted brain, when someone knocked on the post office door.

Not the sharp, confident knock Colby had used earlier. This was gentler, almost apologetic, accompanied by a wavering voice: "Hello? Harper, dear?"

Harper looked up from the mail sorting table, where she'd been trying to organize envelopes by what Colby had called "logical geographic clusters." The result looked more like chaos with good intentions. Through the window in the door, she could see an elderly woman with white permed hair and a covered dish balanced in her hands.

Harper unlocked the door and pulled it open. "Hi, can I help you?"

The woman smiled, and her whole face crinkled with warmth. She was thin, dressed in a cardigan that had probably been fashionable in 1985, with glasses hanging from a beaded chain around her neck. She looked exactly like what Harper imagined when someone said "sweet grandmother type."

"I'm Clara Jenkins," the woman said. "I worked here with your grandmother for thirty years before I retired. I heard you were in town, and I thought..." She lifted the covered dish slightly. "Well, I thought you might need some proper food and maybe some help figuring out Stella's system. If you're interested, that is. I don't want to impose."

Harper felt something loosen in her chest, gratitude mixed with relief. "You're not imposing. Please, come in. I could definitely use the help."

Clara's face brightened as she stepped inside, immediately looking around with the fond expression of someone returning to a beloved place. "Oh, it still smells the same. Paper and vanilla. Stella always kept that coffee brewing." Her eyes misted slightly. "I still can't believe she's gone."

"Me neither," Harper said quietly, taking the dish from Clara's hands. It was warm through the towel, and she caught the scent of chicken and herbs. "Is this...?"

"Chicken and rice casserole," Clara confirmed. "Nothing fancy, but it's filling, and you look like you haven't eaten properly in days." She gave Harper a once-over with the assessing eye of someone who'd probably raised multiple children. "When did you last have a real meal?"

Harper tried to remember. Gas station coffee this

morning. Nothing yesterday except coffee. Before that...
"Tuesday?"

Clara made a disapproving sound. "Well, that won't do. You can't run a post office on coffee and air, dear. Let's get this in the back, and then we'll tackle this mess." She gestured at the sorting table with its haphazard piles of envelopes.

Harper followed Clara to the small back room, where Clara immediately took charge, finding plates and utensils with the ease of someone who knew exactly where everything lived. Within minutes, Harper was sitting at the folding table with a generous portion of casserole in front of her, and Clara was bustling around making fresh coffee.

"Now then," Clara said, settling into the other folding chair with her own small portion. "Eat first, questions later. You look ready to fall over."

The casserole was delicious, comfort food in its purest form, the kind of thing that tasted like someone cared. Harper hadn't realized how hungry she was until the first bite, and then she was eating with focused determination, barely pausing to breathe.

Clara watched with obvious satisfaction, sipping her coffee and letting the silence stretch comfortably. She had that rare quality of being present without being intrusive, content to simply exist in the same space without filling every moment with conversation.

Harper finished her plate and sat back, feeling more human than she had in days. "Thank you. That was exactly what I needed."

"Food always helps," Clara said simply. "Your grandmother taught me that. Whenever someone was having a hard day, Stella would make coffee and find something to feed them. Said you can't solve problems on an empty stomach." She smiled softly. "She was usually right."

Harper felt her throat tighten. "I should have visited more. I should have..." She stopped, unable to finish the sentence.

Clara reached across the table and patted Harper's hand. "Stella knew you loved her, dear. She talked about you all the time, showed everyone pictures of your accomplishments. She was so proud of you."

"I abandoned her," Harper said, the words coming out harsher than she'd intended. "I left and I barely called and I was too busy with my stupid job to come home for the holidays, and now she's gone and I can't..." Her voice broke. "I can't fix it."

"No," Clara agreed gently. "You can't. But you're here now. And Stella left you this place for a reason." She looked around the small room with its ancient coffee maker and worn furniture. "She wanted you to have roots again, I think. Something real to hold onto."

Harper wiped her eyes, frustrated with herself for crying in front of a stranger. "I don't know if I can do this. Run a post office. I'm a marketing consultant. Was a marketing consultant. I create social media campaigns, not... whatever this is."

"This," Clara said, "is about connection. About being the thread that holds a community together. It's not that different from what you did, really. Just more personal." She stood, collecting their plates. "And you don't have to figure it all out today. Let's start with the basics. How to sort mail without losing your mind."

Harper followed Clara back to the main room, where the sorting table waited with its overwhelming collection of envelopes. Clara approached it with the confidence of someone who'd spent three decades mastering this exact chaos.

"Alright," Clara said, pulling on a pair of reading glasses that had been tucked in her cardigan pocket. "Stella had a system, and once you understand it, everything else falls into place. See these dividers?" She pointed to wooden slots along the back of the table. "These are for the routes. Colby Hayes handles the residential route, that's anything on the streets outside downtown. The business route is handled by the federal carrier who comes through twice a week. Everything else is general delivery, which means people come pick it up here."

Harper nodded, trying to absorb the information. "And the brass mailboxes?"

"Those are for the old-timers who've had boxes here for decades. They pay a small annual fee, and they get their own personal box that only they can access. It's traditional, mostly. Very few people actually need them anymore, but it's a point of pride for some folks. The Armstrongs have had box 47 since 1952. Mrs. Patterson has 23, that was her parents' box originally."

Clara moved through the space with practiced ease, demonstrating how to check postage, how to identify priority mail, how to handle packages too large for mailboxes. Harper watched, taking mental notes and trying not to feel completely overwhelmed.

"The key," Clara said, "is to remember that every piece of mail matters to someone. That birthday card might seem insignificant, but to the person waiting for it, it's everything. The bills are annoying, but they keep lives running. The junk mail is tedious, but even that tells you something about a person's life, what they're interested in, what they need."

"Stella saw all that," Harper said slowly, understanding dawning. "That's why people loved her. She paid attention."

"Exactly." Clara smiled. "She knew Mrs. Chen at The Copper Kettle always got her cooking magazine on the third Tuesday of the month, and if it didn't arrive, something was wrong with the postal system. She knew when the Sullivan kids started getting college letters, and she'd always have an encouraging word ready. She knew who was waiting for medical results, who was expecting a letter from deployed family members, who was watching for divorce papers or adoption notices or anything else that might need a gentle touch and a private moment."

Harper felt the weight of it, forty years of bearing witness to people's lives, of being trusted with their most important moments. How had Stella done this without being crushed by the responsibility?

"Did she ever..." Harper hesitated. "Did she ever make mistakes? Miss something important?"

Clara's expression shifted, becoming thoughtful. "Well, everyone makes mistakes, dear. Stella was human. But she took her job seriously. If a letter didn't make it to its destination, it weighed on her." She paused, then added carefully, "Why do you ask?"

Harper debated for a moment, then decided Clara might have answers she needed. "I found letters. In Stella's locked desk drawer. From the seventies. Someone named Jamie writing to someone named Nora Whitfield. They were all marked 'Return to Sender.'"

Clara's hand froze on the envelope she'd been holding. "Nora Whitfield?"

"You know her?"

"Of course I know her. Everyone knows Nora." Clara set down the envelope, giving Harper her full attention. "She was a teacher at the high school for forty years. English and literature. Retired about five years ago, but she still teaches Sunday school at the Methodist church. Lives alone on Maple Street, in that beautiful Victorian with the wraparound porch."

Harper's pulse quickened. "Never married?"

"No." Clara's voice held a note of sadness. "Always said she never found the right person. Though there were plenty who tried over the years. She's a lovely woman, elegant, intelligent, kind. But she always seemed..." Clara searched for the right word. "Waiting. Like she was holding out for something that never came."

Or someone, Harper thought. Someone named Jamie who'd written twenty-five letters that never reached her.

"These letters," Harper said carefully. "They're love

letters. Beautiful, heartbreaking love letters from someone who was moving away for veterinary school. He wrote for over a year, and every single letter came back marked 'Return to Sender.' But the address was correct. I checked."

Clara sank into Stella's stool, her face pale. "That's not possible. If the address was correct and the postage was paid, there's no reason letters would be returned. Unless..." She stopped, looking troubled.

"Unless someone marked them that way intentionally," Harper finished.

They sat in heavy silence, the implications hanging between them. Around them, the post office felt different now, not just a place of connection, but a place where connections could be broken. Where someone, maybe even Stella, had decided that certain letters shouldn't reach their destination.

"Your grandmother wouldn't have done that," Clara said firmly. "Not Stella. She believed in love, in second chances, in fighting for what mattered. She wouldn't have sabotaged someone's relationship."

"Then who?" Harper asked.

Clara shook her head slowly. "I don't know. But..." She hesitated. "In the early seventies, I wasn't working here yet. I didn't start until 1976. So, I don't know what was happening in 1973, or who else might have had access to the mail."

"But Stella locked the letters away," Harper pressed. "She kept them hidden for fifty years. Why would she do that if she wasn't involved?"

"Maybe," Clara said slowly, "she was protecting someone. Or maybe she was waiting for the right time to set things right." She looked at Harper with sudden intensity. "Have you talked to Nora?"

"Not yet. I only found the letters yesterday."

"You should," Clara said. "Before you jump to conclusions about what happened or why. Nora deserves to know that Jamie wrote to her. That he loved her." Her voice caught. "That she wasn't forgotten."

Harper nodded, her mind already planning the approach. How did you tell someone that fifty years of their life had been built on a lie? That the love they'd been waiting for had been trying to reach them all along?

The door rattled, someone trying the handle. Through the window, Harper saw Colby Hayes with his mail satchel, looking surprised to find the door locked. She'd forgotten to flip the sign to "Open."

Harper crossed to the door and unlocked it, pulling it open. "Sorry, I didn't realize..."

"No problem," Colby said, stepping inside. His eyes went to Clara, and his expression brightened immediately. "Mrs. Jenkins! I didn't know you were here."

"Colby Hayes." Clara stood, moving to give him a quick hug. "Look at you, all grown up and official in your uniform. Your father would be so proud."

"Thanks." Colby's ears went slightly pink, and Harper found it unexpectedly endearing. "How have you been?"

"Oh, you know. Busy with grandchildren and church committees. Too much free time and not enough sense to sit still." Clara smiled. "I was just helping Harper understand the sorting system. Stella's system was... unique."

"That's putting it mildly," Colby agreed. He moved to the sorting table, setting down his satchel. "I've got today's delivery. Want me to show you how to integrate it, or should I just..."

"Show me," Harper interrupted. She needed to learn this, needed to understand how the post office actually functioned if she was going to figure out what to do with it. "Please."

Colby glanced at Clara, who nodded encouragingly. "I should get going anyway. My daughter's expecting me for lunch." She squeezed Harper's hand. "You're doing fine, dear. Don't let anyone tell you otherwise."

Clara collected her empty casserole dish and headed for the door, pausing to give Colby a meaningful look that Harper couldn't quite decipher. "Take care of her, Colby. She needs friends right now."

"Yes ma'am," Colby said, holding the door open.

After Clara left, the post office felt different, quieter, more intimate. Harper was suddenly very aware that she and Colby were alone, that he was standing close enough for her to catch the scent of cold air and pine that seemed to follow him, that his blue-gray eyes were watching her with an intensity that made her pulse skip.

"So," Colby said, breaking the moment. "Sorting mail. Clara's right that Stella had a unique system, but it's not complicated once you get the hang of it."

He moved to the table, and Harper joined him, standing close enough to see what he was doing but far enough to maintain what her brain insisted was appropriate professional distance. Colby began pulling envelopes from his satchel, explaining the markings, the codes, the logic behind the organization.

Harper tried to focus on his words, but she kept getting distracted by his hands, strong, capable hands that handled the mail with easy confidence. By his voice, steady and patient, never making her feel stupid for asking questions. By the way he'd push his hair back when he was thinking, leaving it slightly mussed.

This was ridiculous. She was twenty-nine years old, not a teenager with a crush. And she had far more important things to worry about than whether Colby Hayes had nice hands.

"You're not listening," Colby said, amusement coloring his tone.

Harper blinked. "What? No, I'm..."

"You're staring at that envelope like it personally offended you." He held up the letter in question. "This goes in the Rodriguez slot. Lucy's flower shop. Remember?"

"Right. Rodriguez. Flowers." Harper took the envelope, hyper-aware of their fingers brushing. "Sorry. I'm just... there's a lot to remember."

"It takes time," Colby said, his voice gentler. "You don't have to learn everything in one day."

Harper set down the envelope and turned to face him fully. "Clara told me about Nora Whitfield. She still lives here. On Maple Street."

Colby's expression shifted, becoming more serious. "And?"

"And I'm going to talk to her. Show her the letters." Harper crossed her arms, defensive without quite knowing why. "She deserves to know that Jamie wrote to her. That he never forgot her."

"Agreed," Colby said simply. "When?"

"I don't know. Soon. I need to figure out how to approach her without..." Harper trailed off, uncertain.

"Without destroying her?" Colby finished quietly. "Without telling her that the last fifty years of her life might have been different if someone hadn't interfered?"

"Exactly." Harper looked away, staring at the brass mailboxes with their neat little labels. "Clara said Stella wouldn't have done it. Wouldn't have sent the letters back."

"She wouldn't have," Colby agreed. "Stella believed in love stories."

"But she locked them away." Harper turned back to him. "For fifty years, she kept those letters hidden. Why?"

Colby was quiet for a moment, his expression thoughtful. "Maybe she was waiting for the right person to find them. Someone who would know what to do." His eyes met hers. "Someone like you."

Harper felt something flutter in her chest, gratitude, hope, or maybe just the dangerous beginning of trust. "I don't know what I'm doing."

"None of us do," Colby said. "We're all just making it up as we go, hoping we don't screw up too badly." He smiled, and it transformed his whole face, making him look younger and somehow more approachable. "But for what it's worth, I think you're doing okay. Better than okay, actually."

"I snapped at you yesterday," Harper reminded him. "I was defensive and rude."

"You were grieving," Colby corrected. "There's a difference." He hesitated, then added, "And I was being pushy. Showing up to lecture you about civic responsibility when you'd barely been here twenty-four hours. I'm sorry."

Harper felt her defenses crack a little more. "You were trying to protect something you care about. I get it."

"Still," Colby said. "I could have been more patient."

They stood there in the afternoon light filtering through the tall windows, surrounded by decades of other people's correspondence and the quiet hum of a building that had witnessed countless stories. Outside, Willow Creek went about its Friday afternoon business. Inside, something was shifting, some balance between strangers and allies, between suspicion and understanding.

"Can I see them?" Colby asked quietly. "The letters?"

Harper hesitated only briefly before nodding. She walked to the counter where she'd left the bundle, still tied with the faded blue ribbon. She handed them to Colby, watching as he carefully untied the ribbon and selected the first letter.

She already had portions memorized, Jamie's desperation, his love, his gradual acceptance that Nora had chosen silence. But watching Colby read them was different. She could see the emotions crossing his face, sympathy, sadness, anger at the injustice.

"This is..." Colby looked up, his expression raw. "This is the most romantic thing I've ever read. And the most heartbreaking."

"I know." Harper's voice came out softer than she'd intended. "That's why I have to find him. Jamie. If he's still alive, if there's any chance..." She stopped, afraid she'd sound naive or foolish.

"He'd want to know," Colby finished. "That she never rejected him. That the letters just... didn't make it." He looked at the envelope, at the cruel red stamp. "Someone took this from them. Someone stole fifty years."

"I'm going to get it back," Harper said with sudden fierce determination. "However, much time they have left, I'm going to give them the ending they deserved."

Colby met her gaze, and Harper saw something in his eyes that made her breath catch, admiration, maybe, or respect, or something else she didn't want to name.

"I'll help," he said. "Whatever you need, information, introductions, someone to back you up when you talk to Nora. I'm in."

"Why?" Harper asked. "You barely know me."

Colby was quiet for a moment, his gaze dropping to the letters in his hands. "Because everyone deserves a happy ending. And because..." He looked up, meeting her eyes again. "Because you came back. You could have sold this place sight unseen, handled everything through a lawyer, never set foot in Willow Creek again. But you came back, and you're trying. That matters."

Harper felt something warm unfurl in her chest, dangerous and hopeful. "I haven't decided to keep it. The post office. I'm still figuring things out."

"I know," Colby said. "But you're here. That's enough for now."

The moment stretched between them, loaded with things neither of them knew how to say. Then Colby carefully retied the ribbon around the letters and handed them back to Harper.

"Monday," he said. "Let's talk to Nora on Monday. That gives you the weekend to prepare, and it's better than showing up unannounced on a Friday afternoon."

Harper nodded, grateful for the practical direction. "Monday. Okay."

Colby collected his empty satchel and headed for the door. Before leaving, he turned back, his expression serious. "Harper? Whatever you decide about the post office, keep it, sell it, burn it down, I hope you know that Stella was proud of you. She talked about you all the time. About how smart you were, how brave, how you'd gone after your dreams." He paused. "She never blamed you for leaving."

Harper's throat tightened. "Thank you."

Colby nodded once, then left, the door closing softly behind him.

Harper stood in the empty post office, holding fifty-year-old love letters and feeling the weight of all the decisions stretching out before her. Three weeks. She had three weeks to figure out what to do with this building, with these letters, with the unexpected life she'd stumbled into when she'd fled Chicago and her failed career.

Three weeks to decide if she was brave enough to deliver a love story that had been waiting half a century for its ending.

Outside the window, she caught a glimpse of Colby climbing into his mail truck. He looked up, caught her watching, and raised a hand in a small wave.

Harper waved back, then immediately felt foolish.

But she was smiling as she turned back to the sorting table, and for the first time since learning about Stella's death, the grief felt less like drowning and more like swimming, still hard, still painful, but survivable.

Maybe even worth it.

CHAPTER SIX

Saturday morning arrived with the kind of crisp November cold that made Colby grateful for coffee and flannel. He'd promised Dylan he'd meet him at the post office at nine to assess what repairs the building needed, which was perfectly reasonable and had absolutely nothing to do with wanting to see Harper again.

At least, that's what Colby told himself as he parked his truck outside the post office at eight forty-five.

The building looked different in morning light, still old, still showing its age, but somehow more dignified. Like a grand dame who'd seen better days but refused to give up her posture. The brick facade needed repointing in places, and the gutters were definitely past their prime, but the bones were solid. Good bones, his father would have said. Worth saving.

Colby climbed out of his truck just as Dylan's beat-up work van pulled into the lot. His best friend emerged wearing his usual weekend uniform of faded jeans, a Parker's Hardware hoodie, and a tool belt that had seen at least two decades of use. Dylan's blonde hair was messier than usual, sticking up in ways that suggested he'd rolled out of bed twenty minutes ago.

"Morning, sunshine," Dylan called, grabbing a clipboard from his passenger seat. "Ready to play contractor?"

"We're not playing," Colby said. "We're assessing."

"Right. Assessing." Dylan's grin was knowing and infuriating. "And the fact that Harper Delaney will be here has nothing to do with your sudden interest in building maintenance?"

"I've always been interested in building maintenance."

"You literally fell asleep during my presentation on proper ventilation systems last month."

"That was different. That was boring."

Dylan laughed, slapping Colby on the shoulder. "Whatever you say, man. But for the record, I think it's good. You haven't been interested in anyone since Amanda left, and that was three years ago. It's about time."

Colby wanted to argue, but the post office door opened before he could respond. Harper stepped out, and Colby forgot what he'd been about to say.

She wore jeans again, faded in a way that suggested they were actually well-worn favorites, not designer distressed and an oversized sweater in deep green that made her hazel eyes look more gold than brown. Her auburn hair was pulled back in a messy bun with a pencil stuck through it, and she had what looked like a smudge of dust on her cheek. She looked tired, rumpled, and somehow more beautiful than she had in her city business clothes.

"Morning," Harper said, wrapping her arms around herself against the cold. "You must be Dylan. I'm Harper."

"Dylan Parker." Dylan shook her hand with his usual easy charm. "I hear you need someone to tell you everything that's wrong with this building."

"That's the job description, yeah." Harper's smile was small but genuine. "Fair warning: I have a feeling the list is going to be long."

"Nothing I can't handle." Dylan pulled a measuring tape from his tool belt with the flourish of someone who genuinely loved his work. "Mind if we take a look around?"

Harper stepped back, holding the door open. "Be my guest. I've been making my own list, but I don't actually know what half the problems are called."

The three of them entered the post office, and Colby was immediately struck by how much had changed since Friday. The chaos from the sorting table had been organized into neat stacks, each labeled with sticky notes in Harper's precise handwriting. The floor had been swept, the windows cleaned, and someone, Harper, obviously had brought in a space heater that hummed quietly in the corner.

"Wow," Dylan said, looking around. "This is a lot cleaner than when Stella had it."

"Don't let Stella hear you say that," Colby murmured, then caught himself. Stella wasn't here to hear anything anymore.

Harper must have caught the slip because her expression softened. "My grandmother was organized in her own way. I'm just... organized in a different way." She gestured to a legal pad on the counter, covered in neat columns. "I made a list of everything I've noticed so far. The roof leaks in the back room when it rains. The heating system makes concerning noises. The front step is loose. The..."

"Whoa, slow down." Dylan held up a hand, grinning. "Let me do the official assessment first. You're going to give yourself an ulcer trying to fix everything at once."

"I like to be prepared," Harper said, a touch defensively.

"I can see that." Dylan's tone was kind. "But trust me, this building's been standing since 1923. It can handle being evaluated methodically." He turned to Colby. "You coming, or are you just here for moral support?"

"I'm coming," Colby said, shooting Dylan a warning look that his friend cheerfully ignored.

For the next hour, Dylan conducted his inspection with the thoroughness of someone who actually cared about buildings. He poked at walls, tested floorboards, examined the ancient heating system with the focus of a doctor reviewing X-rays. Colby followed, taking notes on Dylan's clipboard and trying not to be too obvious about watching Harper.

She'd pulled out her own notebook and was following them around, asking questions about everything Dylan identified. Why was that crack concerning? How much would it cost to fix the heating system? Was the electrical wiring up to code? Her questions were intelligent and practical, revealing someone who was actually trying to understand rather than just collect estimates.

"You know your stuff," Dylan commented as they examined the roof situation from the attic access point. "Most people just want to know the bottom line."

"I spent five years in marketing," Harper said, peering up at the rafters with a critical eye. "If there's one thing I learned, it's that you can't sell something you don't understand. Or fix it, in this case."

"Are you planning to fix it?" Colby asked before he could stop himself. "The building?"

Harper looked at him, her expression unreadable. "I'm planning to understand what I'm dealing with before I make any decisions."

"Fair enough," Dylan said, easing the sudden tension. "Alright, I've seen enough for the structural assessment. Let's head back down and I'll give you the full report."

Back in the main room, Dylan spread his notes across the counter and launched into an explanation that was somehow both comprehensive and comprehensible. The roof needed patching but not full replacement. The heating system needed updating but was functional for now. The electrical was mostly okay but could use some modernization. The plumbing was ancient but solid. Total estimated cost for necessary repairs: around fifteen thousand. For desired improvements: another ten thousand on top of that.

Harper's expression remained carefully neutral as she took notes, but Colby saw her hand tighten around her pen. Twenty-five thousand dollars. That was a lot of money for someone who'd just quit her job and inherited a building that barely broke even.

"I can give you names of contractors," Dylan offered. "Or..." He glanced at Colby. "If you want to save some money, I could do most of the work myself. Parts plus labor would cut the cost significantly. And Colby here is surprisingly handy with drywall."

"I am?" Colby asked.

"You are now," Dylan said cheerfully. "We did your kitchen renovation, remember? You know how to handle tools."

Harper looked between them, something like hope flickering across her face before she controlled it. "You'd do that? Work on the building?"

"Sure," Dylan said. "I like Stella's post office. Would hate to see it turn into condos." He said it lightly, but the message was clear: he was team Save the Post Office.

"I haven't decided what I'm doing yet," Harper reminded them, but her tone was less defensive than it had been.

"I know." Dylan started packing up his tools. "But if you do decide to keep it, the offer stands. Think about it." He headed for the door, then paused. "Colby, you staying? I can get started on the estimate back at the shop."

"I'll stay," Colby said, perhaps too quickly. "Harper needs help with the mail sorting system. I promised I'd show her the detailed process."

Dylan's grin was absolutely shameless. "Right. The sorting system. Very important." He tipped an imaginary hat at Harper. "Nice meeting you. I'll email the formal estimate by Monday."

After Dylan left, the post office felt quieter. More intimate. Colby could hear the space heater humming, the distant sound of traffic on Main Street, Harper's slightly uneven breathing that suggested she was more stressed than she wanted to admit.

"You okay?" Colby asked.

Harper set down her pen and rubbed her temples. "Twenty-five thousand dollars. That's... a lot."

"Dylan will find ways to bring it down. He's good at creative problem-solving."

"That's not the point." Harper looked around the post office, her expression troubled. "Even with discounts, even with all the goodwill in the world, this place needs money I don't have. And time I don't have. And expertise I definitely don't have."

"But you have people who want to help," Colby said quietly. "That counts for something."

Harper met his gaze, and Colby saw vulnerability there, the kind that made him want to promise things he had no business promising. That they'd figure it out. That she didn't have to do this alone. That Willow Creek would take care of its own, even if she'd been gone for eleven years.

"Come on," Colby said, breaking the moment before he said something stupid. "Let me show you the sorting system properly. Clara gave you the basics, but there are shortcuts that'll save you time."

Harper followed him to the sorting table, and Colby launched into an explanation of the route patterns, the timing of deliveries, the quirks of different neighborhoods. Harper listened with the focused attention he was starting to recognize as her default mode, absorbing information, cataloging it, filing it away for future use.

"Okay, try this one," Colby said, handing her an envelope. "Where does it go?"

Harper studied the address. "Sullivan family, Oak Street. That's... residential route?"

"Right. Which slot?"

She reached for the correct divider, and her hand brushed against Colby's. The contact was brief, accidental, but Colby felt it like an electric shock. Harper froze, her hazel eyes darting to his, and for a suspended moment they just stood there, hands touching, close enough that Colby could count the freckles across her nose.

Harper pulled back first, tucking a stray piece of hair behind her ear with fingers that trembled slightly. "Sorry. I'm...sorry."

"Don't be." Colby's voice came out rougher than intended. He cleared his throat. "You're doing great. Really."

They worked in silence for a few minutes, sorting through sample mail, but the air between them felt charged. Every time Harper reached for a slot, Colby was hyperaware of where her hands were. Every time she leaned close to read an address, he caught the scent of her shampoo, something floral and light that definitely didn't belong in a post office but somehow fit perfectly.

"Why did you quit?" Colby asked abruptly. "Your job in Chicago. You mentioned it yesterday, but you didn't say why."

Harper's hands stilled on an envelope. For a moment, Colby thought she wouldn't answer. Then she set down the mail and leaned against the table, her arms crossed in that defensive posture he was learning meant she was about to be vulnerable.

"I spent five years building someone else's dreams," she said quietly. "Working eighty-hour weeks to make campaigns successful for products I didn't care about, for bosses who took credit for my work. I told myself it was worth it because I was climbing the ladder, making good money, becoming someone important." She laughed, but there was no humor in it. "And then my grandmother died, and I realized I'd spent five years becoming someone I didn't even like. Someone who was too busy to visit the one person who loved me unconditionally. Someone who thought PowerPoint presentations mattered more than showing up."

Colby wanted to reach for her, to offer comfort, but he kept his hands still. "You were building a career. There's nothing wrong with that."

"There is when you lose yourself in the process." Harper

looked at him, her eyes bright with unshed tears. "I became the kind of person who doesn't go home for holidays. Who sends impersonal birthday texts instead of calling. Who prioritizes client meetings over family. And I didn't even realize it until it was too late to fix it."

"You're here now," Colby said. "That's something."

"Is it?" Harper's voice cracked. "Stella's gone. I can't apologize to her. I can't tell her I'm sorry for all the times I chose work over her, or explain why I stopped visiting, or..." She stopped, pressing her hand to her mouth. "I can't fix it."

"No," Colby agreed. "But you can honor her. You can make decisions that Stella would be proud of. You can be the person you want to be going forward, even if you can't change the past."

Harper wiped at her eyes with the back of her hand, smudging the dust on her cheek further. "How did you get so wise?"

"I'm not wise. I'm just someone who spent three years punishing himself for letting Amanda leave." Colby found himself sharing more than he'd intended. "My ex-fiancée. She got a job offer in Seattle, and she wanted me to go with her. Leave Willow Creek, leave my route, leave everything I'd built here."

"And you said no?" Harper asked softly.

"I said I needed time to think about it. Which was code for 'no, but I don't want to admit it.'" Colby picked up an envelope, turning it over in his hands. "She left anyway. Told me she couldn't be with someone who'd choose a small town over her. And for a long time, I thought she was right. That I was selfish for not being willing to give up everything for love."

"But you weren't," Harper said, understanding in her eyes. "You were being honest about what mattered to you."

"Yeah. Took me three years to figure that out, though." Colby set down the envelope and looked at Harper directly. "My point is, we all have things we regret. Choices we wish we could take back. But beating yourself up about them doesn't change anything. The only thing you can control is what you do next."

Harper held his gaze, and Colby saw something shift in her expression, recognition, maybe, or gratitude, or something else he didn't want to name. She took a step closer, and Colby's heart started beating faster.

"Thank you," she said quietly. "For understanding. For not making me feel like an idiot for running away from my life."

"You didn't run away. You ran toward something." Colby's voice dropped lower. "That takes courage."

Harper was close now, close enough that Colby could see the gold flecks in her hazel eyes, close enough that if he just leaned forward a few inches...

The door burst open with a cheerful jingle, and they both jumped apart like guilty teenagers.

Maggie Chen stood in the doorway with a covered dish, her warm brown eyes twinkling with knowledge that Colby really wished she didn't have. "Morning! I brought lunch.

Figured you two might be hungry after all that assessment work with Dylan." Her gaze flicked between them, noting the flushed cheeks and guilty expressions with obvious amusement. "I'm not interrupting anything, am I?"

"No," Colby said at the same time Harper said, "Nothing."

"Mm-hmm." Maggie's smile widened. "Well, I'll just set this in the back. Chicken soup and fresh bread. You both look like you could use it." She disappeared into the back room, humming cheerfully.

Colby and Harper stood in awkward silence, not quite looking at each other. The moment was broken, the almost-kiss that hadn't quite happened hanging between them like a question neither of them knew how to answer.

"I should..." Colby gestured vaguely toward the door.

"Right. Yeah." Harper tucked hair behind her ear again, a nervous gesture he was starting to find endearing. "Thanks for the help. With the sorting."

"Anytime." Colby grabbed his jacket from the chair where he'd left it. "I'll see you Monday? When we talk to Nora?"

"Monday," Harper confirmed. "I'll be ready."

Colby headed for the door, hyper-aware of Maggie still bustling in the back room and probably hearing every word. At the threshold, he turned back.

Harper was watching him, her arms wrapped around

herself again, but she was smiling. Small and uncertain, but genuine.

"Harper?" Colby said.

"Yeah?"

"For what it's worth, I think Stella would be proud of you. Coming back, trying to figure things out, wanting to deliver those letters. That's exactly the kind of thing she would have done."

Harper's smile widened, reaching her eyes. "Thanks, Colby."

He nodded and left before he could do something stupid like cross back to her and finish what they'd almost started.

Outside, the November air was cold and sharp, clearing his head. Colby climbed into his truck and sat there for a moment, hands on the steering wheel, trying to process what had just almost happened.

He'd almost kissed Harper Delaney. Would have kissed her, if Maggie hadn't interrupted. And the terrifying part wasn't that he'd almost done it, it was that he wanted to go back in there and try again.

This was a problem. A serious problem. Harper had been clear that she was only in town for three weeks, that she was still figuring things out, that her life was in chaos. Getting involved with her was asking for heartbreak, the kind he'd spent three years recovering from last time.

But sitting there in his truck, remembering the way Harper

had looked at him, the vulnerability in her eyes, the almost-moment that had felt like possibility, Colby couldn't quite convince himself to stay away.

Three weeks. She had three weeks to decide about the post office.

Three weeks for Colby to figure out if he was brave enough to risk his heart again.

Through the post office window, he could see Harper and Maggie in the back room, probably discussing him with the kind of gleeful detail that made small-town gossip both horrible and comforting. Harper was laughing at something Maggie said, her whole face lighting up.

Colby started his truck and pulled out of the parking lot, but he was smiling despite himself.

This was definitely a problem.

But maybe, just maybe, it was the kind of problem worth having.

CHAPTER SEVEN

Harper had never been particularly good at making friends. In college, she'd been too focused on grades. In Chicago, she'd been too busy climbing the corporate ladder. Friendship required time and vulnerability, two things Harper had spent most of her adult life avoiding.

Which was why, on Sunday afternoon, she found herself standing outside the Willow Creek Public Library, trying to convince herself that asking a complete stranger for help was a perfectly normal thing to do.

The library was housed in a beautiful stone building that looked like it had been transplanted from a New England postcard, ivy climbing the walls, stone steps worn smooth by a century of footsteps, tall windows that promised the kind of natural light libraries in modern buildings could never quite replicate. Harper had spent countless summer afternoons here as a kid, hiding in the stacks with mystery novels while Stella worked at the post office next door.

She'd forgotten how much she'd loved this place.

Harper climbed the steps and pulled open the heavy wooden door. The scent hit her immediately, old books, floor polish, and that indefinable smell that seemed to exist only in libraries, part dust and part magic. The main room was exactly as she remembered: high ceilings, rows of dark wood shelves, reading nooks tucked into corners with overstuffed chairs that had probably been there since 1950.

The circulation desk sat near the entrance, currently occupied by a young woman with black curly hair piled into a messy bun on top of her head. She wore a cardigan covered in embroidered flowers over a bright yellow dress, and her dark brown eyes lit up when she saw Harper.

"Hi! Welcome to the library. Are you looking for anything specific, or just browsing?" Her voice was cheerful, the kind of genuine warmth that couldn't be faked.

"Actually, I was hoping for some help with research," Harper said, approaching the desk. "I'm trying to find information about someone who lived here in the early seventies. I wasn't sure where to start."

The woman's face brightened even more, if that was possible. "Oh, I love research projects! I'm Quinn Torres, head librarian and resident local history nerd. What's your timeline and what do you know so far?"

Harper felt herself relax slightly. Quinn had the kind of energy that made you feel like you'd been friends for years, even though they'd just met. "I'm Harper Delaney. Stella's granddaughter."

Quinn's expression shifted immediately to sympathy. "Oh my god, Harper. I'm so sorry about Stella. She was one of my favorite patrons. Always checking out romance novels and historical fiction." She came around the desk, gesturing for Harper to follow. "Come on, let's sit in the research area. It's more comfortable, and we can spread out."

Harper followed Quinn to a section of the library that had clearly been set up for serious research, large tables, good lighting, and shelves of reference materials within easy reach. Quinn pulled out a chair and settled into it with the ease of someone who spent most of her life in this building.

"So," Quinn said, pulling a notepad from seemingly nowhere. "Who are we looking for?"

Harper hesitated, then decided there was no point in being coy. If she was going to ask for help, she might as well be honest. "Someone named Jamie. First name only, unfortunately. He lived in Willow Creek in 1973, was in his early twenties, and left to go to veterinary school in California. He was in love with Nora Whitfield."

Quinn's pen froze mid-note. "Nora Whitfield? My old English teacher Nora Whitfield?"

"You know her?"

"Everyone knows Ms. Whitfield. She taught at the high school for like forty years before retiring." Quinn's eyes widened. "Wait, Ms. Whitfield had a boyfriend in the seventies?"

"Apparently. But they were separated by..." Harper paused, deciding how much to share. "Circumstances. I found letters he wrote to her. Love letters. They never made it to her, and I'm trying to figure out who he was so I can... I don't know. Set things right, maybe."

Quinn set down her pen and leaned forward, her dark eyes shining with interest. "That is the most romantic thing I've ever heard. You're like a postal Cupid, delivering love fifty years late. I'm obsessed. Tell me everything."

Something in Quinn's enthusiasm made Harper smile, a real smile, the kind that felt rusty from disuse. Before she knew it, she was telling Quinn the whole story: finding the letters, reading Jamie's heartbreak, the mystery of why they'd been returned, Nora's existence in Willow Creek, the plan to visit her tomorrow.

Quinn listened with rapt attention, occasionally interjecting with questions or gasps of sympathy. When Harper finished, Quinn sat back in her chair with a dreamy expression.

"This is incredible. It's like a real-life romance novel. The lost letters, the decades of separation, the mystery..." She grabbed Harper's hand. "We have to find Jamie. We have to reunite them. This is my new life's mission."

Harper laughed, caught off guard by the declaration. "I appreciate the enthusiasm, but I have no idea where to start. All I know is his first name and that he went to veterinary school in California in 1973."

"That's more than you think." Quinn stood, already moving toward the reference section with purpose. "Come on. Let's see what we can dig up."

For the next two hours, Harper and Quinn worked

together like they'd been doing this for years. Quinn pulled out yearbooks from the early seventies, local newspaper archives, city directories. They made lists of every Jamie, James, or Jacob who would have been the right age in 1973, cross-referencing against veterinary school enrollment records that Quinn somehow managed to access through the library's database.

It was tedious work, but Quinn made it fun, providing running commentary, making wild theories about what might have happened, and periodically declaring that they were definitely going to reunite a lost love if it was the last thing she did.

"Okay, so we've got three strong possibilities," Quinn said, tapping her notes with a pen decorated with tiny cats. "James Whitfield...wait, Whitfield? Like Nora?"

"Could be a relative," Harper said. "Maybe that's why the relationship was complicated."

"Ooh, forbidden love between relatives. Very Gothic romance." Quinn made another note. "Then we have James Mitchell, who graduated from Willow Creek High in 1971 and according to this newspaper clipping, won a scholarship for pre-veterinary studies. And James Parker, who worked at his father's hardware store before leaving for college."

Harper felt a flutter of excitement. "Parker? As in Parker's Hardware?"

"The very same. Dylan Parker's family has owned that store since forever." Quinn's eyes gleamed. "And you know who's best friends with Dylan Parker?"

"Colby Hayes," Harper said slowly, understanding

dawning.

"Exactly!" Quinn grinned. "Which means your hottie mail carrier can probably help us narrow down the search."

Harper felt her cheeks heat. "He's not my hottie anything."

"Please. Maggie told me all about how he's been at the post office every day since you arrived. And Dylan said Colby volunteered to help with renovations, which is very unlike our boy Colby, who usually avoids construction projects like the plague." Quinn's grin widened. "Face it, Harper. He's into you."

"He's being helpful," Harper protested. "He cares about the post office."

"Mm-hmm. And I'm sure that's the only reason he brought you coffee yesterday morning. And stayed to help with sorting for three hours. And looked at you like you hung the moon when you weren't looking."

Harper's face was definitely red now. "You weren't even there. How do you know any of this?"

"Small town, remember? Also, Maggie is very observant and loves to share." Quinn leaned forward conspiratorially. "So? Are you interested?"

"I..." Harper stopped, unsure how to answer. Was she interested in Colby? Yesterday's almost-kiss had certainly suggested something was happening. The way her heart sped up when he was around suggested it too. But admitting it felt dangerous, like opening a door she wasn't sure she could close again. "It doesn't matter. I'm only here for three weeks."

"That's not a no," Quinn observed. "And three weeks is plenty of time to fall in love. Some people know in three days. My parents knew in three hours."

"I'm not falling in love," Harper said firmly. "I'm figuring out what to do with a post office I inherited and trying to deliver letters to a woman who's been waiting fifty years for them. Romance is not on my agenda."

"Romance is never on anyone's agenda," Quinn said wisely. "That's what makes it romance instead of a business plan." She tapped her pen against her notes. "But fine, we'll table the Colby discussion for now. Back to the mystery. I think James Mitchell is our best bet. The scholarship for pre-vet studies, the right age, the timing all works."

Harper pulled the 1971 yearbook closer, flipping to the senior class photos. There...James Mitchell, with kind brown eyes and a gentle smile. The caption read: *James "Jamie" Mitchell, Future Veterinarian, Drama Club, 4-H.*

"Jamie," Harper breathed. "It's really him."

Quinn squeezed her shoulder. "We found him. Now we just need to figure out where he is now."

They spent another hour trying to track James Mitchell's current location, but the trail went cold after he graduated from veterinary school in 1978. No social media presence, no recent news articles, no obvious forwarding addresses. It was like he'd vanished into thin air, or simply lived a quiet life that didn't generate much digital footprint.

"Don't worry," Quinn said as they packed up their research. "We'll find him. I have connections at the California veterinary association. I'll make some calls tomorrow." She paused. "You're still visiting Ms. Whitfield tomorrow, right?"

"That's the plan. Colby's going with me for moral support."

"Of course he is." Quinn's grin was shameless. "Make sure to wear something cute."

"It's not like that," Harper protested.

"Sure, it's not." Quinn handed Harper a business card with the library's information. "Here's my number. Text me after you talk to Ms. Whitfield. I want to know everything."

Harper took the card, feeling something warm settle in her chest. "Thanks for helping today. You didn't have to spend your Sunday afternoon researching with a stranger."

"You're not a stranger. You're Stella's granddaughter, which basically makes you Willow Creek royalty." Quinn's expression softened. "Plus, I like you. You're real in a way that's hard to find. No pretense, no small-town judgment about the girl who left and came back. Just... real."

Harper felt her throat tighten unexpectedly. "I like you too."

"Good. Because you're stuck with me now." Quinn pulled Harper into a quick hug that smelled like vanilla and books. "I'm claiming you as my new friend, and I'm very possessive of my friends. Fair warning."

Harper hugged back, surprised by how much she needed exactly this, someone who expected nothing from her except honesty, someone who was enthusiastic instead of judgmental, someone who saw a mystery and wanted to solve it instead of questioning whether it was worth solving.

"Deal," Harper said.

They left the library together, stepping out into the late afternoon cold. The sun was already setting, November days were short this far north and Main Street was quiet, most shops closed for Sunday.

"So," Quinn said as they paused on the library steps. "What are you doing for dinner? Because if you say eating takeout alone at the post office, I'm dragging you to my place for pasta and wine."

Harper started to decline automatically, she had work to do, mail to sort, decisions to make, but then she stopped. What was she really going to do? Sit alone in the post office, staring at Stella's belongings and drowning in guilt? Or spend an evening with someone who seemed determined to be her friend?

"Pasta and wine sounds great," Harper heard herself say.

Quinn's face lit up. "Perfect! My apartment's right above the flower shop. Come on, I'll show you the most amazing painting I just finished. It's a series of vintage stamps reimagined as abstract art. Very meta for a librarian, I know, but I contain multitudes."

As Harper followed Quinn down Main Street, listening to her new friend chatter about art and books and the best places to eat in Willow Creek, she felt something she hadn't felt in years: the simple joy of connection. Not networking, not social climbing, not carefully curated professional relationships designed to advance her career. Just... friendship.

Quinn's apartment was exactly what Harper would have imagined—eclectic, colorful, covered in books and paintings and quirky decorative objects that all somehow worked together. Quinn put on music, poured generous glasses of red wine, and proceeded to tell Harper stories about growing up in Willow Creek while she cooked.

"So, then Mrs. Patterson's cat got stuck in the tree, again, and Sheriff Mitchell had to call the fire department. But the fire department was dealing with the Johnson barn incident, so it was just Colby who happened to be delivering mail and had a ladder in his truck." Quinn stirred the pasta sauce with theatrical gestures. "He climbed up, got the cat, and Mrs. Patterson declared him her hero. She still gives him homemade cookies every Christmas."

Harper laughed, taking a sip of wine. "That sounds very Colby."

"Right? He's like terminally helpful. It's both his best and most frustrating quality." Quinn shot Harper a sly look. "Also, he's been single for three years. Just throwing that out there."

"I thought we were tabling the Colby discussion."

"That was hours ago. The table has been un-tabled." Quinn drained the pasta and started plating. "Look, I'm just saying, if you're interested, the man is interested. And you deserve something good after quitting your terrible job and dealing with all this inheritance stress and trying to deliver decades-old love letters."

Harper accepted the plate Quinn handed her, the pasta fragrant with garlic and herbs. "I don't know if I'm ready for something good. I'm still figuring out what I'm doing with my life."

"Those two things aren't mutually exclusive." Quinn settled onto the couch, tucking her legs under her. "You can figure out your life and be open to connection at the same time. In fact, sometimes connection helps you figure out your life."

Harper thought about yesterday, standing close to Colby at the sorting table, feeling that electric moment when their hands brushed, the almost-kiss that had left her breathless and confused and wanting. She thought about how he'd shared his story about Amanda, how he'd understood her guilt about Stella without making her feel weak for it.

"Okay, fine," Harper admitted. "He's attractive. And kind. And I may have thought about kissing him. Multiple times."

Quinn literally squealed, nearly dropping her wine glass. "I knew it! This is perfect. You're perfect together. Small-town mail carrier and reformed city girl, bonding over lost love letters while renovating a historic post office. It's like a Hallmark movie, but better because it's real."

"We almost kissed yesterday," Harper confessed, the wine loosening her tongue. "And then Maggie walked in."

"Of course she did." Quinn shook her head. "Maggie has the worst timing and the best timing simultaneously. She definitely knew what she was doing."

"We're visiting Nora together tomorrow. To show her the letters."

"That's so romantic!" Quinn bounced slightly on the couch. "You're literally delivering love together. If that's not a sign from the universe, I don't know what is."

Harper couldn't help but smile at Quinn's enthusiasm. "You're very invested in this."

"I'm a librarian and an artist. Romance is literally part of my job description. Plus, Colby's my friend, and he's been sad for way too long. And you seem like you could use someone who looks at you the way he does, like you're interesting and complicated and worth figuring out."

"How does he look at me?" Harper asked before she could stop herself.

Quinn's expression softened. "Like you matter. Like he wants to know all your stories. Like he's trying really hard not to fall for you and failing spectacularly."

Harper set down her wine glass, feeling something flutter in her chest that might have been hope or fear or both. "I'm only here for three weeks. Maybe less, if I decide to sell the post office."

"Are you going to sell it?"

Harper thought about the question she'd been avoiding for days. "I don't know. It needs so much work. It barely makes money. And I don't know anything about running a post office."

"But?" Quinn prompted gently.

"But every time I think about selling it, I remember reading Jamie's letters. I remember Clara explaining how Stella paid attention to everyone's lives. I remember Colby telling me the post office is about connection, not just mail." Harper stared at her wine glass. "And I wonder if maybe there's something here worth keeping. Not just the building, the whole thing. The purpose."

Quinn reached over and squeezed Harper's hand. "That's not nothing, Harper. That's actually everything."

They talked late into the evening, about art and books, about Quinn's dreams of having her own gallery someday, about Harper's realization that five years of marketing had taught her more about manipulation than connection. Quinn told stories about Willow Creek with the affection of someone who'd lived her whole life in a place she genuinely loved, and Harper found herself seeing the town differently through Quinn's eyes.

When Harper finally left Quinn's apartment around ten, stepping out into the cold November night, she felt lighter than she had in weeks. Maybe months. She had a friend, a real friend who wasn't a work contact or a strategic networking opportunity. She had a plan for tomorrow. She had leads on Jamie Mitchell. She had a purpose, even if it was temporary.

And maybe, just maybe, she had the beginning of something else. Something that involved a blue-eyed mail carrier who made her laugh and listened when she needed to talk and looked at her like she mattered.

Harper walked back to the post office slowly, taking in Main Street at night. Most of the shops were dark, but a few had left their window displays lit, the flower shop with its arrangements, the bookstore with its featured new releases, The Copper Kettle with its cozy interior visible through large windows. Everything looked peaceful, settled, like a town that knew exactly what it was and had no desire to be anything else.

At the post office, Harper let herself in and locked the door behind her. The building was dark except for the security light in the back room, casting long shadows across the mail sorting table. Tomorrow, she'd visit Nora Whitfield. Tomorrow, she'd start the process of delivering letters that had waited fifty years for their destination.

But tonight, Harper allowed herself a moment of hope. Hope that some love stories did get their happy endings, even if they took five decades to arrive. Hope that maybe she was exactly where she was supposed to be. Hope that three weeks might be enough time to figure out who she wanted to become, even if it wasn't enough time for everything else her heart was starting to want.

Harper climbed the stairs to Stella's apartment above the post office, her apartment now, she supposed, and got ready for bed. As she drifted off to sleep, she thought about tomorrow. About Nora's face when she saw the letters. About Colby standing beside her, offering support.

About the possibility that delivering someone else's love story might help her understand what she wanted for her own.

CHAPTER EIGHT

S unday evening found Colby at his mother's bakery, ostensibly helping with prep work for Monday morning but really just avoiding his own apartment and the thoughts that seemed to chase him there. He'd spent most of the day finishing his route, running errands, and absolutely not thinking about Harper Delaney standing close enough for him to count her freckles.

He was failing spectacularly at the not-thinking part.

The bakery kitchen smelled like cinnamon and vanilla, warm and comforting in the way only his mother's baking could be. Rosie Hayes moved through the space with the efficiency of someone who'd been doing this for forty years, measuring flour with practiced precision while Colby chopped apples for tomorrow's turnovers.

"So," his mother said casually, not looking up from her mixing bowl. "Harper Delaney."

Colby's knife slipped slightly. "What about her?"

"You've mentioned her approximately seventeen times since you got here an hour ago." Rosie glanced over with those warm blue eyes that missed absolutely nothing. "Harper said this. Harper's trying to figure out that. Harper needs help with the other thing." She smiled. "It's nice to hear you talk about someone with actual interest for the first time in three years."

"I'm being helpful," Colby said, focusing very intently on the apples. "She's new in town, trying to deal with an inherited post office, grieving her grandmother. Someone needs to help her."

"Mm-hmm. And the fact that she's beautiful has nothing to do with your sudden dedication to postal education?"

Colby set down the knife. "Did Dylan tell you about yesterday?"

"Dylan didn't have to tell me anything. Maggie saw the way you two looked at each other before she interrupted." Rosie's smile widened. "You should have seen her face when she came into the café this morning. Pure delight. Said you two were about to kiss and she felt like a chaperone at a middle school dance."

"We weren't..." Colby stopped. They had been about to kiss. Would have kissed, if Maggie hadn't arrived with perfect terrible timing. "It's complicated."

"Love usually is." Rosie started measuring sugar, her movements methodical and soothing. "But that doesn't mean it's not worth pursuing."

"It's not love," Colby protested. "I've known her for less than a week."

"Your father knew he loved me after three days." Rosie's expression softened with memory. "Said he saw me at The Copper Kettle, pouring coffee and laughing at something Mrs. Patterson said, and he just knew. Walked right up and asked me to dinner. I said no."

This was a story Colby had heard before, but he let his mother tell it anyway. She needed the telling as much as he needed the hearing, a reminder that good love stories existed, even when your own felt broken.

"He asked me every day for two weeks," Rosie continued. "And every day I said no, because I was scared. Scared of getting hurt, scared of trusting someone, scared that if I let him in, he'd eventually leave. And then one day, he showed up with flowers he'd picked from Mrs. Rodriguez's garden, with permission, mind you, and he said, 'Rosie, I can't promise I won't hurt you sometimes, because we're human and humans hurt each other. But I can promise I'll never leave. I can promise I'll choose you every single day. Is that enough?'" She paused, wiping at her eyes with the back of her flour-dusted hand. "And I realized that being scared of getting hurt was keeping me from something beautiful. So I said yes."

Colby's chest felt tight. His father had died four years ago, heart attack, sudden and devastating, but he'd kept his promise. Forty years of marriage, forty years of choosing Rosie every single day.

"Harper's only here for three weeks," Colby said quietly. "Maybe less. She hasn't decided if she's keeping the post office or selling it. And even if she stays, she's made it clear she's still figuring her life out. Getting involved with her would be asking for heartbreak."

"Or it would be giving yourself a chance at happiness." Rosie set down her measuring cup and turned to face Colby fully. "Baby, I know Amanda hurt you. I know she made you feel like you weren't enough, like choosing Willow Creek meant choosing against her. But Harper isn't Amanda."

Colby flinched at his ex-fiancée's name. Three years, and it still stung. "How do you know? She's from the city, she has a career somewhere else, she's only here because she inherited a building. That sounds pretty similar to Amanda to me."

"Amanda left because she wanted something you couldn't give her, a different life, in a different place, with different priorities." Rosie's voice was gentle but firm. "She made you feel like you had to choose between loving her and being yourself. That was never a choice you should have had to make." She moved closer, resting her flour-dusted hand on Colby's shoulder. "Harper came back. She could have handled everything through a lawyer and never set foot in Willow Creek, but she came back. She's trying to understand what Stella built, trying to deliver those letters to Nora, trying to figure out if this town has a place for her. That's not someone who's already decided to leave. That's someone who's trying to decide if she can stay."

Colby wanted to believe that. Wanted to believe that the way Harper looked at him meant something, that the almost-kiss had been the beginning of something instead of just a moment that would dissolve into regret. But believing it meant risking everything again, risking his heart, his carefully rebuilt defenses, the comfortable safety of staying alone.

"I don't know if I can do it again," Colby admitted, the words coming out raw. "Amanda leaving nearly broke me, Ma. For months after, I kept expecting to see her everywhere. I'd smell her perfume on someone passing by and my heart would just..." He stopped, pressing the heel of his hand against his chest. "I spent a year being angry, another year being sad, and the last year trying to convince myself I was fine alone. And now Harper shows up, and I feel like I'm sixteen again, nervous and hopeful and terrified all at once. What if I let myself feel something and she leaves? What if I'm just setting myself up for the same thing all over again?"

Rosie pulled him into a hug, the kind of hug only mothers can give, all-encompassing and unconditionally loving. Colby let himself lean into it, breathing in the familiar scent of vanilla and home.

"You can't live your life protecting yourself from pain, sweetheart," Rosie said against his shoulder. "Because when you do that, you're also protecting yourself from joy. And I didn't raise you to play it safe. I raised you to be brave."

"I don't feel brave," Colby muttered.

"Brave people never do. That's what makes them brave." Rosie pulled back, holding Colby's face between her hands the way she used to when he was small. "I've watched you these past few days. You're different when you talk about Harper. Lighter. More like yourself than you've been in years. And maybe it won't work out, maybe she'll decide to leave, or maybe you'll decide you're not right for each other. But maybe she'll stay. Maybe you'll build something wonderful together. And you'll never know unless you try."

Colby thought about Harper in the post office, dust on her cheek and determination in her eyes. Harper reading Jamie's letters with tears streaming down her face. Harper standing close enough to kiss, looking at him like he might be worth the risk. Harper admitting she'd quit her job and didn't know what came next, but was here anyway, trying.

"She's complicated," Colby said.

"Good. You deserve complicated." Rosie smiled. "Simple is boring, and you've never been interested in boring."

"She might leave."

"She might stay. And the only way to find out is to give her a reason to." Rosie released his face and returned to her mixing, but her voice remained warm. "You know what I think? I think Harper Delaney came to Willow Creek looking for something, even if she doesn't know what yet. Maybe it's a place to belong. Maybe it's a purpose. Maybe it's a person who looks at her the way you do, like she's worth figuring out, even when she's messy and uncertain."

"How do I look at her?" Colby asked, echoing Harper's question to Quinn that he'd never heard.

Rosie's smile turned knowing. "Like she's the best part of your day. Like you want to know all her stories. Like you're trying not to fall in love with her and losing that battle completely."

Colby leaned against the counter, feeling something shift

in his chest, a loosening of the tight grip he'd kept on his heart for three years. "We're visiting Nora Whitfield tomorrow. To give her the letters."

"I heard. The whole town's heard." Rosie's eyes sparkled. "Maggie says it's the most romantic thing she's seen in forty years. Delivering fifty-year-old love letters to their intended recipient. Like something out of a movie."

"It was Harper's idea. She's determined to make it right."

"Of course she is. She's Stella's granddaughter." Rosie started folding the dough with practiced movements. "Stella never gave up on people. Never stopped believing that connection mattered more than convenience. Harper has that same quality, you can see it in how she's trying to understand the post office instead of just selling it to the highest bidder. She cares, even when she's trying to convince herself she doesn't."

Colby thought about Victor Brennan and his aggressive interest in the property. Thought about the twenty-five thousand dollars in repairs the building needed. Thought about how easy it would be for Harper to accept an offer, take the money, and go back to whatever life she'd built in Chicago.

And then he thought about the way she'd looked at those letters. The way she'd said, "Someone deserves to get the letters that were meant for them, even if it's fifty years too late."

"I want to do something," Colby said suddenly. "For her. To show her that..." He trailed off, unsure how to finish.

"That you care?" Rosie supplied gently. "That she matters to you? That you're willing to take a chance even though it scares you?"

"All of that," Colby admitted.

Rosie studied him for a moment, then smiled. "Bring her breakfast tomorrow. Before you go to see Nora. Something simple, coffee, pastries, maybe those lemon scones she mentioned liking when she was here with Clara last week."

"She mentioned lemon scones?"

"She mentioned a lot of things. I pay attention." Rosie's expression softened. "Baby, here's what I know: Harper Delaney is grieving, overwhelmed, trying to figure out where she fits in a world that suddenly looks nothing like she planned. What she needs right now isn't grand gestures or declarations. She needs someone who shows up. Someone who pays attention to the small things, like which pastries she likes. Someone who supports her without asking for anything in return. Someone who makes her feel like she's not facing everything alone."

"I can do that," Colby said.

"I know you can. That's who you are." Rosie reached over and patted his cheek. "You're a good man, Colby. You're patient and kind and you notice things most people miss. Those are the exact qualities someone like Harper needs right now. Don't hide those qualities because you're scared of getting hurt. Use them. Show her what it looks like when someone chooses to show up."

Colby felt his resolve solidify. "Okay. I'll bring her breakfast tomorrow."

"And maybe tell her how you feel?" Rosie suggested hopefully.

"Let's not get ahead of ourselves."

"Fine. Baby steps." Rosie's smile was both fond and exasperated. "But Colby? Don't wait too long. Three weeks isn't much time, and I'd hate to see you lose something good because you were too busy being cautious."

They worked in comfortable silence for a while, Colby finishing the apples while Rosie moved through the familiar choreography of baking. The kitchen was warm and smelled like everything good about home, and for the first time in days, Colby felt like he could breathe properly.

"Ma?" he said after a while.

"Hmm?"

"Thank you. For not letting me hide."

Rosie looked over at him with so much love it made his chest ache. "That's what mothers do, sweetheart. We see through the walls you build and we love you anyway. And sometimes, we give you a little push toward the things that scare you, because we know you're brave enough to face them."

"What if I'm not?" Colby asked quietly. "What if I try and it all falls apart?"

"Then you pick yourself up, and you remember that trying was still worth it. That the possibility of joy is always worth the risk of pain." Rosie wiped her hands on her apron and came to stand beside him. "Your father and I had forty good years together. But I'd take those forty years even knowing how they'd end, even knowing I'd spend the rest of my life missing him. Because the love was worth it. It's always worth it."

Colby pulled his mother into another hug, holding tight. "I miss him."

"I know, baby. I do too." Rosie's voice was thick with emotion. "But he'd want you to be happy. He'd want you to take chances and fall in love and build a life that feels full. He'd tell you that hiding from heartbreak is the same as hiding from happiness, and neither of us raised you to hide."

They stayed like that for a long moment, two people who'd lost someone irreplaceable but were still standing, still trying, still believing that good things could happen even after devastating loss.

When they finally separated, Rosie's eyes were bright with unshed tears, but she was smiling. "Now. Let's finish these turnovers so I can send you home with a dozen lemon scones for tomorrow morning. And maybe some of those chocolate croissants Harper mentioned liking. And coffee, I'll give you the good beans, the Ethiopian blend she said reminded her of Stella."

"You really do pay attention to everything," Colby marveled.

"Someone has to." Rosie's smile turned mischievous. "Besides, I'm invested now. I told Maggie you two would be dating by Thanksgiving. I have money on this."

"Ma!"

"What? I'm a businesswoman. I have to diversify my

income streams." Rosie laughed at his expression. "I'm teasing. Mostly. Now help me with these turnovers before you get all broody again. You have a girl to win over tomorrow, and you need your sleep."

Colby helped his mother finish the baking, feeling lighter than he had in years. Tomorrow, he'd bring Harper breakfast. Tomorrow, they'd visit Nora Whitfield together and deliver letters that had waited fifty years for their destination. Tomorrow, he'd show Harper, in small, quiet ways, that she didn't have to face any of this alone.

And maybe, if he was brave enough, he'd start to show her that Willow Creek wasn't just a town she was passing through. It was a place where she could belong. Where someone could see all her complications and uncertainties and still think she was worth choosing.

Where someone was already halfway to falling in love with her, even if he was still trying to convince himself he wasn't.

By the time Colby left the bakery, it was late, and Main Street was dark except for the streetlights casting their warm glow. He carried a box of pastries and a bag of coffee beans, both chosen specifically for Harper, both representing his mother's certainty that he was doing the right thing.

As he drove past the post office, Colby saw a light on in the second-floor window. Harper was still awake, probably working through mail or making lists or reading Jamie's letters again. He wanted to stop, to knock on the door, to tell her that she didn't have to carry everything alone.

But tomorrow would come soon enough. Tomorrow, he'd show up with breakfast and support and the kind of patience that said *I'm not going anywhere.*

Tomorrow, he'd start being brave.

Colby drove home, already counting down the hours until morning.

CHAPTER NINE

Monday morning arrived with frost on the windows and butterflies in Harper's stomach. She'd been awake since five, unable to sleep, rehearsing what she'd say to Nora Whitfield. *I found letters that were meant for you fifty years ago. The man who wrote them never forgot you. Your whole life might have been different if these had been delivered.*

No pressure or anything.

Harper was standing at the post office window, watching Main Street wake up, when she heard a knock at the door. Through the glass, she saw Colby holding a cardboard box and two paper cups that were definitely from his mother's bakery.

She opened the door, and the cold November air rushed in along with the scent of coffee and fresh pastries.

"Morning," Colby said, his breath clouding in the cold.

"I thought you might need breakfast before we..." He gestured vaguely, and Harper realized he was nervous too. "Before we visit Nora."

Harper felt something warm unfurl in her chest. "You didn't have to do that."

"I know." Colby stepped inside, setting the box on the counter. "But my mother insisted, and you don't argue with Rosie Hayes when she's on a mission." He pulled out pastries wrapped in wax paper. "Lemon scones, chocolate croissants, and Ethiopian coffee. She said those were your favorites."

Harper stared at the carefully chosen items, her throat suddenly tight. "She remembered that?"

"She remembers everything." Colby handed her one of the coffee cups. "It's her superpower. Also, her curse, according to my teenage years."

Harper took the coffee, holding the warmth between her hands. "Thank you. Really. I was too nervous to eat earlier, but this is..." She stopped, unsure how to finish. *Perfect? Thoughtful? Exactly what I needed without knowing I needed it?*

"It's breakfast," Colby said simply, but his eyes were soft. "You shouldn't face this on an empty stomach."

They ate standing at the counter, neither of them quite looking at each other, both of them hyperaware of the almost-kiss from Saturday that hung between them like a question. Harper bit into a lemon scone and nearly moaned, it was perfect, buttery and tart and exactly right.

"Your mother is a magician," Harper said.

"She's something," Colby agreed. "Probably why half the town is addicted to her cinnamon rolls." He paused, then added more quietly, "She's also convinced we're going to be dating by Thanksgiving. Just so you know. She may have mentioned it. Multiple times."

Harper nearly choked on her coffee. "Dating?"

"I told her it was complicated," Colby said quickly, his ears going slightly pink in that way Harper was starting to find adorable. "That you're only here for a few weeks, that you're dealing with a lot, that we barely know each other..."

"But?" Harper prompted, because there was clearly a but.

Colby met her gaze directly. "But she said that three weeks is plenty of time to know if something's worth pursuing. And that complicated is just another word for interesting." He took a breath. "And that I shouldn't let fear keep me from something that could be good."

Harper's heart was beating too fast. "Your mother is very wise."

"She really is." Colby's expression turned serious. "Harper, I know the timing is terrible. I know you're grieving and overwhelmed and trying to figure out your entire life. But I also know that I can't stop thinking about you, and I don't want to. And if that makes things more complicated, I'm sorry. But I think you should know."

Harper set down her coffee carefully, buying herself a moment to process. Colby was being honest, vulnerable and brave in a way she recognized cost him something. The least she could do was return the favor.

"I can't stop thinking about you either," she admitted. "Which is inconvenient, because you're right, the timing is terrible and I have no idea what I'm doing with my life. But every time you show up with coffee or offer to help or look at me like..." She stopped, feeling her cheeks heat.

"Like what?" Colby asked softly.

"Like I matter," Harper finished. "Like I'm not just some mess you're trying to clean up out of obligation to my grandmother."

Colby moved closer, and Harper's breath caught. "You're not a mess. You're someone dealing with an impossible situation and somehow still trying to do right by people you've never met. That's not mess. That's..." He paused, searching for the right word. "That's brave."

They stood there, close enough that Harper could see the flecks of darker blue in his gray eyes, close enough that if she just leaned forward a few inches...

Harper's phone alarm went off, shattering the moment. Nine o'clock. Time to visit Nora.

"Right," Harper said, stepping back and fumbling for her phone. "We should... Nora's expecting us at nine-thirty."

"Yeah." Colby looked like he wanted to say more, but he just nodded. "Let me grab the letters?"

Harper retrieved the bundle from where she'd left them in

Stella's locked drawer, tied with the faded blue ribbon. Looking at them now, she felt the weight of what they represented, fifty years of missed chances, of love that had waited patiently in darkness, of a story that deserved better than the ending it had gotten.

"Just one," Harper decided, carefully untying the ribbon and selecting the first letter Jamie had written. "I'll show her one letter first. If she wants to see the rest, we can bring them."

Colby nodded his approval. "Easier to process that way."

They drove to Nora Whitfield's house in Colby's truck, Harper clutching the single letter in her lap like it might dissolve if she held it too loosely. Colby filled the silence with small talk about the neighborhood they were passing through, clearly trying to ease Harper's nerves. It worked, mostly.

Nora's house was exactly as Quinn had described, a beautiful Victorian on Maple Street with a wraparound porch and gardens that, even in November, showed signs of meticulous care. The house was painted a soft dove gray with white trim, and smoke curled from the chimney, promising warmth inside.

"It's beautiful," Harper said.

"Nora's maintained it herself since her parents died," Colby said. "The whole town offered to help over the years, but she's proud. Independent." He paused. "This is going to break her heart, you know. Finding out what she missed."

"I know," Harper said quietly. "But wouldn't you want to know? If you'd spent fifty years wondering?"

"Yeah," Colby agreed. "I would."

They climbed the porch steps together, and Harper knocked before she could lose her nerve. The sound seemed too loud, too final, the knocking that would change everything for the woman on the other side of the door.

Footsteps approached, and then the door opened to reveal a woman who took Harper's breath away.

Nora Whitfield was eighty-one years old and absolutely stunning. Her white hair was styled in elegant waves that framed her face, and her blue eyes were sharp with intelligence. She wore a lavender cardigan over a white blouse, and vintage pearl earrings that probably dated back to the 1960s. Everything about her spoke of dignity, grace, and a life well-lived, but there was something in her eyes, some quality of sadness or longing, that suggested not everything had gone as planned.

"Miss Delaney?" Nora's voice was cultured, the kind that came from years of teaching literature to skeptical teenagers. "And Colby. What a pleasant surprise. Please, come in."

Harper and Colby entered a home that looked like it had been frozen in time, not in a dusty, neglected way, but in a carefully preserved way. Vintage furniture, shelves filled with books, photographs in ornate frames. Everything was immaculate, everything was beautiful, and everything felt just slightly too perfect, like a museum display of how life used to be.

"I made tea," Nora said, leading them into a sitting room with bay windows that overlooked the garden. "I hope you don't mind. I rarely have visitors on Monday mornings, and I confess I'm curious about why you wanted to see me."

Harper sat in the chair Nora indicated, a Victorian-era piece that was somehow both elegant and comfortable. Colby sat beside her on the loveseat, close enough that his presence was reassuring.

"Thank you for seeing us," Harper said, her rehearsed speech evaporating. "I... this is going to sound strange, but I found something at the post office. Something that belonged to you, I think."

Nora's expression shifted, becoming more alert. "Belonged to me?"

Harper pulled the envelope from her bag, holding it carefully. "Letters. From 1973. They were in my grandmother's desk, locked away. They're addressed to you, but they were marked 'Return to Sender.' I don't think they ever reached you."

Nora's face went very still. "Letters from 1973?"

"From someone named Jamie." Harper watched Nora's face carefully. "Do you... did you know a Jamie?"

The teacup in Nora's hand began to tremble. She set it down with a soft clink, her eyes fixed on the envelope Harper held. "May I see it?"

Harper handed over the letter, and Nora took it with shaking fingers. She stared at the envelope for a long moment, not opening it, just tracing the handwriting with one fingertip.

"I know this hand," Nora whispered. "I know every loop, every slant." She looked up at Harper, her blue eyes suddenly bright with unshed tears. "Where did you get this?"

"In my grandmother's desk. There are more, twenty-five letters total, all from 1973 and 1974. All marked 'Return to Sender,' but the address is correct. Someone sent them back deliberately."

Nora's hands were shaking so badly she almost dropped the envelope. "James Mitchell," she said, her voice breaking on the name. "Jamie. He... these are from Jamie?"

"You knew him," Harper said gently.

"Knew him?" Nora let out a sound between a laugh and a sob. "I loved him. He was my whole world." She pressed the unopened letter to her chest. "He left for veterinary school in California in May of 1973. We were going to write, going to make long distance work until he came back. But after a few months, the letters stopped coming. I waited and waited, and finally I called the school. They said he'd withdrawn, that he'd left California. I thought..." Her voice cracked. "I thought he'd met someone else. Thought he'd decided I wasn't worth the distance."

Harper felt tears sliding down her own cheeks. "He didn't stop writing. Someone sent the letters back. Someone made sure you never received them."

"Who?" Nora demanded, sudden fire in her eyes. "Who would do that?"

"I don't know," Harper admitted. "But these letters, they're love letters, Ms. Whitfield. Beautiful, heartbreaking love letters from someone who never stopped thinking about you."

Nora's hands trembled as she opened the envelope, pulling out the thin paper inside. Harper watched as Nora's eyes moved across Jamie's words, watched as tears began streaming down her elegant face, watched as fifty years of wondering and longing and grief converged into one devastating moment of understanding.

When Nora finished reading, she looked up at Harper with eyes that held decades of pain. "He loved me," she whispered. "All this time, he loved me."

"He did," Harper confirmed. "He wrote twenty-five letters over more than a year. He was heartbroken when you didn't respond. He thought you'd chosen not to answer."

"But I never received them," Nora said, her voice rising. "I never knew he was writing. I spent fifty years thinking he'd forgotten me, thinking I wasn't enough to keep him, and he was..." She pressed the letter to her chest again. "He was waiting to hear from me."

Colby leaned forward. "Ms. Whitfield, do you know why your family might have intercepted the letters?"

Nora's laugh was bitter. "My father. It had to be my father." She set down the letter carefully, as if it might break. "He never approved of Jamie. Said he was unsuitable, that veterinarians didn't make enough money, that I could do better. When Jamie left for California, my father was relieved. He probably saw the letters coming and..." She stopped, covering her mouth with one hand. "Oh God. My father stole fifty years from us. From both of us."

"I'm so sorry," Harper said, the words feeling inadequate.

"Don't apologize." Nora wiped at her tears with trembling fingers. "You brought me the truth. After all these years, you gave me the truth." She looked at Harper with sudden intensity. "Where is he? Jamie. Is he... is he still alive?"

"I don't know," Harper admitted. "We've been trying to find him. We know he graduated from veterinary school in 1978, but after that, the trail goes cold. No social media, no recent news articles. I'm sorry...I know that's not what you want to hear."

Nora stood abruptly, walking to the bay window and staring out at her garden. I never stopped thinking about Jamie. Never stopped wondering what might have been if he'd just written to me, if I'd just known he still wanted me."

"He wanted you," Harper said. "Every letter makes that clear."

Nora turned back, her face composed but her eyes still wet. "I need to see them. All of them. Every letter Jamie wrote."

"Of course." Harper stood. "I'll bring them this afternoon. All twenty-five."

"And you'll keep looking for him?" Nora asked, her voice desperate now. "Even if it's too late, even if fifty years is too long, I need to know. I need to tell him that I never stopped either. That I waited, even when I didn't know I was waiting."

"We'll find him," Colby promised. "I'll call every veterinary clinic in California if I have to. We'll find him, Ms. Whitfield."

Nora crossed the room and took Harper's hands in hers. Her grip was strong despite the trembling. "Thank you. You're Stella's granddaughter, of course you are. She would have done the same thing. She believed in love, in second chances, in delivering what needed to be delivered, no matter how long it took." Her voice caught. "Thank you for not giving up on us."

Harper hugged Nora impulsively, feeling the older woman cling to her like she was afraid to let go. When they separated, Nora was crying again, but she was smiling too, a fragile, hopeful smile that made Harper's heart ache.

"I'll bring the rest this afternoon," Harper repeated. "And I promise, we won't stop looking until we find him."

"Fifty years," Nora said, touching the letter again. "Fifty years I could have been with him. Fifty years stolen by fear and control and someone else's decision about what was best for me." She looked at Harper. "Don't let anyone steal your time, dear. If you love someone, fight for them. Don't let fear or propriety or other people's expectations keep you from something real."

Harper felt Colby's gaze on her, felt the weight of Nora's words settling over both of them. "I'll remember that."

They left Nora standing in her perfect Victorian sitting room, clutching a letter that had waited half a century to reach her, finally understanding why the man she loved had never come back.

In the truck, Harper let herself cry, for Nora, for Jamie, for fifty years of missed chances and stolen possibilities. Colby drove in silence, occasionally reaching over to squeeze Harper's hand, offering comfort without words.

"We have to find him," Harper said when she could speak again. "Even if he's remarried, even if it's too late, she deserves to tell him the truth. He deserves to know she never stopped loving him."

"We'll find him," Colby said with quiet certainty. "Quinn's already making calls to California veterinary boards. Dylan's checking alumni records. We'll find him, Harper."

Harper looked at Colby, patient, steady Colby who'd shown up with breakfast and held her hand and promised to help find a man he'd never met for a woman who'd waited fifty years for truth.

"Thank you," she said. "For coming with me. For... everything."

Colby pulled the truck to a stop in front of the post office and turned to face her fully. "Harper, I need you to understand something. I'm not doing this out of obligation to Stella, or because I feel sorry for you, or because I'm trying to save the post office." He reached over and tucked a strand of her auburn hair behind her ear, his fingers lingering. "I'm doing this because I care about you. Because watching you try to fix a fifty-year-old love story is one of the most beautiful things I've ever seen. Because you make me believe in second chances again."

Harper's breath caught. "Colby..."

"I know the timing's terrible," he continued. "I know you're leaving in a few weeks, I know everything's complicated. But I also know that life is short and chances are rare, and I don't want to waste whatever time we have being too scared to try." He met her gaze steadily. "So, I'm trying. I'm here, I'm helping, and I'm hoping that maybe, maybe you'll decide that three weeks is long enough to see if this is something worth staying for."

Harper felt like her heart might burst through her chest. "I don't know what I'm doing with my life. I don't know if I can keep the post office, or if I even want to. I don't know..."

"I know," Colby interrupted gently. "And I'm not asking you to have all the answers. I'm just asking you to let me be here while you figure it out."

Harper looked into his blue-gray eyes and saw everything she'd been afraid to want, patience, understanding, someone who saw her mess and complications and chose to stay anyway. She thought about Nora, about fifty years of wondering, about stolen chances and delivered letters.

About how sometimes the bravest thing you could do was admit you wanted something.

"Okay," Harper whispered.

"Okay?"

"Okay." Harper smiled, feeling something shift in her chest, fear transforming into possibility. "Let's see what happens."

Colby's answering smile was like sunrise, slow, warm, and absolutely beautiful. "Yeah?"

"Yeah." Harper squeezed his hand. "But first, we need to

bring Nora the rest of those letters. And find Jamie Mitchell. And figure out what the hell I'm doing with a post office that needs twenty-five thousand dollars in repairs."

"Priorities," Colby agreed, but he was still smiling. "One love story at a time."

Harper climbed out of the truck feeling lighter than she had in weeks. Behind her, Colby followed, and together they walked into the post office to retrieve twenty-five letters that had waited fifty years to complete their journey.

Some deliveries, Harper was learning, were worth the wait.

CHAPTER TEN

Colby spent Monday afternoon finishing his route with Harper on his mind, which, admittedly, was becoming a pattern. He kept replaying the moment in his truck when she'd said "okay," when she'd agreed to see what might happen between them despite all the very logical reasons why it was complicated.

He was still smiling about it when he pulled up to the post office around three o'clock to drop off the afternoon delivery.

Through the window, he could see Harper at the counter, surrounded by stacks of mail she was attempting to sort. She looked focused, determined, and slightly overwhelmed, pretty much her default state since arriving in Willow Creek. Colby grabbed his satchel and headed inside.

The door chimed, and Harper looked up, her face brightening when she saw him. "Hey. How was the route?"

"Long. Cold. The usual November complaints." Colby set down his satchel and noticed the bundle of letters on the counter, tied with their faded blue ribbon. "You haven't taken these to Nora yet?"

Harper's expression shifted. "I went back at noon. Spent two hours with her while she read every single letter." Her voice caught. "Colby, it was... watching her read them, seeing her realize that Jamie never stopped loving her, that he wrote for over a year hoping she'd respond..." She pressed her hand to her mouth. "I've never seen someone experience that much grief and hope simultaneously."

Colby moved around the counter instinctively, pulling Harper into a hug. She came willingly, resting her forehead against his shoulder, and Colby held her, feeling the tremors that suggested she'd been holding this emotion in all afternoon.

"She kept saying 'thank you,'" Harper mumbled against his shirt. "Over and over. Like I'd given her something precious instead of breaking her heart with fifty years of missed chances."

"You gave her truth," Colby said quietly. "That's precious."

Harper pulled back enough to look at him, her hazel eyes red-rimmed but fierce. "We have to find him, Colby. Quinn called earlier, she has leads on veterinary clinics in California, some alumni associations that might have contact information. We're getting close."

"We'll find him," Colby promised. "And when we do, you'll deliver one more letter, the most important one. The one that says it's not too late."

Harper smiled, wobbly but genuine. "When did you become such a romantic?"

"About a week ago," Colby admitted. "When a woman showed up in town with a mess of inherited problems and decided that delivering fifty-year-old love letters was more important than anything else." He brushed a strand of auburn hair from her face, his fingers lingering. "You make it hard not to be romantic."

Harper's breath caught, and Colby saw her gaze drop to his mouth. They were close again, too close, not close enough, exactly the right amount of close that made his heart beat faster and his brain shut down. This time, there was no Maggie arriving with casseroles, no alarms interrupting, just Harper looking at him like...

The door burst open with such force it crashed against the wall.

Victor Brennan stood in the doorway, immaculate in his expensive suit despite the November cold, his phone in one hand and an expression that suggested he was deeply unimpressed with what he saw.

Harper jumped back from Colby like they'd been caught doing something far more scandalous than almost kissing. Colby stayed where he was, positioning himself slightly between Harper and Victor in a move that was probably too obvious but that he couldn't help.

"Miss Delaney," Victor said, his tone professionally pleasant in a way that didn't reach his cold gray eyes. "I apologize for the interruption. I tried calling, but it went to voicemail."

"I was with a friend," Harper said, her voice steadier than Colby expected. "What can I do for you, Mr. Brennan?"

Victor stepped fully inside, letting the door close behind him. He surveyed the post office with the assessing gaze Colby had seen before, calculating square footage, evaluating potential, seeing dollar signs where other people saw history.

"I'll be direct," Victor said. "I'm prepared to make you an offer for this property. A very generous offer that I think you'll find addresses all your current concerns."

"I'm not interested in selling," Harper said immediately.

Victor smiled, the kind of smile that suggested he'd expected this response and had prepared for it. "You haven't heard the offer yet. One hundred and fifty thousand dollars. Cash, closing in thirty days, all legal fees paid. And I'll match any competing offers within that timeframe."

Colby felt his stomach drop. One hundred and fifty thousand dollars. That was more than the property was worth, even with its prime location. That was enough to solve Harper's problems, set her up somewhere else, give her a fresh start without the burden of a building that needed twenty-five thousand in repairs.

That was enough to make leaving very attractive.

Harper's face had gone pale. "That's... that's a lot of money."

"It's a fair offer for prime real estate on Main Street," Victor corrected. "And before you refuse, consider your situation. You've inherited a building that needs extensive repairs, roof, heating, electrical. Your contractor gave you an estimate of twenty-five thousand dollars, I believe?" He pulled out his phone, scrolling through something. "And the post office barely breaks even. According to public records, it generated less than thirty thousand in revenue last year. After expenses, you're looking at maybe ten thousand in profit annually. That's not a viable business, Miss Delaney. That's a money pit."

"How do you know about the repair estimate?" Colby demanded.

Victor's smile widened. "Small town. People talk. And Dylan Parker's secretary is my cousin." He turned back to Harper. "I'm offering you a solution. Take the money, go back to Chicago or wherever you want to build your life, and let me turn this building into something that actually serves the community, mixed-use space, boutique hotel, something that brings tourism and revenue instead of nostalgia."

"The post office serves the community," Colby said, his voice harder than he'd intended. "It's been the heart of this town for nearly a century."

"The heart of the town should be profitable," Victor shot back. "Should generate jobs and tax revenue and growth. Not barely survive on federal subsidies and the goodwill of people who remember the good old days." He looked at Harper. "You're a smart woman, Miss Delaney. You spent five years in marketing, you understand business. This building is a bad investment. I'm offering you a way out."

Harper's hands were clenched into fists at her sides, and Colby could see her jaw working. "I appreciate the offer, Mr. Brennan. But I'm not selling."

"Not today," Victor agreed smoothly. "But you're only here for three weeks, correct? That's what I heard. Three weeks to decide what to do with an inherited property you don't really want, in a town you left eleven years ago, while trying to honor your grandmother's memory." He tucked his phone away. "I'm a patient man, Miss Delaney. My offer stands. And when you realize that keeping this place means staying in Willow Creek, investing money you don't have, and giving up whatever life you planned for yourself back in Chicago, when you realize all that, you'll call me."

He pulled a business card from his wallet and set it on the counter. "My private cell is on the back. Call anytime. The offer's good through the end of the month."

Victor nodded once to Colby, a gesture that managed to be both polite and dismissive, and left, the door closing softly behind him this time.

The silence he left was heavy, oppressive. Colby watched Harper stare at the business card like it might bite her.

"Harper..." he started.

"He's right," Harper interrupted, her voice flat. "About all of it. The building needs repairs I can't afford. The business barely makes money. I have three weeks to decide, and I don't know what the hell I'm doing." She looked up at Colby, and the uncertainty in her eyes made his chest ache. "What if he's right? What if I'm being stupid and sentimental, trying to save something that's already dead?"

"It's not dead," Colby said firmly. "It's struggling, yeah. It needs work. But it's not dead, Harper. You've seen what this place means to people. Clara, Maggie, Nora, even me. The post office is where connections happen. Where stories get delivered, literally and metaphorically."

"But is that enough?" Harper asked, her voice breaking. "Is sentiment and nostalgia enough to justify turning down life-changing money? Is it enough to stay in a town that's not really my home anymore, working a job I'm not qualified for, hoping that somehow it all works out?"

Colby wanted to say yes. Wanted to promise her that staying would be worth it, that the post office would thrive, that Willow Creek could be her home again if she just gave it a chance. But he couldn't make those promises. He couldn't guarantee that choosing this town, this building, this life, choosing him, would be the right decision.

All he could offer was the truth.

"I don't know," Colby admitted. "I don't know if it's enough. But I know that walking away from something that matters because it's hard or uncertain or financially risky, that's not who you are. The Harper who quit her job because it was empty? The Harper who's spending her time trying to reunite a fifty-year-old love story? The Harper who stood up to Victor Brennan even though he was offering her an easy out? That Harper doesn't give up just because things are complicated."

Harper pressed her hands to her face, muffling a sound

that might have been a laugh or a sob. "You have a lot of faith in someone you've known for less than a week."

"Yeah," Colby agreed. "I do. Because you've shown me who you are every single day since you got here. And I like who you are, Harper. I like that you care about things that don't make logical sense. I like that you're here, trying, even though it would be easier to walk away."

Harper lowered her hands, and Colby saw tears tracking down her cheeks. "What if I fail? What if I try to keep this place and it falls apart anyway? What if I stay and..." She stopped, seeming to catch herself.

"And what?" Colby prompted gently.

"And you realize I'm not worth it," Harper finished quietly. "That I'm too much work, too much mess, too much complication for three weeks in a small town to fix."

Colby's heart cracked. He closed the distance between them, taking Harper's face in his hands, making her look at him. "Listen to me. You're not too much of anything. You're exactly enough. And I'm not here because I think you need fixing. I'm here because I think you're extraordinary, messy and complicated and worth every single second."

Harper's eyes were wide, vulnerable in a way that made Colby want to promise things he had no business promising. But before he could say anything else, Harper's phone rang, loud and jarring in the quiet post office.

Harper pulled back, wiping at her eyes. "Sorry, I should..." She grabbed her phone, and her expression changed when she saw the screen. "It's Quinn."

"Answer it," Colby said, even though he wanted nothing more than to finish what they'd started.

Harper answered, putting the phone on speaker. "Hey, Quinn."

"Harper! Oh my god, I found him!" Quinn's voice was high with excitement. "James Mitchell! He's alive, he's in Wisconsin, not California, Wisconsin! and he owns a veterinary clinic in the next county over. Forty-five minutes from Willow Creek. I have an address, a phone number, everything!"

Harper's hand flew to her mouth. "He's here? In Wisconsin?"

"He came back," Quinn said. "I called the clinic pretending to need a reference for vet school applications, totally plausible, by the way, and the receptionist was super chatty. Said Dr. Mitchell opened the clinic in 1980 after working in California for a few years. He's been here ever since. Harper, he came back to be near where Nora was. He came home."

Colby watched Harper's face cycle through shock, hope, and determination. "Quinn, you're a genius. Send me the address. We're going tomorrow."

"Already sent! Check your email. And Harper? Make sure you bring tissues. This is going to wreck him." Quinn paused. "In the best way. But still. Tissues."

After they hung up, Harper stood frozen, staring at her phone. "He came back," she whispered. "After everything, after thinking she didn't want him, he still came back to Wisconsin. To be near her, even if he couldn't have her."

"That's real love," Colby said. "The kind that doesn't give up, even when it should."

Harper looked at him, and Colby saw something shift in her expression, resolve settling into place, fear transforming into determination. "I'm not selling the post office."

"No?"

"No." Harper picked up Victor's business card and dropped it in the trash. "He's right that it's a bad investment. He's right that it would be easier to take the money and leave. But he's wrong about it being dead. And he's wrong about me not being able to do this." She squared her shoulders. "I'm staying. At least through the three weeks. Maybe longer. I'm going to deliver Jamie's truth to him, I'm going to figure out how to make this place work, and I'm going to prove that some things are worth more than their market value."

Colby felt his smile widen. "Yeah?"

"Yeah." Harper stepped closer to him. "And I'm going to stop letting fear make my decisions for me. Fear of failure, fear of staying in one place, fear of..." She stopped, seeming to lose her nerve.

"Fear of what?" Colby asked, though he thought he knew.

"Fear of wanting something I might not get to keep," Harper admitted.

Colby reached for her hand, threading their fingers together. "What if you do get to keep it?"

"Then I'll be the luckiest person in Willow Creek,"

Harper said softly.

They stood there, hands clasped, the post office quiet around them except for the old building's familiar creaks and sighs. Outside, the November afternoon was fading toward evening, Main Street preparing for another night. Tomorrow, they'd drive to the next county and deliver fifty years of undelivered truth to a man who'd been waiting his whole life to hear it.

But tonight, tonight was about this moment, this decision, this choice to stay and fight for something that mattered.

"We should close up," Harper said eventually. "Tomorrow's going to be a long day."

"Yeah," Colby agreed, but neither of them moved.

"Colby?"

"Hmm?"

"Thank you. For showing up today. For all the days." Harper squeezed his hand. "For making me believe I can do this."

"You can," Colby said. "And I'll be here, showing up, for as long as you'll let me."

Harper smiled, a real smile, the kind that lit up her whole face. "That might be a while."

"Good," Colby said. "I'm counting on it."

They separated reluctantly, Colby collecting his satchel while Harper started locking up. But before he left, he turned back.

"Harper? One more thing."

"Yeah?"

"Victor was wrong about something else too. This town is your home. It always has been. You're the one who forgot that for a while."

Harper's eyes glistened with fresh tears, but she was smiling. "Maybe you're right."

"I usually am," Colby said with a grin. "Ask my mother."

Harper laughed, and the sound filled the post office with warmth. Colby left reluctantly, climbing into his truck with the knowledge that tomorrow would change everything. Tomorrow, they'd reunite a love story that had waited fifty years for completion.

And maybe, just maybe, they'd figure out their own story along the way.

CHAPTER ELEVEN

Tuesday morning arrived gray and cold, the kind of November day that promised snow but hadn't quite delivered. Harper stood outside the post office at seven-thirty, clutching a manila envelope that contained photocopies of Jamie's letters. The originals were safely locked in Stella's desk, Nora had insisted Harper keep them there until Jamie could see them himself, but Harper had made copies of every page, every word, every declaration of love that had waited fifty years to reach its destination.

Today, they were finishing the delivery.

Colby's truck pulled into the lot, and Harper felt her stomach flip. She'd barely slept, running through scenarios in her mind. What if Jamie was married? What if he'd moved on so completely that these letters would only bring pain? What if Harper was about to ruin his life instead of fixing it?

"Morning," Colby said, climbing out of the truck. He

took one look at Harper's face and immediately pulled her into a hug. "You're overthinking."

"I'm appropriately thinking," Harper protested against his chest. "This is huge, Colby. I'm about to tell a man that he spent fifty years believing a lie. That the woman he loved never rejected him. That his entire life could have been different."

"That's exactly why we're going," Colby said gently. "Because he deserves the truth, no matter how much time has passed. Because Nora deserves for him to know. Because some love stories don't get endings, they get second chances."

Harper pulled back enough to look at him. "When did you become so wise?"

"I had a good teacher." Colby smiled. "My mother. Who, by the way, insisted I bring you breakfast again. She's apparently decided that feeding you is her new mission in life."

He handed Harper a travel mug of coffee and a paper bag that smelled like cinnamon and butter. Inside were fresh cinnamon rolls, still warm, with Rosie's signature cream cheese frosting.

"Your mother is a saint," Harper said.

"She's something," Colby agreed. "Ready?"

Harper looked at the manila envelope in her other hand. "As ready as I'll ever be."

The drive to the next county took them through rural Wisconsin at its November finest, bare trees against gray skies, farm fields lying fallow, the occasional house with smoke curling from chimneys. Colby drove while Harper picked at her cinnamon roll and tried not to think about all the ways this could go wrong.

"Tell me about Chicago," Colby said after about fifteen minutes of silence.

Harper glanced at him. "What about it?"

"I don't know. What did you love about it? What made you stay there for so long?"

Harper considered the question. A week ago, she would have rattled off all the things she was supposed to love, the career opportunities, the culture, the restaurants, the energy. But now, with distance and perspective, she wasn't sure any of that had been real.

"I loved the anonymity," Harper admitted. "In a city of three million people, you can be anyone or no one. Nobody knows your history or your family or what you were like in high school. You just... exist. And for a while, that felt freeing."

"But?" Colby prompted.

"But eventually, being no one felt the same as being lonely." Harper stared out the window at the passing landscape. "I spent five years building a career, making money, checking boxes on some invisible list of what success was supposed to look like. And the whole time, I felt like I was playacting. Like I was pretending to be the kind of person who belonged in that world."

"What kind of person do you actually want to be?" Colby asked.

Harper didn't answer right away. A week ago, she wouldn't have known. But now, after delivering letters and meeting Nora and watching her grandmother's community rally around a struggling post office, the answer felt obvious.

"The kind who shows up," Harper said quietly. "The kind who pays attention to people's stories. The kind who thinks a fifty-year-old love story matters more than a six-figure salary." She looked at Colby. "The kind who's brave enough to stay in one place long enough to build something real."

Colby's hand found hers across the console, squeezing gently. "That's exactly who you are."

"I'm working on it," Harper said. "Still have some recovering-corporate-drone tendencies to unlearn."

"Like what?"

"Like thinking everything needs to be optimized for efficiency. Like measuring success in metrics and KPIs instead of..." She gestured vaguely. "Whatever you measure it in when you're not trying to impress people you don't actually like."

Colby laughed. "I measure success in whether Mrs. Patterson's cat stays out of trees and whether Dylan stops trying to set me up with his cousin's friend's sister."

"How's that going?"

"The cat's doing great. Dylan's hopeless." Colby's thumb traced circles on the back of Harper's hand. "Although I'm pretty sure he's stopped with the setups since you arrived. Maggie told him he didn't need to bother anymore."

Harper felt her cheeks heat. "Did she?"

"Small town," Colby said with a shrug. "Everyone knows everything. Usually before you know it yourself."

"And what exactly does everyone know?" Harper asked, trying for casual and missing by a mile.

Colby glanced at her, his expression soft. "That I'm falling for Stella's granddaughter who showed up with a mess of problems and somehow made me believe in second chances again. That she's staying in Willow Creek for at least three weeks, maybe longer. That she makes me smile more than I have in three years." He paused. "That I'm probably going to ask her on an actual date once we finish delivering fifty-year-old love letters to their rightful recipient."

Harper's heart was doing something complicated in her chest. "An actual date?"

"Dinner. Maybe a movie if the theater in Ashland is showing something decent. Definitely holding hands and possibly kissing without being interrupted by well-meaning townspeople or aggressive real estate developers."

"That sounds..." Harper struggled to find words. "Really nice, actually."

"Yeah?" Colby's smile widened.

"Yeah." Harper squeezed his hand. "I'd like that. The date, I mean. All of it."

They drove in comfortable silence for a while, hands still linked, the morning gradually brightening as they left Willow

Creek further behind. Harper watched the landscape change, more commercial buildings appearing, the spacing between houses decreasing as they approached the county seat.

"Do you ever think about leaving?" Harper asked eventually. "Willow Creek, I mean. Going somewhere bigger, seeing what else is out there?"

Colby was quiet for a moment. "I did once. When Amanda wanted to go to Seattle. I thought about it seriously, about what it would be like to start over somewhere new, to build a different kind of life." He paused at a stoplight, looking over at Harper. "But I realized I didn't want a different life. I wanted my life, in my town, with my people. I wanted to wake up knowing everyone on my route, wanted to walk into The Copper Kettle and have Maggie already pouring my coffee, wanted to be able to help Mrs. Patterson with her gutters because I happened to be nearby and have a ladder." He shrugged. "That's not settling. That's choosing what matters to me."

"And Amanda didn't understand that," Harper said.

"No. She thought I was being small-minded. Afraid to take risks." Colby pulled through the intersection. "But staying somewhere because you love it, that's not fear. That's faith. Faith that the place and the people and the life you've built are worth choosing, even when something shinier is on offer."

Harper thought about Victor's offer, $150,000 and an escape from responsibility. She thought about her Chicago apartment, still technically hers, waiting for her to come back. She thought about the post office with its peeling paint and needed repairs and the way it smelled like paper and vanilla and home.

"I'm starting to understand that," Harper said. "The difference between running away and running toward something."

"Yeah?" Colby's expression was hopeful.

"Yeah." Harper looked at the manila envelope in her lap. "I spent eleven years running away from Willow Creek because I thought leaving made me successful. Thought distance made me sophisticated. But maybe I was just scared."

"Of what?"

"Of staying and being ordinary." Harper laughed at herself. "Like there's something wrong with ordinary. Like building a life in a small town where everyone knows your name is somehow less than building a career in a city where no one does."

"For what it's worth," Colby said, "you're not ordinary. You're extraordinary in the most ordinary ways, which is the best kind of extraordinary."

Harper felt tears prick her eyes. "That might be the nicest thing anyone's ever said to me."

"Then the people in Chicago were idiots," Colby said matter-of-factly.

The GPS announced their turn, and suddenly they were on a tree-lined street with a mix of residential houses and small businesses. Harper's stomach clenched as she saw the sign: *Mitchell Veterinary Clinic - Dr. James Mitchell, DVM.*

Colby pulled into the parking lot and turned off the engine. Through the window, Harper could see a modest building with a painted sign featuring a dog and cat. The parking lot had a few cars, staff, probably, or early morning appointments.

"He's in there," Harper whispered. "Right now. Jamie Mitchell. The man who wrote those letters."

"The man who loved Nora Whitfield for fifty years," Colby added. "Even when he thought she didn't love him back."

Harper looked at the envelope in her lap, at the photocopied words that represented a lifetime of heartbreak and hope. "What if I make things worse? What if he's happy now, and I'm about to destroy that?"

Colby reached over and took Harper's face in his hands, making her look at him. "Harper. Listen to me. That man has spent fifty years wondering why the woman he loved didn't write back. Fifty years thinking he wasn't enough to make her want him. Fifty years living with a question that had no answer." He brushed his thumb across her cheek. "You're not destroying anything. You're giving him the truth. And maybe, maybe, you're giving him a chance at the happiness he should have had all along."

"But what if..."

"No what-ifs," Colby interrupted gently. "We're here. He's here. Nora is waiting forty-five minutes away, probably staring out her window wondering if today's the day. You can't turn back now, and you don't want to. You want to finish what you started."

Harper took a shaky breath. "You're right."

"I usually am. Ask my mother."

Harper laughed despite her nerves. "You already used that line."

"It's a good line. I'm keeping it in rotation." Colby released her face but took her hand instead. "Come on. Let's go reunite a love story."

They climbed out of the truck into the cold morning air. Harper clutched the envelope like a lifeline as they walked toward the clinic door. Through the window, she could see a waiting room with the standard setup, chairs, magazines, a reception desk where a young woman sat typing.

"Wait," Harper said, stopping just before the door. "Should we have called ahead? Made an appointment or something?"

"To tell someone their entire life is about to change?" Colby shook his head. "I don't think there's a protocol for that."

"What if he has patients? What if he can't see us?"

"Then we wait." Colby's voice was calm, steady. "Harper, you've been carrying these letters since last week. You've cried over them, researched them, delivered them to Nora, and driven forty-five minutes to find their author. You don't give up now because you're scared. You see it through."

Harper looked at him, patient, supportive Colby who'd

shown up with breakfast and driven her here and somehow made her believe she could do impossible things like reunite fifty-year-old lovers and run a failing post office and stay in a town she'd spent eleven years avoiding.

"What if I mess this up?" Harper asked quietly.

"Then we mess it up together," Colby said. "But Harper? I don't think you're capable of messing this up. I think you're capable of delivering the most important message Jamie Mitchell has ever received. And I think that's exactly what you're going to do."

Harper took one more deep breath, squared her shoulders, and pulled open the clinic door.

The waiting room was clean and warm, decorated with photos of happy pets and their owners. It smelled like antiseptic and dog treats. The receptionist, a woman probably in her thirties with bright red hair and a friendly smile, looked up as they entered.

"Good morning! Do you have an appointment?" she asked cheerfully.

Harper's mouth went dry. "No, we... I need to speak with Dr. Mitchell. It's personal. About..." She stopped, unsure how to finish that sentence.

The receptionist's smile shifted to curious concern. "Dr. Mitchell's between appointments right now. Let me check if he has a few minutes." She picked up the phone, pressed a button. "Dr. Mitchell? There's a young woman here who needs to speak with you. Says it's personal." A pause. "Okay, I'll send her back."

She hung up and gestured to a door marked "Staff Only." "Through there, second door on the left. He said he can give you ten minutes before his next appointment."

Harper looked at Colby, who nodded encouragingly. "I'll wait here," he said. "You've got this."

Harper walked through the door on shaking legs, counting doors. One. Two. The second door on the left had a nameplate: *Dr. James Mitchell, DVM.*

She knocked.

"Come in," called a voice from inside, a man's voice, aged but still strong.

Harper pushed open the door and stepped into a small office lined with veterinary textbooks and framed certificates. Behind the desk sat a man in his early eighties with silver hair and kind brown eyes that looked up from paperwork with polite curiosity.

"Can I help you?" he asked.

Harper looked at James Mitchell, Jamie, the man who'd written twenty-five love letters that never reached their destination, and her voice came out as barely a whisper.

"Dr. Mitchell, my name is Harper Delaney. I'm Stella Delaney's granddaughter, from the Willow Creek Post Office." She held up the manila envelope with shaking hands. "And I have something that belongs to you. Something that should have been delivered fifty years ago."

Jamie's expression changed, confusion shifting to

something Harper couldn't quite read. He set down his pen slowly.

"I don't understand," he said.

Harper stepped closer to the desk, her heart pounding so hard she could hear it in her ears. "Letters, Dr. Mitchell. Twenty-five letters you wrote to Nora Whitfield between 1973 and 1974. Letters that were marked 'Return to Sender' but never actually returned to you. Letters that never reached her."

The color drained from Jamie's face. He stood abruptly, knocking papers off his desk. "What did you say?"

"Nora Whitfield," Harper repeated, her voice stronger now. "She never received your letters, Dr. Mitchell. Someone sent them back before they could reach her. She's been waiting fifty years to hear from you, not knowing that you'd been writing to her all along."

Jamie gripped the edge of his desk like he might fall without it. "That's... that's not possible. I wrote to her for over a year. She never responded. I thought..." His voice broke. "I thought she'd chosen not to answer."

"She never got them," Harper said gently. "But she does now. I delivered them to her two days ago. And she asked me to find you. To tell you the truth. To bring you these."

Harper set the envelope on the desk.

Jamie stared at it like it might explode. Then slowly, with trembling hands, he reached for it.

"Nora," he whispered. "After all this time. She... she

didn't forget me?"

"She never forgot you," Harper said, tears streaming down her face now. "She's been waiting, Dr. Mitchell. For fifty years. And she's still waiting. Just forty-five minutes away. Waiting to tell you that she never stopped loving you either."

Jamie sank back into his chair, the envelope clutched against his chest, and began to cry.

CHAPTER TWELVE

Colby sat in the veterinary clinic waiting room, watching the clock tick away minutes while Harper was somewhere in the back with Dr. James Mitchell, delivering news that would either destroy or restore a man's faith in love.

He'd been sitting for exactly twelve minutes when the receptionist, her nameplate read "Amy", looked over at him with concern.

"Are you okay? You look like you're about to be sick."

"Just worried about my... about Harper," Colby said. "She's delivering some difficult news to Dr. Mitchell."

Amy's expression shifted to curiosity. "You're her boyfriend?"

Colby considered the question. Were they dating? They'd held hands, almost kissed twice, admitted feelings, planned an actual date. "Yes," he said, and the word felt right. "I'm her boyfriend."

Amy smiled. "That's sweet. Dr. Mitchell's a good man. Whatever the news is, he can handle it. He's tough as nails under all that kindness."

Colby hoped she was right. Because from everything Harper had told him about those letters, what Jamie was about to learn would shake the foundation of his entire life.

The door to the back opened, and Harper appeared. Her eyes were red and her mascara was smudged, but she was smiling, sort of. A wobbly, emotional smile that suggested she'd just witnessed something profound.

"Colby?" Harper's voice cracked. "Dr. Mitchell wants to meet you. And he... he wants to read all the letters. The originals. He's canceling his appointments for the rest of the day."

Amy stood immediately. "I'll call the patients. Tell them we have a family emergency." She looked at Harper with knowing eyes. "Dr. Mitchell doesn't cancel appointments. Not in the fifteen years I've worked here. Whatever you told him, it's important."

Harper nodded, unable to speak. Colby crossed to her and pulled her into a hug. She clung to him, shaking.

"He's reading them," Harper whispered against Colby's chest. "The photocopies. And he's... Colby, he's completely destroyed. Fifty years. He thought she didn't want him for fifty years."

"Come on," Colby said gently. "Let's go be with him."

They followed Amy through the door marked "Staff Only," past examination rooms and what looked like a small surgical suite, to Dr. Mitchell's office. Amy knocked once and opened the door.

Jamie Mitchell sat at his desk, holding one of the photocopied letters in trembling hands, tears streaming down his face. When he looked up and saw Colby, he tried to compose himself, swiping at his eyes with the back of his hand.

"I'm sorry," Jamie said, his voice rough with emotion. "I'm not usually so... I just..." He gestured helplessly at the letters spread across his desk.

"Don't apologize," Colby said, moving into the office with Harper. "I'm Colby Hayes. I'm here with Harper."

"Colby brought me," Harper added, her voice still shaky. "He's been helping me find you. He's been..." She stopped, seeming unable to find the right words.

"He's been her support," Jamie finished, looking at Colby with the kind of understanding that came from experience. "You love her."

It wasn't a question, but Colby answered anyway. "Yes, sir. I do."

Harper's head snapped toward him, eyes wide. They'd said "falling for" and "care about" but never the actual word. Never the commitment that "love" implied.

Jamie's smile was sad and knowing. "That's good.

Everyone should have what I thought I'd lost." He looked back at the letters. "Miss Delaney, Harper, she told me that Nora's father intercepted these. That Nora never received them. That she's been waiting in Willow Creek all these years, thinking I'd abandoned her."

"She's been waiting," Harper confirmed. "Never married. Never stopped thinking about you."

Jamie's face crumpled again. "I need to read them. All of them. I need to... I need to understand what I lost. What we both lost." He looked at Colby and Harper. "Would you stay? I don't want to be alone for this."

"Of course," Colby said immediately.

Amy appeared in the doorway. "Dr. Mitchell, I've cleared your schedule. Should I lock up?"

"Please," Jamie said. "And Amy? Thank you. For everything. I know this is strange."

"Family emergency," Amy said firmly. "That's all anyone needs to know." She squeezed his shoulder as she passed. "Take all the time you need."

After Amy left, closing the door softly behind her, Jamie reached for the stack of photocopies. His hands were still shaking as he organized them by date, creating a chronological timeline of a love story that had been stolen from both writer and recipient.

"I wrote the first one from a motel in Indiana," Jamie said quietly, staring at the May 1973 date. "I was on my way to California for veterinary school. Nora and I had just said goodbye, and I already missed her so much I couldn't sleep." He looked up at Harper and Colby. "I thought I was being dramatic. Thought I'd get to school and meet new people and the missing would fade. But it never did."

He began to read aloud, his voice breaking over words he'd written half a century ago:

"*My dearest Nora, I'm writing this from a motel room in Indiana, somewhere between everything I've ever known and a future I'm not sure I want...*"

Colby watched Jamie's face as he read his own declarations of love, watched the way his expression shifted from nostalgia to pain to something deeper, a grief that had been waiting fifty years to be fully felt. When Jamie reached the part about the flickering neon sign and the cigarette smell, he stopped.

"I can still see that room," Jamie whispered. "Can still remember how the walls looked red then dark, red then dark. I thought if I could just make Nora understand how much I loved her, how much I needed her, she'd wait for me. That we'd find a way." He looked at the letter. "But she never read these words. She never knew."

"She knows now," Harper said gently. "I showed her the letters two days ago. She's read every single one."

Jamie's head dropped into his hands. "Fifty years. She's known for two days that I loved her, and I've known for..." he checked his watch "...thirty minutes that she loved me back. Thirty minutes to rewrite half a century of believing I wasn't enough."

He picked up the second letter, dated three weeks later. As he read, Colby watched the progression of emotion, the hope in those early letters gradually transforming into desperation, then into resignation. By the time Jamie reached the letters from California, his tears were falling onto the pages, smudging the photocopied ink.

"*I saw a girl today who looked like you from behind,*" Jamie read, his voice barely audible, "*and for a moment I thought maybe you'd changed your mind, maybe you'd come to find me. But when she turned around, she was a stranger, and I felt like an idiot for hoping.*"

He stopped, pressing his fist against his mouth. "I saw so many girls who looked like Nora. For years. I'd see dark hair and blue eyes and my heart would stop, thinking maybe this time, maybe now, maybe she'd come." He looked at Colby. "Does she still have dark hair? Or is it white now, like mine?"

"White," Harper said softly. "But beautiful. She's beautiful, Dr. Mitchell. Elegant and kind and she's been teaching Sunday school for decades, probably to keep herself from going crazy waiting for someone who never came."

"I came back," Jamie said suddenly. "In 1980, after I finished school and did a few years in California. I came back to Wisconsin. Opened a clinic one county over from Willow Creek because I couldn't bring myself to be in the same town, seeing her with someone else. But I needed to be close. Needed to know she was near, even if I couldn't have her." He laughed bitterly. "I've been forty-five minutes away from her for forty-five years. And I never knew she was waiting."

Colby felt his own throat tighten. "She'll be glad you came

back. That you never left completely."

Jamie continued reading, working through the letters methodically, chronologically, experiencing his own heartbreak from both sides now, the writing and the not-being-received. When he reached the final letter, dated December 1974, his hands were shaking so badly he could barely hold the page.

"*This is the last one,*" Jamie read. "*I promise. I'll stop haunting your mailbox and your memory. I'll finish school, I'll build a career, I'll probably even get married someday to someone practical and appropriate.*"

"I did marry," Jamie interrupted himself. "Ellen. She was a veterinary technician, kind and patient and good. We had thirty years together before she died of cancer." He looked at Harper. "I loved her. I did. But she knew, she always knew, that part of me was somewhere else. With someone who'd chosen not to answer my letters. And she loved me anyway."

He returned to the letter:

"*But I'll never love anyone the way I loved you. I don't think I'm capable of it anymore. You took that part of me with you when you let me go.*"

Jamie set down the final letter and sat in silence for a long moment. Then he looked up at Harper with red-rimmed eyes.

"I need to see her. Today. Now. I need to..." His voice broke completely. "I need to tell her that I never stopped. That every word in those letters was true. That I've been waiting too, even when I didn't know I was waiting."

"She's ready," Harper said. "I called her from the parking lot before coming in. She knows you're reading the letters. She's waiting at her house on Maple Street."

Jamie stood abruptly, knocking over his chair. "Maple Street. The same house? Her parents' house?"

"The same house," Harper confirmed. "Victorian, gray with white trim, wraparound porch."

"I know that house," Jamie said, his voice distant with memory. "I used to pick her up there for dates. Her father would glare at me from the window, like he was daring me to be worthy of his daughter." Jamie's expression hardened. "He did this. He's the one who sent the letters back. He decided we weren't meant to be together, and he stole fifty years from us."

"He's dead," Harper said quietly. "Nora told me. He died twenty years ago."

"Good," Jamie said with sudden vehemence. "I know I'm supposed to forgive, to be the bigger person, but that man robbed us of half our lives. He decided his daughter's happiness was less important than his pride, and I..." He stopped, collecting himself. "I'm sorry. That's not fair to say to strangers."

"We're not strangers," Colby said. "We're the people who found you. Who brought you the truth. Who are about to drive you back to Willow Creek to reunite you with the woman who's been waiting fifty years." He stood, offering his hand. "And Dr. Mitchell? Forgiveness can wait. Right now, you just need to get to Nora."

Jamie shook Colby's hand with a grip that was

surprisingly strong for a man in his eighties. "Thank you. Both of you. I don't know why you did this, why you cared enough to find me, to drive out here, to tell me something that must have been difficult to say, but thank you."

"My grandmother believed in second chances," Harper said. "And in delivering what needs to be delivered, no matter how long it takes. This is what she would have wanted."

"Stella Delaney," Jamie said, recognition dawning. "I remember her. She ran the post office when I was young. Kind woman with red lipstick and a laugh that carried."

"That was her," Harper said, smiling through her tears.

Jamie gathered the letters carefully, handling them like the precious artifacts they were. "May I keep these copies? Until I can see the originals?"

"They're yours," Harper said. "The originals are locked in my grandmother's desk, waiting for you."

"Then let's go," Jamie said. "I've waited fifty years. I'm not waiting another minute."

They helped Jamie close up the clinic, turning off lights, locking doors, leaving a note for Amy about tomorrow's schedule. Jamie moved with the kind of focused energy that came from having a singular purpose, the kind of determination that had carried him through veterinary school and thirty years of marriage and half a century of not understanding why the woman he loved had never written back.

In the parking lot, Jamie paused at his car, a practical sedan that looked exactly like what a sensible octogenarian veterinarian would drive.

"Should I follow you?" Jamie asked. "Or..."

"You should ride with us," Colby said impulsively. "That way you're not alone with your thoughts for forty-five minutes. And Harper can tell you about Nora—what she's like now, what she told us."

Jamie's relief was visible. "Yes. Please."

He locked his car and climbed into the back seat of Colby's truck with a spryness that belied his age. As Colby pulled out of the parking lot, heading back toward Willow Creek, Harper turned in her seat to look at Jamie.

"Do you want to know about her?" Harper asked. "Or do you want to be surprised?"

"Tell me," Jamie said. "Tell me everything. I've imagined her for fifty years; I want to know if I was right."

So, Harper told him. About Nora's elegant white hair and sharp blue eyes, about her posture that came from years of commanding teenagers' attention, about the way she quoted classic literature and maintained her parents' Victorian house with meticulous care. About how she'd never married, how she'd dedicated her life to teaching, how she'd created a full and meaningful life despite the hole at its center.

"She sounds exactly like I remembered," Jamie said softly. "And nothing like I imagined. I pictured her with someone else, with children and grandchildren, with a life so full there was no room for a boy she'd loved at twenty-two."

"She had a full life," Harper said. "But you were always part of it. She told me, she said she was waiting, even when she didn't know she was waiting."

Jamie wiped at his eyes again. "What do I say to her? After fifty years, what words are enough?"

"The truth," Colby said, catching Jamie's eyes in the rearview mirror. "You tell her the truth. That you loved her then, you love her now, and you're sorry it took fifty years to say it to her face."

"I'm eighty-three years old," Jamie said. "We're both in our eighties. How do you build a relationship when you're running out of time?"

"The same way you build one at any age," Harper said. "One day at a time. One honest conversation at a time. One moment of choosing to show up."

Jamie was quiet for a while, watching the landscape pass—the same route he'd driven away from all those years ago, leaving behind a girl who'd promised to wait and then seemingly changed her mind.

"I used to dream about this," Jamie said eventually. "Finding out I'd been wrong, that she'd loved me after all. But in my dreams, we were young. We had our whole lives ahead of us. Now..." He trailed off.

"Now you have whatever time you have left," Colby said. "And you can spend it knowing the truth, being together, making up for what was stolen. That's not nothing, Dr. Mitchell. That's everything."

As they crossed back into Willow Creek, passing the familiar landmarks that marked Harper's hometown, Jamie sat forward in his seat, gripping the headrest in front of him.

"I'm nervous," he admitted. "I'm eighty-three years old and I'm as nervous as I was at twenty-two, waiting for her to answer her door for our first date."

"She's nervous too," Harper said. "I've called her twice today. She's changed her outfit four times and she's been pacing her living room since breakfast."

Jamie laughed, a sound that was half sob, half genuine amusement. "Some things don't change."

Colby pulled onto Maple Street, and Jamie's breathing became audibly faster. "There. That's the house. I'd know it anywhere."

The gray Victorian sat beautiful and solid, smoke curling from the chimney, lights glowing in the windows. And on the front porch, barely visible from the street, stood a figure in lavender, Nora Whitfield, waiting.

Jamie saw her at the same moment she saw the truck. Even from a distance, Colby could see the way she straightened, the way her hand went to her throat.

"She's there," Jamie whispered. "She's really there."

Colby pulled to the curb and put the truck in park. For a moment, nobody moved. Then Jamie reached for the door handle with shaking hands.

"Dr. Mitchell?" Harper said.

Jamie paused, looking back.

"She loved you," Harper said. "The whole time. She never stopped. Remember that."

Jamie nodded, unable to speak, and climbed out of the truck.

Colby and Harper watched as James Mitchell, eighty-three years old, walked up the path to Nora Whitfield's house. Watched as Nora came down the porch steps to meet him halfway. Watched as they stopped a few feet apart, just staring at each other, fifty years of longing and loss and love suspended in the November cold.

And then Nora spoke, Colby couldn't hear the words, but he saw Jamie's face crumple. Saw Nora reach for him. Saw fifty years dissolve as they came together in an embrace that looked like coming home.

Harper was crying. Colby was crying. And on Maple Street, two people who'd been waiting half a century were finally, finally together.

"We did it," Harper whispered.

"You did it," Colby corrected. "You found the letters, you found Nora, you found Jamie. You delivered a love story that everyone said was over."

Harper turned to him, tears streaming down her face. "We should go. Give them privacy."

"Yeah," Colby agreed, but neither of them moved. They sat watching as Jamie and Nora held each other, as Nora pulled back to touch Jamie's face, as Jamie spoke words that made Nora laugh through her tears.

"Colby?" Harper said quietly.

"Yeah?"

"You told Jamie you loved me."

Colby's heart stopped. "I did."

"Did you mean it?"

Colby looked at Harper, beautiful, complicated Harper who'd shown up in Willow Creek with a mess of problems and somehow made him believe in second chances and delivered letters and love stories worth fighting for.

"Yes," he said simply. "I meant it."

Harper's smile was tremulous and bright. "Good. Because I love you too."

Colby felt something click into place in his chest, something that had been waiting three years to heal, something that Harper had fixed just by being exactly who she was.

"Yeah?" he said, his voice rough.

"Yeah." Harper leaned across the console. "And I know we said we'd wait for an official date, but..."

Colby kissed her.

Finally, with no interruptions from well-meaning townspeople or aggressive developers, Colby Hayes kissed Harper Delaney in the front seat of his truck while fifty yards away, another couple was having their own first kiss fifty years late.

When they broke apart, both breathless, Harper was smiling.

"Worth the wait?" she asked.

"Absolutely," Colby said. "Though next time, let's not wait fifty years between kisses."

Harper laughed and kissed him again.

On the porch, Nora and Jamie had their arms around each other, walking toward her front door. Going inside. Going home.

And in Colby's truck, Harper rested her head on his shoulder, both of them watching the house where a love story was finally getting its proper beginning.

"Thank you," Harper whispered.

"For what?"

"For showing up. For every single day. For making me believe that staying could be better than running."

Colby kissed the top of her head. "Always."

CHAPTER THIRTEEN

Harper sat in Colby's truck, her lips still tingling from their kiss, watching Nora's house fade in the rearview mirror. Inside that Victorian, two people were getting a second chance at a love story that had waited fifty years. And in this truck, Harper was getting her own second chance, at believing in staying, at trusting someone with her mess, at love itself.

"We should probably talk about what just happened," Colby said after a few blocks of comfortable silence.

Harper turned to look at him. "Which part? The part where we delivered fifty-year-old love letters and reunited two people who'd been separated by a cruel twist of fate? Or the part where you told Dr. Mitchell you loved me and then we had our first kiss while watching said reunion?"

Colby's ears went pink in that way Harper was starting to find completely adorable. "All of it?"

"Okay." Harper shifted in her seat to face him more fully. "Let's start with the big one. You love me."

"I do." Colby kept his eyes on the road, but his voice was steady. "I know it's fast. I know we've only known each other for a week and a half. I know all the logical reasons why I should wait to say it. But watching Jamie read those letters, watching him realize he'd wasted fifty years not knowing the truth, I just thought, what's the point of waiting? What's the point of pretending I don't know exactly how I feel?"

Harper felt tears prick her eyes again. She'd cried so much today that she was probably dehydrated. "I love you too. And you're right, it's fast, it's probably crazy, but it's also the most certain thing I've felt in years. Maybe ever."

Colby reached over and took her hand, threading their fingers together. "So, we're doing this? For real?"

"We're doing this," Harper confirmed. "No more almost-kisses, no more pretending it's complicated when it's actually pretty simple. I'm staying in Willow Creek, at least for now, and I want to be with you while I'm here."

"At least for now," Colby repeated, his voice careful.

Harper heard the worry beneath the words. "Colby, I can't promise forever. I can't promise I won't fail at running the post office or that Victor won't eventually wear me down or that I won't wake up one day and panic about giving up my Chicago life. But I can promise I'm not running away. Not from you, not from Willow Creek, not from what we might be building together."

Colby was quiet for a moment, processing. Then he

squeezed her hand. "That's enough. That's more than enough. We'll figure out the rest as we go."

Harper leaned her head against his shoulder, breathing in the scent of him, soap and coffee and something uniquely Colby. "Did you see their faces? When they first saw each other?"

"Yeah." Colby's voice was soft with wonder. "Fifty years and they looked at each other like no time had passed at all. Like they were still those kids who fell in love in the seventies."

"Do you think they'll be okay?" Harper asked. "I mean, they're in their eighties. They've lived entire lives without each other. What if the reality doesn't live up to fifty years of imagining?"

"I think," Colby said slowly, "that they'll have exactly what they always should have had, the truth, and time together, and the knowledge that they were always loved. Even if it's only for a few years, or months, or however long they have left, it'll be worth it."

Harper thought about that. About how her grandmother Stella had lived alone for twenty years after Harper's grandfather died, but she'd had those forty good years first. About how Jamie had married Ellen knowing part of him would always belong to someone else, but he'd loved her anyway. About how Nora had built a full life teaching and serving her community, but she'd still kept every memory of Jamie alive in her heart.

"Love is weird," Harper said finally.

Colby laughed. "That's your profound takeaway from

reuniting a fifty-year-old love story?"

"It's messy and complicated and it doesn't follow any logical rules." Harper lifted her head to look at him. "Two people fall in love, get separated by circumstances they can't control, spend five decades apart, and somehow the love survives. That shouldn't work. It defies everything rational."

"And yet it does work," Colby said. "Because love isn't rational. It's stubborn and impossible to kill and it waits even when it shouldn't." He glanced at her. "Kind of like someone I know who quit her corporate job and inherited a failing post office and decided that delivering decades-old letters was more important than taking an easy buyout."

"Are you calling me stubborn?" Harper asked, mock-offended.

"I'm calling you someone who knows what matters, even when the world tells you you're being impractical." Colby brought her hand to his lips and kissed it. "I'm calling you someone worth waiting for, worth believing in, worth loving even when it's complicated."

Harper felt her heart swell dangerously. "You're good at this."

"At what?"

"Saying exactly the right thing to make me want to kiss you again."

"Good thing we're dating now," Colby said with a grin. "Kissing is allowed. Encouraged, even."

They drove through downtown Willow Creek, past The Copper Kettle where Maggie was probably already gossiping about why Colby's truck was parked at the post office all morning, past Dylan's hardware store where tools and supplies waited for the renovations Harper had decided to tackle, past the library where Quinn had helped research Jamie Mitchell's location.

"Oh God, Quinn," Harper said suddenly. "I have to call Quinn. She's been texting me all morning asking for updates."

"Call her from the post office," Colby suggested. "Better yet, invite her over. She deserves to hear this story in person."

Harper pulled out her phone and saw approximately fifteen texts from Quinn, each more excited and impatient than the last. The most recent one, sent ten minutes ago, read: *If you don't call me in the next hour I'm driving to that clinic myself and I don't even know where it is!!!*

Harper typed quickly: *We found him. Reunited them. Coming back to post office now. Can you meet us there? Bring tissues.*

Quinn's response was immediate: *OMG OMG OMG YES. Leaving library NOW. This better be the greatest love story I've ever heard or I'm disowning you as my best friend.*

Harper smiled and tucked her phone away. "Quinn's meeting us at the post office. Fair warning, she's going to completely lose her mind when we tell her everything."

"Everything including us?" Colby asked.

"Everything including us," Harper confirmed. "Is that

okay?"

"Harper, the entire town is going to know we're together by tomorrow morning regardless of what we tell Quinn. Maggie saw us almost-kiss on Saturday. Mrs. Patterson probably has binoculars trained on the post office at all times. Dylan will take one look at my face and know something's changed." Colby shrugged. "Small towns don't have secrets. They have delayed announcements."

"I'm still getting used to that," Harper admitted. "In Chicago, you could date someone for six months and your neighbors wouldn't know. Here, we kiss once and it's breaking news."

"Do you hate it?" Colby asked, and Harper heard the real question underneath: *Are you going to run when you realize what small-town life actually means?*

"No," Harper said honestly. "It's different, and sometimes it'll probably be annoying, but it's also kind of nice. People caring, people paying attention, people invested in each other's happiness." She squeezed his hand. "In Chicago, I was invisible. Here, I matter. That's worth the gossip."

Colby pulled into the post office parking lot, and Harper saw Quinn's car already there, she'd clearly broken several speed limits to arrive first. Quinn stood on the front steps, practically vibrating with anticipation, her black curly hair escaping from its messy bun in the cold wind.

"Finally!" Quinn called as they climbed out of the truck. "I've been waiting for seven whole minutes and I'm dying!"

Harper and Colby walked up the steps together, and

Quinn's eyes immediately zeroed in on their joined hands. Her mouth dropped open.

"Oh my God," Quinn breathed. "Oh my GOD. You're holding hands. You're..." She looked at their faces more closely. "You kissed. You definitely kissed. I can tell from the way Colby looks all smug and the way Harper looks all glowy. You kissed!"

"We reunited two people who'd been separated for fifty years," Harper said, unlocking the post office door. "That seems like the headline here."

"That's the co-headline," Quinn corrected, following them inside. "But seriously, you have to tell me everything. Every single detail. Starting with whether Jamie is as romantic and wonderful as I've been imagining, because I've been picturing him like a vintage movie star who speaks in poetry."

Harper laughed and gestured for Quinn to sit in one of the chairs near the counter. Colby perched on the counter itself while Harper made tea, a calming ritual that felt necessary after the emotional intensity of the morning.

"Jamie Mitchell is eighty-three years old," Harper began, handing out mugs. "Silver hair, kind brown eyes, gentle voice. He's a veterinarian who came back to Wisconsin in 1980 and opened a clinic one county over, forty-five minutes from Willow Creek, because he couldn't bring himself to be in the same town as Nora, seeing her with someone else, but he needed to be close."

Quinn's hand flew to her mouth. "He came back?"

"He came back," Colby confirmed. "Spent forty-five

years forty-five minutes away from her, not knowing she was waiting for him."

Harper continued the story, walking into Jamie's office, showing him the letters, watching him read his own words from fifty years ago and realizing the truth. Quinn cried through the entire telling, and when Harper got to the part about Jamie and Ellen, Quinn actually sobbed.

"He loved someone else but she knew," Quinn whispered. "She knew part of him belonged to someone he thought had rejected him, and she loved him anyway. That's, that's, I can't even..."

"It gets better," Harper said. "We drove him back to Willow Creek. To Nora's house. And Quinn, when they saw each other..." Her own voice broke. "Fifty years just disappeared. They came together like they'd been waiting their whole lives, because they had been."

"I'm going to need another tissue box," Quinn announced, wiping at her streaming eyes. "Where are they now?"

"Nora's house," Colby said. "Getting their second chance."

Quinn set down her tea with shaking hands. "And you two? Because I'm picking up some serious couple energy here, and you're holding hands, and you both have that look that people get when they've said important things to each other."

Harper glanced at Colby, who nodded encouragingly. "We're together. Officially. We said..." She stopped, feeling suddenly shy.

"We said I love you," Colby finished for her. "While we were watching Jamie and Nora's reunion. And then we kissed. First real kiss. No interruptions."

Quinn's squeal could probably be heard in the next county. "I KNEW IT! I knew from the moment I saw you two that this was happening! This is the best day! Jamie and Nora got their happy ending, and you two get yours, and I get to witness all of it!" She jumped up and pulled Harper into a hug, then Colby, then tried to hug them both at once. "I'm so happy I could literally explode."

"Please don't explode in my post office," Harper said, laughing through her own tears. "I just cleaned."

The door chimed, and all three of them turned to see Victor Brennan standing in the doorway, expensive coat spotless despite the cold, expression carefully neutral.

"Miss Delaney," Victor said, his tone pleasant but firm. "We need to talk."

Harper felt Colby tense beside her, but she stepped forward, meeting Victor's gaze directly. "Mr. Brennan. I thought I made my position clear yesterday. I'm not selling."

"I heard you had an eventful morning," Victor said, moving into the post office uninvited. "Driving to the next county, reuniting old lovers, playing postal matchmaker." He smiled, but it didn't reach his eyes. "Very sweet. Very sentimental. But while you've been focused on delivering half-century-old love letters, you've missed some important developments."

"What developments?" Harper asked warily.

Victor pulled out his phone and showed her a document. "The Willow Creek town council is meeting next week to discuss the future of Main Street. Several business owners have expressed interest in redevelopment, updating the aesthetic, attracting more tourism, bringing in chains that could generate actual revenue. Your post office, as the oldest building with the most prime location, is central to those plans."

"The town council can't force me to sell," Harper said, her voice stronger than she felt.

"No," Victor agreed. "But they can make things difficult. Increase property taxes, enforce codes that haven't been touched in decades, require expensive updates to bring the building up to current commercial standards." He tucked his phone away. "I'm not trying to threaten you, Miss Delaney. I'm trying to help you see reality. That building is a liability. The town wants progress. And you're standing in the way of both."

"She's standing in the way of your profit margin," Colby said, his voice hard. "Let's be honest about what this is, Victor. You want to buy the post office cheap, flip it for triple, and turn Main Street into another generic shopping district. That's not progress. That's erasure."

Victor's expression cooled. "Mr. Hayes. I didn't realize this was your business."

"Harper's my business," Colby said flatly. "And the post office matters to this community. So yeah, it's my business."

"How romantic," Victor said, sarcasm evident. "The small-town mail carrier defending his girlfriend's inherited property. I'm sure that'll pay the bills when the roof needs replacing." He turned back to Harper. "My offer still stands. One hundred and fifty thousand dollars. But it won't stand forever. The town council meeting is next Tuesday. After that, the landscape changes. Think carefully about what you want your future to look like."

He left without waiting for a response, the door closing firmly behind him.

The silence he left was heavy with tension. Quinn spoke first.

"I hate that guy," she announced. "He's like a cartoon villain, except less subtle."

"He's not wrong about the town council," Harper said quietly, sinking into a chair. "If they decide to enforce code updates, I could be looking at way more than twenty-five thousand in repairs. I could be looking at losing the building entirely if I can't afford the upgrades."

"Then we fight," Colby said. "We go to the town council meeting. We remind everyone what the post office actually means. We show them that history and connection and community matter more than potential tourist revenue."

"And if they don't care?" Harper asked.

"Then we make them care," Quinn said fiercely. "Harper, you just reunited a fifty-year-old love story. You think this town doesn't value that? You think people won't show up to defend something that matters?"

Harper looked at her two friends, Quinn, who'd only known her for a week but was ready to go to war for her, and

Colby, who'd somehow made her believe that staying was braver than running. She thought about Nora and Jamie, getting their second chance because Harper had refused to give up on delivering those letters.

Maybe some things were worth fighting for, even when the odds were bad.

"Okay," Harper said. "We fight."

Colby's smile was proud and warm. "That's my girl."

Quinn clapped her hands together. "Town council meeting. Next Tuesday. We're going to show them exactly why the Willow Creek Post Office matters." She pulled out her phone. "I'm texting Maggie and Clara and Dylan. We need a strategy session. And probably snacks. Fighting corporate villains requires excellent snacks."

As Quinn started typing furiously, Colby moved to sit beside Harper, taking her hand.

"You okay?" he asked quietly.

Harper leaned against his shoulder, feeling the solid warmth of him. "Yeah. Scared, but okay. Is this what it's like? Staying in one place? Fighting for things instead of just moving on when they get hard?"

"Pretty much," Colby said. "But you're not fighting alone. That's the difference."

Harper turned to kiss him, a quick, sweet kiss that felt like a promise. "Thank you for showing up today. For all the days."

"Always," Colby said.

And Harper believed him.

CHAPTER FOURTEEN

Colby had seen Harper Delaney in a lot of states over the past week and a half, overwhelmed, determined, vulnerable, brave. But he'd never seen her like this: standing at the post office counter with a notepad, organizing a town meeting with the confidence of someone who'd finally figured out where she belonged.

It was seven o'clock on Tuesday evening, and the post office had become campaign headquarters.

Maggie Chen had arrived first, bringing enough coffee and pastries from The Copper Kettle to fuel an army. "If we're going to war with Victor Brennan, we're doing it caffeinated and well-fed," she'd announced, setting up a spread on the sorting table.

Clara Jenkins came next, moving slowly but with fierce determination in her eyes. "I worked in this post office for forty-three years," she'd said when Harper tried to tell her she didn't need to come. "Victor Brennan can pry it from my cold, dead hands."

Dylan showed up with building code books and contractor friends' phone numbers. Quinn arrived with poster board and markers, ready to make visual aids. And Rosie Hayes, Colby's mother, swept in with her warmth and organizational skills honed from running a bakery for four decades.

Now they were all gathered in a circle of mismatched chairs, looking at Harper like she was about to lead them into battle. Which, Colby supposed, she was.

"Okay," Harper said, consulting her notes. "The town council meeting is next Tuesday at seven. Victor's going to argue for redevelopment, updating Main Street, bringing in chain stores, turning the post office into something more 'profitable.'" She looked around at the assembled group. "We need to show them why that's the wrong choice. Why this building, this institution, matters more than potential tax revenue."

"We need testimonials," Maggie said immediately. "Real stories about what the post office means to people. Not just nostalgia, actual impact on their lives."

"I can talk about Stella," Clara offered. "How she knew everyone's story. How she'd hold mail when someone was going through a rough time, or make sure birthday cards arrived on the actual day. How this place was about connection, not just delivery."

"I'll talk about how the post office is central to small

business," Dylan added. "Hardware store depends on shipping supplies, getting orders from manufacturers. If this becomes some boutique hotel or whatever Victor's planning, where do those services go?"

Quinn raised her hand like she was in school. "I'll talk about the historical preservation angle. This building is part of Willow Creek's identity. Once you tear that down, you can't get it back."

Colby watched Harper scribble notes, her auburn hair falling forward to hide her face. He could see the tension in her shoulders, the way she was holding herself together through sheer will.

"What about you, Colby?" Rosie asked, her knowing eyes moving between her son and Harper. "What are you going to say?"

Colby hadn't really thought about speaking at the meeting. He'd been so focused on supporting Harper that he hadn't considered his own testimony. But looking at her now, at this woman who'd shown up in town with nothing but inherited problems and had somehow made them matter, he knew exactly what he'd say.

"I'll talk about what it means to deliver more than just mail," Colby said quietly. "About how a good postal worker knows when Mrs. Patterson's packages are getting heavier because she's stress-shopping again, or when the Johnsons stop getting their usual magazine subscriptions because they're having money trouble. I'll talk about how Stella taught me that this job isn't about efficiency, it's about paying attention. And how Harper's proven she understands that in ways most people never will."

Harper looked up, her hazel eyes bright with unshed tears. "Colby…"

"It's true," he interrupted gently. "You spent the last week and a half delivering letters that didn't have to be delivered. You tracked down a man you'd never met to tell him a truth that could have broken him. You reunited a love story that everyone else had forgotten about. That's what this place is for. That's what we're fighting to preserve."

The room was quiet for a moment. Then Rosie spoke, her voice warm with approval.

"My son's right. This isn't about a building. It's about what the building represents, a place where people matter more than profit, where stories get delivered, where connections happen." She looked at Harper. "And you've reminded everyone of that. Victor can threaten all he wants with his code enforcement and his tax increases, but he can't threaten what this place means to people who actually live here."

"Unless the town council sides with him," Harper said, voicing the fear they were all thinking. "If they decide that progress and revenue matter more than history and connection, we lose. No matter how good our testimonials are."

"Then we make sure the council meeting is packed," Maggie said firmly. "We get every person in this town who's ever received mail at this post office to show up. We remind the council that they work for us, not for Victor Brennan's development plans."

"We could also do a social media campaign," Quinn

suggested. "Local news loves this kind of story, small town fighting corporate development, historic building in danger, elderly woman's legacy at stake. I know people at the Willow Creek Gazette. Let me make some calls."

Dylan nodded. "And I'll talk to other business owners. Make sure they understand that if Victor gets what he wants with the post office, their buildings could be next. This sets a precedent."

Harper wrote everything down, but Colby could see the doubt creeping into her expression. "What if it's not enough? What if we do all this and the council decides Victor's right, that the building is a liability, that progress is more important than preservation?"

"Then we fight harder," Clara said, her elderly voice surprisingly strong. "Harper, dear, I've lived in this town for eighty-two years. I've seen buildings come and go, businesses open and close, people move away and move back. But some things, some things are worth fighting for even when you're not sure you can win. This is one of those things."

"Stella would be proud of you," Rosie added gently. "The way you're standing up for this place, for what it represents. That takes courage."

Harper wiped at her eyes quickly. "I'm terrified I'm going to fail. That I'm going to disappoint everyone who's counting on me."

"You won't," Colby said with absolute certainty. "Because you're not doing this alone. That's what you keep forgetting, Harper. You're not some corporate drone making decisions in isolation anymore. You've got a whole town backing you up."

"A whole town that I left eleven years ago and barely stayed in touch with," Harper pointed out.

"A whole town that doesn't care about that," Maggie countered. "Because you're here now, and you're trying, and that's what matters. Willow Creek forgives prodigal granddaughters who come home and fight for what's right."

Harper laughed wetly. "Is that the official policy?"

"It is now," Maggie said with a grin.

They spent the next two hours planning strategy, who would speak at the meeting, what order, what points to emphasize. Quinn volunteered to create a presentation with historical photos of the post office. Dylan offered to pull together data on small-town post offices that had been preserved successfully. Maggie promised to coordinate with other Main Street businesses to ensure a strong turnout.

By nine o'clock, they had a solid plan and a shared sense of purpose. As people started gathering their coats and saying goodnight, Rosie pulled Colby aside in the post office kitchen.

"That girl is special," Rosie said quietly.

"I know," Colby replied.

"And she's scared. Not just of failing at the post office, scared of staying, scared of letting herself be happy here, scared that if she puts down roots they'll strangle her." Rosie squeezed his shoulder. "Be patient with her. She'll get there."

"What if she doesn't?" Colby asked, voicing his own fear. "What if she realizes that small-town life isn't what she wants, that I'm not enough to make her stay?"

"Then you'll have loved her anyway," Rosie said simply. "And that will have been worth it. But Colby? I don't think that's going to happen. I think that girl is already falling in love with this town all over again. She just hasn't admitted it to herself yet."

Rosie kissed his cheek and left, calling out a goodbye to Harper on her way out. One by one, the others followed, Quinn with a fierce hug for Harper, Dylan with a promise to stop by tomorrow with contractor estimates, Maggie with a reminder that The Copper Kettle always had a table for them, Clara with a gentle pat on Harper's arm and a whispered "You're doing Stella proud."

And then it was just Colby and Harper, alone in the post office with coffee cups and scattered notes and the weight of what they were trying to accomplish.

Harper sank into a chair, suddenly looking exhausted. "That was a lot."

"That was amazing," Colby corrected, moving to sit beside her. "You just organized a town meeting and got six people to commit to fighting for something they all believe in. You're a natural leader, Harper."

"I'm a terrified woman who has no idea what she's doing," Harper said, but she was smiling slightly.

"Those aren't mutually exclusive." Colby reached over and took her hand. "How are you really doing? And don't say fine, I can see you're not fine."

Harper was quiet for a moment, staring at their joined hands. "I'm overwhelmed. And scared. And also..." She looked up at him. "Also, happier than I've been in years. Which is insane, because my life is objectively a mess right now. I'm running a failing post office, fighting off a persistent developer, trying to rally a town I barely reconnected with, and falling in love with someone I've known for less than two weeks."

Colby's heart stuttered at the words "falling in love." "That does sound complicated."

"But it doesn't feel complicated," Harper continued. "When I'm here, with you, planning how to save this place with people who actually care, it feels right. It feels like maybe I've been running toward this my whole life and I just didn't know it." She squeezed his hand. "Does that make sense?"

"Complete sense," Colby said. "I felt the same way when I came back from Seattle. Like I'd been trying to be someone else, somewhere else, and the whole time the life I actually wanted was right here waiting for me."

Harper shifted in her chair to face him more fully. "Colby, I need to tell you something. And I need you to be honest with me about how you feel."

Colby's stomach clenched, but he nodded. "Okay."

"I can't promise I'm staying forever," Harper said, the words tumbling out quickly. "I can't promise I won't get scared and want to run, or that I won't fail at this post office thing and have to sell anyway, or that Chicago won't call with some amazing opportunity I can't refuse. I want to promise those things, I want to be the kind of person who can commit to forever without qualification, but I can't. Not yet."

Colby absorbed this, feeling the familiar fear of abandonment try to claw its way up his throat. Amanda had said similar things, about keeping options open, about not making promises she couldn't keep. And then she'd left.

But Harper wasn't Amanda.

"Okay," Colby said slowly. "Then here's what I can promise: I'm not going to punish you for being honest. I'm not going to hold it against you that you can't see your whole future yet. And I'm not going to love you any less because you're still figuring things out."

Harper's eyes widened. "You're not?"

"No." Colby moved closer, bringing his other hand up to cup her face. "Harper, I don't need forever right now. I just need you to be here, trying, for as long as you can. Whether that's three more weeks or three months or three years, I'll take whatever you can give me. Because being with you, even temporarily, is better than not being with you at all."

"That's the most romantic thing anyone's ever said to me," Harper whispered, tears sliding down her cheeks.

"Yeah?" Colby smiled. "I've got more where that came from. My mother says I'm emotionally articulate."

Harper laughed through her tears. "Your mother is right about everything, isn't she?"

"Pretty much." Colby wiped at her tears with his thumbs.

"Harper, I love you. Not the hypothetical future version of you who has everything figured out, I love the messy, uncertain, currently-fighting-a-real-estate-developer version of you who's sitting in front of me right now. That's the person I'm choosing. Every day."

Harper's breath caught. Then she leaned forward and kissed him, slow and sweet and full of promise. When they broke apart, both breathing heavily, Harper rested her forehead against his.

"I love you too," she whispered. "And I'm going to try. I'm going to try so hard to be brave enough to stay."

"That's all I'm asking," Colby said.

They sat like that for a while, holding each other in the quiet post office, surrounded by the ghosts of delivered letters and the possibility of futures not yet written. Outside, Willow Creek was settling into night, shops closing, lights dimming, the November cold pressing against windows.

"We should close up," Harper said eventually, though she didn't move.

"We should," Colby agreed, also not moving.

Harper pulled back enough to look at him, her expression soft and open in a way that made Colby's chest ache. "Stay? Just for a little while longer? I don't want to be alone tonight."

"I'll stay as long as you want," Colby promised.

They moved upstairs to Stella's apartment, Harper's apartment now, which still felt more like Stella's space than

Harper's. Colby had only been up here once before, helping Harper carry boxes. It was exactly what he'd expected: vintage furniture, family photos on every surface, books lining the walls, the lingering scent of the vanilla candles Stella had loved.

Harper put on the kettle for tea while Colby looked at the photographs, Stella and her late husband, young and in love. Stella with a toddler Harper on her lap. Harper's mother at various ages, smiling that same smile Harper had.

"My grandmother kept every picture," Harper said from the kitchen. "Even the ones of my mother after she left. Even the ones of me from Chicago when I barely visited. She kept all of us here, in this apartment, like we never really left."

She brought Colby his tea and sat beside him, looking at the photographs. "My mom worked at this post office every summer as a teenager. She loved it, apparently. Then she turned eighteen and couldn't leave fast enough. Minneapolis, a fresh start, a life that was 'bigger' than Willow Creek." Harper touched the edge of one photo, her mother at seventeen, standing in front of the post office, smiling. "I never understood why she ran until..." Harper gestured around the apartment, at the small-town life contained within these walls. "Actually, I'm still not sure I do."

"She loved you," Colby said simply.

"She did." Harper sat on the couch, tucking her legs under her. "I didn't appreciate it enough when she was alive. I was so busy being successful and sophisticated and proving I didn't need Willow Creek that I forgot to just... love her back."

Colby sat beside her, close enough that their shoulders

touched. "She knew. Parents and grandparents always know, even when we're too stubborn to say it."

They drank their tea in comfortable silence, the kind that only came when two people were comfortable enough not to fill every moment with words. Eventually, Harper set down her mug and curled into Colby's side, her head on his shoulder.

"Thank you," she said quietly.

"For what?"

"For showing up. For organizing tonight's meeting. For believing I could do this when I didn't believe in myself. For loving me even though I'm a mess." She tilted her head to look up at him. "For being exactly who you are."

Colby kissed the top of her head. "That's what you do when you love someone. You show up. Every day. In all the small, ordinary ways that somehow add up to everything."

Harper's arm tightened around his waist. "I want to be worthy of that. Of you."

"You already are," Colby said. "You were worthy the moment you decided that a fifty-year-old love story mattered more than your convenience. Everything since then has just been proof."

They stayed like that, Harper curled against Colby, Colby's arms around her, as the night deepened and the old building creaked and settled around them. Tomorrow, they'd face Victor's threats and town politics and all the practical problems of saving a historic post office. But tonight was just for them, for choosing to be together, for believing that sometimes the bravest thing you could do was simply stay.

"Colby?" Harper murmured, half-asleep.

"Hmm?"

"I'm glad you're here. I'm glad you showed up that first day and offered to help and kept showing up even when I was difficult."

"You were never difficult," Colby said. "You were just scared. There's a difference."

"I'm still scared," Harper admitted.

"I know. But you're not letting the fear stop you anymore. That's what matters."

Harper's breathing evened out, and Colby realized she'd fallen asleep. He should probably wake her, suggest she move to her actual bed, but he couldn't bring himself to disturb her. She looked peaceful, the worry lines that had become permanent fixtures on her face finally smoothing out.

So, Colby stayed, holding the woman he loved in the apartment above the post office they were both fighting to save, and let himself believe that some stories really did have happy endings.

Even the ones that started with almost-kisses and inherited problems and love letters that had waited fifty years to reach their destination.

CHAPTER FIFTEEN

Harper stood in front of Stella's full-length mirror Wednesday evening, trying to remember the last time she'd been this nervous about a date. Probably never, if she was being honest. In Chicago, dates had been strategic, networking disguised as romance, career advancement with a side of wine. She'd gone to expensive restaurants with men in expensive suits and felt absolutely nothing.

But tonight, tonight she was going on a real date with Colby Hayes, and she felt everything.

She'd changed outfits three times before settling on a deep green dress that Quinn had insisted she borrow ("It brings out your eyes and Colby is going to DIE when he sees you"). It was simple but elegant, hitting just above her knees, with long sleeves that made it appropriate for November in Wisconsin. Harper had paired it with boots and the vintage necklace Stella had left her, a small silver locket that felt like bringing her grandmother along for the evening.

Her phone buzzed. Colby: *Downstairs whenever you're ready. No rush.*

Harper took one last look in the mirror, barely recognizing the woman staring back. Two weeks ago, she'd been a corporate drone in designer suits, running from failure. Now she was someone who fought developers and reunited fifty-year-old love stories and was about to have dinner with a man who looked at her like she hung the moon.

She grabbed her coat and headed downstairs.

Colby was waiting by his truck, and Harper's breath caught when she saw him. He was wearing dark jeans and a navy button-down that made his blue-gray eyes even more striking, and his hair looked like he'd actually tried to tame it for once. When he saw Harper, his expression shifted into something that made her feel beautiful and wanted and absolutely terrified.

"Wow," Colby said, his voice slightly rough. "You look... wow."

Harper laughed, feeling her cheeks heat. "Very articulate."

"Give me a minute. My brain stopped working." Colby crossed to her and took her hands. "Harper, you look incredible."

"You clean up pretty nice yourself," Harper said, taking in the sight of him. "Though I kind of miss the mail carrier uniform."

"I can wear it to dinner if you want. Really set the tone."

"Please don't." Harper squeezed his hands. "Where are we going?"

"There's a restaurant in Ashland, about thirty minutes away, that I've been wanting to try. Italian place, supposed to be excellent. No one from Willow Creek will be there to gossip about us, and they have actual cloth napkins." Colby smiled. "I figured for our first official date, we should do it right."

"Cloth napkins," Harper said solemnly. "Very fancy."

"I'm pulling out all the stops." Colby opened the passenger door for her with exaggerated chivalry. "Your chariot awaits, m'lady."

Harper slid into the truck, feeling lighter than she had in years. As Colby drove out of Willow Creek toward Ashland, Harper watched the landscape pass, familiar fields and forests painted silver by the nearly-full moon. She'd made this drive countless times growing up, heading to Ashland for movies or shopping or anything that felt more sophisticated than small-town life.

But tonight, she wasn't running from Willow Creek. She was just taking a break from it, with someone who made her want to come back.

"Penny for your thoughts," Colby said after a few minutes of comfortable silence.

Harper turned to look at him. "I was thinking about how different everything feels now. Two weeks ago, I was terrified of this town, of this post office, of staying in one place long enough to fail at it. And now..." She trailed off, unsure how to finish.

"And now?" Colby prompted gently.

"And now I'm going on a date with the mail carrier who's somehow convinced me that staying might be braver than running. And I'm not terrified anymore." Harper paused. "Well, I'm terrified of different things. But not of being here."

"What are you terrified of now?" Colby asked.

Harper considered the question. "Failing. Disappointing everyone who's counting on me. Losing the town council vote and having to sell anyway. Falling so completely in love with you and this town that I forget who I was supposed to be." She looked at him. "Is that too honest for a first date?"

"No," Colby said firmly. "That's exactly honest enough. Harper, I don't want the filtered version of you. I want the version who's scared and uncertain and still shows up anyway."

"Even when I'm a mess?"

"Especially when you're a mess. Those are the moments when you're most yourself." Colby reached over and took her hand. "Besides, I like your mess. It makes my mess feel less lonely."

Harper laughed. "We're quite a pair, aren't we?"

"The best kind," Colby agreed.

The restaurant was exactly as advertised, intimate lighting, soft jazz playing, and yes, actual cloth napkins. The hostess seated them at a corner table with a flickering candle and a view of Ashland's small downtown through the window.

It felt impossibly romantic, like something out of the movies Harper used to watch and not believe in.

"This is perfect," Harper said as they settled into their seats.

"Wait until you try the food," Colby said. "Dylan recommended this place. Said he brought his girlfriend here for their anniversary and she actually cried over the carbonara."

"High praise from Dylan, who I've watched eat gas station hot dogs without complaint."

"Exactly. If Dylan says it's good, it's transcendent."

They ordered wine and pasta, falling into easy conversation about everything and nothing. Colby told her stories about growing up in Willow Creek, the time he and Dylan accidentally started a small fire in the hardware store trying to build a potato cannon, the year his mother entered him in the county fair pie-eating contest without his knowledge, the summer he'd worked as a lifeguard at the public pool and spent most of his time rescuing the same kid who kept jumping in the deep end despite not being able to swim.

Harper told him about Chicago, not the polished version she'd presented to colleagues, but the real version. The loneliness of living in a city of millions. The way she'd sometimes go entire weekends without speaking to anyone except through screens. The corporate happy hours where everyone smiled and networked and went home feeling emptier than when they'd arrived.

"Do you miss it?" Colby asked. "Chicago, I mean. The career, the sophistication, all of it?"

Harper twirled pasta on her fork, thinking. "I miss the version of myself who thought she was supposed to want those things. Does that make sense? Like I miss the certainty of having a clear path, even if it was the wrong path." She set down her fork. "But do I miss the actual life? No. That life was about becoming someone impressive. This life, here, with the post office, with you, is about becoming someone real."

Colby's expression was soft with understanding. "My mother always says that growing up is learning the difference between who you thought you'd be and who you actually are. And being brave enough to choose the real version."

"Your mother is basically a walking fortune cookie of wisdom, isn't she?"

"She really is." Colby took a sip of his wine. "Can I ask you something?"

"Anything."

"What do you want? Not what you think you should want, not what would make sense or be practical, what do you actually want for your life?"

Harper felt the question settle over her like a weight. No one had asked her that in years. Her entire adult life had been about should: should get this degree, should take this job, should climb this ladder, should want this promotion. Want had never factored into it.

"I want," Harper said slowly, "to wake up excited about the day ahead instead of dreading it. I want to know my neighbors' names and their stories. I want to do work that matters to people, even if it doesn't pay much or impress anyone at cocktail parties." She looked at Colby. "I want to fall asleep next to someone who loves me exactly as I am, mess and all. I want to stop running from the possibility of failure and start running toward the possibility of happiness."

"That sounds like a good life," Colby said quietly.

"It sounds terrifying," Harper admitted. "Because it's so different from everything I planned. But also... also it sounds perfect."

Colby reached across the table and took her hand. "For what it's worth, I think you're already living that life. You just haven't admitted it to yourself yet."

Harper felt tears prick her eyes. "When did you get so wise?"

"I had a good teacher." Colby squeezed her hand. "And I've had three years to figure out what actually matters. Turns out, it's not the big impressive things. It's the small everyday things that add up to a life you don't want to escape from."

They finished dinner slowly, talking and laughing and stealing bites of each other's desserts. Harper couldn't remember the last time she'd felt this present, this aware of every moment. In Chicago, she'd been constantly looking ahead, to the next meeting, the next promotion, the next milestone that would finally make her feel successful. But here, with Colby, she just wanted to stay exactly where she was.

After dinner, Colby suggested a walk through downtown Ashland. The November air was cold but not unbearable, and the small downtown was decorated with early Christmas lights that reflected off the shop windows. They walked hand-in-hand, looking at displays and talking about nothing important.

"Can I tell you something?" Harper said as they paused in front of a bookstore window.

"Always."

"I'm really happy right now. Like, stupidly, unreasonably happy." Harper turned to face him. "And it's scaring me a little, because every time I've been this happy in the past, something's come along to ruin it. Like the universe doesn't want me to get too comfortable."

Colby pulled her closer, his hands on her waist. "The universe doesn't work like that. Happiness isn't something you have to earn or that can be taken away as punishment. It's just... something you choose, every day, even when it's scary."

"Is that what you're doing? Choosing this? Choosing me, even though I'm a flight risk?"

"Every single day," Colby said firmly. "And I'll keep choosing you, Harper. For as long as you'll let me."

Harper stretched up and kissed him, right there on the sidewalk in downtown Ashland with the Christmas lights glowing around them. It was different from their first kiss, less desperate, more certain. A kiss that felt like a promise instead of a question.

When they broke apart, both breathing a little harder, Colby rested his forehead against hers.

"Best first date ever," he said.

"We should probably have a second one," Harper

suggested. "Just to make sure the first wasn't a fluke."

"Tomorrow?"

"You don't want to seem too eager?"

"I am too eager," Colby said with a grin. "I've been waiting to take you on an actual date for two weeks. I'm not playing it cool now."

Harper laughed and kissed him again, feeling something settle in her chest, something that felt a lot like belonging.

They drove back to Willow Creek with Harper's head on Colby's shoulder, his arm around her, both of them quiet but content. When they pulled up to the post office, Harper didn't want the evening to end.

"Come up?" Harper asked. "Just for a little while? I don't want to say goodnight yet."

"Yes," Colby said immediately.

They climbed the stairs to Stella's apartment, and Harper put on the kettle more out of habit than desire for tea. Colby settled on the couch, looking comfortable and right in the space that was slowly becoming Harper's instead of her grandmother's.

"Thank you for tonight," Harper said, sitting beside him. "For dinner and walking and making me feel like maybe I'm not completely crazy for wanting to stay here."

"You're not crazy," Colby said. "You're brave. There's a difference."

Harper curled into his side, feeling his warmth and solidity and the steady rhythm of his heartbeat. "Can I ask you something?"

"Anything."

"What do you see when you look at me? I mean, really see, not the potential version or the fixed version, but the actual me right now?"

Colby was quiet for a moment, and Harper could feel him thinking. "I see someone who's been running for so long she forgot she could stop. I see someone who thinks vulnerability is weakness when it's actually the strongest thing about her. I see someone who drove forty-five minutes to tell a stranger that he'd been loved for fifty years, because she believed that truth mattered more than convenience." He tilted her face up to look at him. "I see someone extraordinary pretending to be ordinary. And I see someone I love, exactly as she is right now, mess and uncertainty and all."

Harper's throat was tight with emotion. "How do you always know exactly what to say?"

"I'm just telling the truth," Colby said simply. "It's easy when the truth is this obvious."

They stayed like that for a long time, holding each other in the quiet apartment, the November wind rattling the windows and the old building creaking around them. Harper thought about the town council meeting next Tuesday, about Victor's threats, about the twenty-five thousand dollars in repairs and the uncertain future of the post office.

But tonight, none of that mattered. Tonight was just about

this, about choosing to be happy, about choosing to stay, about choosing to believe that maybe, just maybe, she deserved something good.

"Colby?" Harper said eventually.

"Hmm?"

"I'm glad you showed up that first day. I'm glad you kept showing up."

"Me too," Colby said, pressing a kiss to the top of her head. "Best decision I ever made."

Harper tilted her face up and kissed him, slow and sweet and full of promise. When they broke apart, she settled back against his chest, listening to his heartbeat and feeling more at peace than she had in years.

Outside, Willow Creek was quiet, the small town settling into sleep. Inside, Harper was wide awake, finally understanding what it meant to be home.

Not a place. Not a building. Not even a town.

Home was this: someone's arms around you, someone's heartbeat under your ear, someone who chose you every single day and made you want to choose them back.

Harper had spent eleven years running from Willow Creek, thinking home was something she'd left behind.

Turns out, home had been waiting for her all along. She just needed to be brave enough to stay and claim it.

"Stay?" Harper asked quietly. "Just to sleep. I don't want

to be alone tonight."

"I'll stay as long as you want," Colby promised.

And Harper believed him.

CHAPTER SIXTEEN

Colby was delivering mail to the library Thursday afternoon when Quinn grabbed his arm with barely contained excitement.

"Is it true?" she demanded, steering him toward the reference section where they could talk without disturbing patrons. "Did you take Harper on an actual date? Like a real one, with dinner and everything?"

"Good afternoon to you too, Quinn," Colby said, unable to keep the smile off his face. "Yes, we went to dinner last night. In Ashland. It was nice."

"Nice?" Quinn looked personally offended. "Colby Hayes, you take the woman you're in love with on your first official date and all you can say is 'nice'? I need details. Maggie's already creating a timeline of your relationship on her café chalkboard and I need to verify her facts."

"She's doing what?"

"Don't change the subject. How was it? Was it romantic? Did you kiss? Obviously you kissed. Did she like the restaurant? What did you talk about? When's the next date?"

Colby laughed at Quinn's rapid-fire questions. "It was perfect. Yes, we kissed. She loved the restaurant. We talked about everything. And the next date is tomorrow, we're just going to grab pizza and work on post office stuff, but it still counts."

Quinn squealed quietly, mindful of the library setting. "You're doing the casual-date-that's-actually-spending-all-your-time-together thing. That's so cute I could die."

"I'm glad our relationship provides you with entertainment," Colby said dryly.

"It provides the entire town with entertainment," Quinn corrected. "Harper Delaney comes home after eleven years, falls in love with the mail carrier, and fights a real estate developer for the soul of Willow Creek? This is better than any book I could shelve. We're all invested now."

"No pressure or anything."

"Oh, tons of pressure. If you two don't end up together, the whole town will riot." Quinn's expression turned more serious. "But Colby? I think everyone can see how good you are for each other. Harper's different since she met you. Lighter. Like she finally figured out where she belongs."

Colby felt warmth spread through his chest. "I hope so. She's still scared, but she's staying. For now, that's enough."

"It's more than enough. It's everything." Quinn handed him a stack of mail she'd been holding for the library. "Oh, before you go, Nora Whitfield called this morning. She wants to come to the post office tomorrow to talk to Harper. Said she has something important to say and wants the community there to hear it."

Colby's interest sharpened. "Did she say what about?"

"Just that it was time to tell her story publicly. And that she wanted to do it before the town council meeting." Quinn's smile was knowing. "I think she's going to be your secret weapon, Colby. A woman who's been waiting fifty years for love letters that finally arrived? That's the kind of story that reminds people what the post office is really for."

By Friday afternoon, the post office was packed.

Colby stood near the sorting table, watching the community gather. Word had spread fast, Nora Whitfield was going to speak, and anyone who wanted to support Harper's fight to save the post office should come hear what she had to say.

Maggie had closed The Copper Kettle early to attend, bringing coffee and pastries for everyone. Clara sat in a place of honor near the front, her walker parked beside her. Dylan and several other business owners lined the walls. Quinn had brought half the library board. Even Sheriff Mitchell had stopped by, technically on his lunch break but clearly invested in what was happening.

And there, at the center of it all, was Harper, looking nervous and beautiful and completely overwhelmed by the number of people crammed into her grandmother's post office.

Colby caught her eye and smiled, and she smiled back, some of the tension leaving her shoulders. They'd only been officially together for three days, but Colby could already read her moods, knew when she needed encouragement and when she needed space.

Right now, she needed to know she wasn't alone.

The door opened, and Nora Whitfield entered, elegant as always in a navy dress and pearls, her white hair perfectly styled. But it was the man beside her who made the room collectively gasp, James Mitchell, silver-haired and distinguished in a cardigan and slacks, his hand clasped firmly in Nora's.

They looked at each other, and Colby saw fifty years of longing transform into fifty years of gratitude. They were together. Finally, impossibly, beautifully together.

"Thank you all for coming," Nora said, her cultured voice carrying easily through the crowded space. "I know this is unusual, gathering like this on a Friday afternoon. But I wanted to tell you a story before Tuesday's town council meeting. A story about love and loss and the importance of what happens in this building."

The room fell completely silent. Colby saw Harper press her hand to her mouth, eyes already shining with tears.

Nora took a breath and began.

"In 1973, I fell in love with Jamie Mitchell." She squeezed the hand she was holding. "We were young, I was twenty-two, he was twenty-four. We met at a church potluck, of all places. I'd brought my mother's famous potato salad, and he spilled punch on my dress trying to reach for a second helping."

Soft laughter rippled through the room.

"He apologized about fifty times, offered to pay for dry cleaning, and asked if he could take me to dinner to make up for it. I said yes. We dated for six months, six perfect, wonderful months. And then Jamie got accepted to veterinary school in California. We promised to write, to make long distance work, to wait for each other."

Nora's voice wavered slightly, and Jamie's arm went around her waist, supporting her.

"I waited," Nora continued. "For months, I waited for letters that never came. I thought, I was certain, that Jamie had met someone else. That I wasn't worth the distance, wasn't worth the effort of a simple letter. I spent fifty years believing that the man I loved had forgotten me. That I wasn't enough."

Harper made a small sound of distress, and Colby moved closer to her, offering silent support.

"But two weeks ago," Nora said, her voice strengthening, "Harper Delaney found twenty-five letters in her grandmother's desk. Letters Jamie had written to me. Letters someone had marked 'Return to Sender' and hidden away. Letters I'd never received."

The room erupted in shocked murmurs. Colby saw people's faces shift from curiosity to outrage to sympathy as they understood what had been stolen.

"My father intercepted them," Nora said clearly. "He didn't approve of Jamie, thought a veterinarian wasn't good enough for his daughter. So, he made sure I never knew that Jamie had been writing. And he made sure Jamie never knew I'd been waiting."

"Jesus," someone muttered from the back. Colby thought it was Dylan.

"Harper found those letters," Nora continued, looking directly at Harper now. "And she didn't just file them away as interesting historical artifacts. She didn't just think 'how sad' and move on with her day. She tracked down Jamie. She drove to the next county. She told him the truth, a truth that was fifty years old but still mattered."

Colby watched Harper's face as Nora spoke, saw the tears streaming down her cheeks, saw the way her hands were clasped together like she was holding herself upright through sheer will.

"Because of Harper," Nora said, "Jamie and I found each other again. Because of this post office, because of what it represents, what it's always represented, a love story that should have ended in 1973 got its second chance in 2025."

Nora turned to address the whole room now, her blue eyes fierce with conviction.

"That is what this building does. It doesn't just deliver packages and letters. It delivers hope. It delivers truth. It delivers connection between people who are separated by distance or time or cruel circumstance. Stella Delaney understood that. She ran this post office for forty years with the knowledge that sometimes a letter isn't just a letter, it's a lifeline. It's proof that someone cares enough to write. That someone remembers you exist."

The room was completely silent now, everyone hanging on Nora's words.

"Next Tuesday, the town council will decide whether this building, this institution, is worth preserving. Victor Brennan will tell you it's not profitable enough, not modern enough, not worth the investment. He'll tell you that progress means tearing down the old to make room for the new." Nora's voice hardened. "But I'm telling you that some things are worth more than their profit margin. Some things matter because of what they represent, not what they earn. And this post office matters."

Clara stood, her walker scraping against the floor as she leveraged herself up. "Nora's right. I worked here for forty-three years. I saw what Stella did, how she knew everyone's story, how she held mail when someone was going through a divorce because she knew they weren't ready to face bills yet. How she made sure birthday cards arrived on time, how she noticed when someone stopped getting letters from their kids and made quiet phone calls to check on them. That's not something you can put in a spreadsheet. That's not something Victor Brennan's development plan can replace."

More people started speaking up, sharing their own stories about Stella, about what the post office had meant to them over the years. Mrs. Patterson talked about how Stella had held packages for her when her husband was sick, saving her trips into town. Dylan mentioned how the post office was the first place his grandfather had taken him as a child, teaching him that community meant showing up for each other. Maggie shared how Stella had been the first person to congratulate her when she opened The Copper Kettle, appearing with a bouquet of flowers and a promise to order coffee supplies through the post office's business services.

Colby watched Harper listen to each testimony, saw the way understanding was dawning on her face. This wasn't just about a building or even about her grandmother's legacy. This was about what happened when people chose connection over convenience, when they valued relationships over revenue.

Finally, Quinn spoke up from her spot near the window. "I'm going to the town council meeting on Tuesday. And I'm going to tell them that the Willow Creek Post Office is part of our historical identity. That once you tear down history, you can't get it back. That some things are worth fighting for even when the odds are bad." She looked directly at Harper. "And I'm going to fight because Harper showed us how. She could have sold this building to Victor Brennan two weeks ago. Taken the money and walked away. But she stayed. She fought. She delivered letters that didn't have to be delivered and reunited a love story that everyone else had forgotten about. If she can do that, if she can be that brave, then we can be brave enough to show up on Tuesday and tell the council that this place matters."

The room erupted in agreement, people clapping, calling out affirmations, promising to attend the meeting.

Harper looked completely overwhelmed. She stood frozen, tears streaming down her face, as person after person came up to thank her, to promise their support, to tell her they'd be there Tuesday.

Colby made his way to her side, and she immediately grabbed his hand like a lifeline.

"I can't believe this is happening," Harper whispered.

"Believe it," Colby said. "This is what community looks like when someone reminds them what matters."

After everyone had left, after final promises and hugs and Clara's fierce declaration that Victor Brennan would have to "pry this post office from her cold, dead hands" (her new favorite phrase), it was just Harper, Colby, Nora, and Jamie remaining.

Nora approached Harper with tears in her eyes. "Thank you. I can never thank you enough for what you've done. You gave me my life back."

Harper shook her head, crying too hard to speak. Nora pulled her into a hug, and Harper clung to her, both women crying, both understanding something profound about second chances and delivered truths.

When they separated, Jamie stepped forward. "Miss Delaney, I don't have eloquent words like Nora. But I want you to know, you changed my life. I spent fifty years living with a question that had no answer. And you gave me the answer. You gave me peace. And more than that, you gave me Nora." He smiled at the woman beside him. "That's a debt I can never repay."

"You don't owe me anything," Harper managed. "I just

delivered what was supposed to be delivered. I just... I just did what was right."

"That's exactly what your grandmother would have said," Jamie replied. "Stella had the same philosophy, do what's right, even when it's not convenient. Even when no one's watching. Even when it's been fifty years." He extended his hand. "Thank you for being Stella's granddaughter. The world needs more people like you two."

After Nora and Jamie left, holding hands, still looking at each other like they couldn't quite believe they were together, Harper sank into a chair, emotionally exhausted.

"That was intense," she said.

Colby sat beside her, pulling her close. "That was incredible. Nora just gave you the strongest testimonial possible. When she speaks at the town council meeting on Tuesday, there won't be a dry eye in the room."

"What if it's not enough?" Harper asked quietly. "What if Victor's right about the building being a bad investment? What if the council decides that profit matters more than history?"

"Then we'll deal with it," Colby said firmly. "But Harper, you saw what just happened. You saw this community rally around you, around this place. That's not nothing. That's everything."

Harper leaned her head on his shoulder. "I'm scared."

"I know. But you're not alone. You keep forgetting that." Colby kissed the top of her head. "Whatever happens Tuesday, we face it together. The whole town faces it together."

Harper was quiet for a moment, then lifted her head to look at him. "Colby, if we lose, if the council sides with Victor and I have to sell...I'm still staying. In Willow Creek, I mean. I'll find another job, another way to contribute. But I'm not running anymore."

Colby felt his heart expand in his chest. "Yeah?"

"Yeah. Because this..." Harper gestured around the post office, then took Colby's hand "...this is home now. Not the building. The people. You. And I'm not leaving that behind, no matter what happens with Victor Brennan."

Colby pulled her into a kiss that felt like a promise, like a celebration, like everything good he'd been hoping for since the moment Harper Delaney had arrived in Willow Creek with her mess of inherited problems.

When they broke apart, both breathless, Harper was smiling.

"We should probably actually do some post office work," she said. "Since we're fighting to save it and all."

"Probably," Colby agreed. "Or we could just sit here and appreciate the fact that Nora Whitfield just gave the most moving speech about mail delivery in the history of Wisconsin."

Harper laughed, a real laugh, full and genuine. "That too."

They stayed like that, holding each other in the quiet post

office, while outside Willow Creek went about its business. In four days, they'd face the town council. In four days, they'd find out if community and history could triumph over profit and progress.

But today, today they had this. They had each other, they had a community that believed in them, and they had a love story that had waited fifty years for completion and had somehow led to their own.

Some deliveries, Colby thought, took longer than others. But they were always worth the wait.

CHAPTER SEVENTEEN

Saturday morning arrived with clear skies and temperatures just warm enough that working outside wouldn't be miserable. Harper stood in front of the post office at seven a.m., coffee in hand, watching pickup trucks pull into the parking lot one by one.

Dylan's truck came first, loaded with paint supplies, brushes, drop cloths, and what looked like enough equipment to renovate an entire city block. Quinn's car followed, music blasting from her open windows. Then Maggie's van, Rosie's sedan, and at least a dozen others, people Harper barely knew, all showing up to help fix a building that most of them probably hadn't thought about in years.

"Ready to get your hands dirty?" Colby asked, appearing at her side with two more coffees and a grin that made Harper's heart do complicated things.

"I've never painted anything in my life," Harper admitted.

"In Chicago, you just call someone to do that."

"Well, welcome to small-town living, where 'calling someone' means calling your friends and offering them pizza in exchange for labor." Colby handed her a coffee. "Don't worry. I'm an excellent teacher. And by excellent, I mean I'll probably get more paint on you than on the walls."

Harper laughed, feeling some of her nervousness ease. "That's weirdly reassuring."

Dylan hopped out of his truck and immediately started directing traffic like a general commanding troops. "Okay, people! We've got two days to make this place look like something worth saving. Painting crew, you're with me. Repair crew, see the list I posted on the door. Cleaning crew, Maggie's in charge of you. Let's move!"

Within minutes, the post office had transformed into organized chaos. Harper watched, amazed, as people she'd seen around town but never really talked to claimed tasks and got to work. Mrs. Patterson, who had to be in her seventies, was scrubbing windows with the vigor of someone half her age. Sheriff Mitchell and two of his deputies were repairing the front steps that had been loose for as long as Harper could remember. Quinn and several library volunteers were cleaning out the storage room, sorting through decades of accumulated mail supplies and paperwork.

And Colby, true to his word, was teaching Harper how to paint the exterior trim.

"Long, even strokes," Colby demonstrated, his brush gliding smoothly across the white trim. "Don't overload the brush or you'll get drips. And try not to paint the windows. That's harder to fix."

Harper dipped her brush carefully and attempted to mimic his technique. Paint immediately dripped onto her jeans.

"I think I'm bad at this," she said.

"You're doing great," Colby lied cheerfully. "Look, you only got minimal paint on the window. That's progress."

"You're a terrible teacher."

"I'm an excellent teacher with a terrible student. There's a difference."

Harper tried to elbow him and accidentally smeared paint on his shirt. They both froze, then burst out laughing.

"That was assault with a deadly paintbrush," Colby said. "I could have you arrested. My best friend is literally the sheriff."

"Your best friend is too busy fixing my steps to care about your shirt," Harper retorted.

They painted in comfortable silence for a while, the sounds of work happening all around them, hammers, laughter, music from Quinn's portable speaker, Dylan's occasional directions shouted over the noise. Harper had never been part of something like this before. In Chicago, community meant networking events where everyone had ulterior motives. Here, community meant showing up on a Saturday morning to paint someone's building for free because it was the right thing to do.

"What are you thinking about?" Colby asked after a

while.

Harper set down her brush. "I'm thinking about how different this is from anything I've ever experienced. In Chicago, if I needed something done, I'd pay someone. It was a transaction, money for services, no relationship required. But this..." She gestured at the people working all around them. "This is something else entirely."

"This is what happens when people actually care about each other," Colby said. "When a place isn't just where you live, but where you belong."

"I'm starting to understand that," Harper said quietly. "For the first time in my adult life, I feel like I'm part of something bigger than myself. Like I matter to people, not because of what I can do for them, but just because I'm here."

Colby set down his own brush and pulled her close, apparently unconcerned about getting paint on both of them. "You do matter. You've always mattered. You just didn't have anyone around to remind you."

Harper leaned into him, breathing in the scent of paint and coffee and Colby. "Thank you for reminding me."

"Always," Colby said, and kissed her, a quick, sweet kiss that somehow felt more intimate than any of the longer kisses they'd shared.

"Hayes! Delaney! Less kissing, more painting!" Dylan shouted from across the parking lot, grinning.

Harper and Colby broke apart, both laughing. "He's bossy when he's in contractor mode," Colby said.

"I heard that!" Dylan called. "And yes, I am. Now get back to work!"

By lunchtime, the transformation was already visible. The exterior trim was halfway painted, the steps were repaired and solid, the windows sparkled in the sunlight. Inside, the cleaning crew had uncovered the beautiful original wood floors that had been hidden under decades of grime. The storage room was organized for the first time in probably thirty years.

Rosie and Maggie had organized a lunch setup on folding tables in the parking lot, sandwiches, salads, cookies, and enough coffee to fuel a small army. Everyone took a break, eating and laughing and admiring their progress.

Harper sat on the newly-repaired steps with Colby, Quinn, and Dylan, feeling more content than she could remember being in years.

"This is amazing," Quinn said through a mouthful of sandwich. "The building actually looks like something worth saving now."

"It always was worth saving," Clara said, making her way over with her walker. She'd been supervising from a chair Maggie had set up for her, offering historical context and occasionally shouting corrections. "But I'll admit, it's nice to see it looking loved again. Stella would be proud."

Harper felt her throat tighten. "I hope so. I keep wondering what she'd think about all this, me fighting to keep it, the community showing up like this, everything."

"She'd think you were finally figuring out what she knew all along," Clara said. "That this place isn't about mail. It's about the people mail connects. And you, Harper Delaney, have reminded everyone of that."

After lunch, they got back to work with renewed energy. Harper was reassigned to interior painting, apparently her exterior technique needed "more practice," according to Dylan's diplomatic assessment. She ended up working with Rosie on the customer service area, painting the walls a warm cream color that made the whole space feel brighter and more welcoming.

"So," Rosie said casually as they painted, "you and my son seem pretty serious."

Harper nearly dropped her paint roller. "We, um. We're together, yes."

"I can see that." Rosie's smile was warm and knowing. "I've watched Colby date over the years. I've seen him interested, I've seen him infatuated, I've even seen him engaged. But I've never seen him look at someone the way he looks at you."

"How does he look at me?" Harper asked, curious despite her embarrassment.

"Like you're home," Rosie said simply. "Like after three years of wandering, he finally found where he belongs. And Harper? He looks at you that way because you look at him the same way."

Harper's hand stilled on the wall. "I do?"

"You do. You light up when he walks in a room. You relax when he's near you. You trust him in a way that tells me you haven't trusted many people in your life." Rosie paused in her painting to look directly at Harper. "My son is a good man. He's patient and kind and he'll show up for you every single day. But he's also been hurt badly. Amanda left him questioning everything about himself. So I'm asking you, as his mother, are you staying? Not just in Willow Creek, but with him? Because if you're not sure, if there's a chance you'll run when things get hard, it's kinder to tell him now."

Harper set down her roller, meeting Rosie's gaze directly. "I'm staying. I'm terrified, and I don't have everything figured out, but I'm staying. For the post office, for this town, and absolutely for Colby. I love him, Rosie. I know it's fast and probably sounds crazy, but I love him. And I'm not running."

Rosie's eyes filled with tears. "That's all I needed to hear." She pulled Harper into a paint-splattered hug. "Welcome to the family, dear. You're stuck with us now."

"I'm okay with that," Harper said, hugging back.

By late afternoon, the transformation was remarkable. The exterior was freshly painted, the trim gleaming white against the brick. The interior walls were a warm, inviting cream. The floors were clean and polished. The storage room was organized. Even the old postal boxes that lined one wall had been cleaned and polished until they shone.

Harper stood in the middle of the customer service area, turning in a slow circle, barely able to believe this was the same space she'd walked into two weeks ago.

"It's beautiful," she whispered.

"It really is," Colby said, appearing beside her. He was

covered in paint and dust, his hair sticking up at odd angles, and Harper had never found him more attractive. "Your grandmother would love what you've done here."

"We've done," Harper corrected. "Colby, I couldn't have done any of this without you. Without everyone." She gestured at the people still working around them. "Two weeks ago, I was ready to sell this place to Victor Brennan and run back to Chicago. Now I can't imagine leaving. This building, this town, you, it's all become home somehow."

Colby took her hand. "You know, when I came back from Seattle after Amanda left, I felt like I'd failed. Like choosing Willow Creek meant choosing small, choosing safe, choosing less. But watching you these past two weeks, watching you choose this town not because you have to, but because you want to, I've realized that choosing small isn't failure. It's courage. It's choosing what matters over what impresses."

Harper squeezed his hand, unable to speak past the lump in her throat.

"Harper!" Quinn called from the doorway. "Come see what we found in the storage room!"

Harper and Colby followed Quinn to the newly-organized storage room, where she was holding a dusty photo album.

"I found this on the top shelf," Quinn said, carefully opening it. "Look...it's photographs of the post office through the decades."

Harper leaned over to look. There was the post office in the 1940s, looking almost exactly as it did now, with a young man in a postal uniform standing proudly in front. The 1950s, with Stella as a young woman, already working behind the counter. The 1960s, 70s, 80s...decade after decade of postal workers, of customers, of community gathered in this exact space they were standing in now.

"Stella kept records of everyone who worked here," Quinn said softly, turning pages. "Look, there's Clara in 1965. And here's a customer appreciation day from 1978. Harper, this place has been the center of this town for over a century. That's not just history. That's legacy."

Harper stared at the photographs, at the faces of people who'd stood where she was standing, who'd delivered mail and connected community and made this space matter to generations of people. And suddenly, Tuesday's town council meeting didn't feel scary, it felt necessary. This building deserved to be saved, not just for what it was, but for what it had always been: proof that connection mattered more than convenience, that relationships were worth more than revenue.

"We're going to save it," Harper said with sudden conviction. "On Tuesday, we're going to show the town council exactly why this place matters. And we're going to win."

"Damn right we are," Quinn said fiercely.

By the time the sun set Saturday evening, everyone was exhausted, covered in paint and dust, and enormously proud of what they'd accomplished. Harper stood outside with Colby, watching the last volunteers pack up their supplies.

"Same time tomorrow?" Dylan called. "We've still got the exterior back wall to paint and some trim work to finish."

"We'll be here," Harper promised.

As people drove away, calling out goodbyes and promises to return tomorrow, Harper leaned against Colby, feeling the weight of the day settle into her bones.

"Tired?" Colby asked.

"Exhausted. But it's a good tired. The kind that comes from actually doing something meaningful instead of just talking about it in meetings." Harper looked up at the building, at the fresh paint glowing in the streetlights. "Colby, do you think we have a chance on Tuesday? Really?"

"I think," Colby said carefully, "that we have a better chance than Victor Brennan expects. We have Nora's story, we have the community's support, we have this building looking beautiful and cared-for. We have you, standing up and fighting for something you believe in. That's not nothing, Harper. That's everything."

"But what if it's not enough?"

"Then we'll deal with it together. But I don't think it's going to come to that. I think you're going to walk into that meeting on Tuesday and remind everyone why some things are worth more than their profit margin."

Harper turned to kiss him, pouring all her gratitude and love and hope into it. When they broke apart, both breathless, Colby rested his forehead against hers.

"Whatever happens Tuesday," Harper said, "thank you. For showing up that first day. For every day since. For making me believe that staying could be better than running."

"Thank you for staying," Colby replied. "For being brave

enough to stop running and build something here. With me. With all of us."

They stood like that for a long moment, holding each other outside the transformed post office as Willow Creek settled into Saturday night. Tomorrow, they'd paint more. Tuesday, they'd face the town council.

But tonight, tonight was for this. For believing in possibilities. For choosing hope over fear. For standing together in front of a building that had become so much more than bricks and mortar.

Harper had spent two weeks learning what her grandmother already knew: that a post office wasn't just about delivering mail. It was about delivering connection, truth, second chances, and hope. It was about showing up, day after day, for the people and places that mattered.

And Harper was finally ready to show up.

For the post office. For Willow Creek. For Colby. For herself.

She was ready for Tuesday.

CHAPTER EIGHTEEN

Sunday evening found Colby standing in his kitchen, staring at the ingredients he'd laid out on the counter and wondering if he'd lost his mind. He was about to cook dinner for the woman he loved, a woman who'd spent five years in Chicago eating at restaurants he probably couldn't afford to look at the menu for. And he was making spaghetti.

Very fancy spaghetti, but still. Spaghetti.

His phone buzzed. Harper: *Be there in 10. Should I bring anything?*

Colby: *Just yourself. And low expectations for my cooking.*

Harper: *Your cooking got me to fall in love with you. Expectations already exceeded.*

Colby smiled at his phone like a lovesick teenager, which, he supposed, he basically was. Two weeks with Harper Delaney and he was completely gone, making her dinner at his place, planning futures he'd given up on three years ago, believing in possibilities he'd thought Amanda had killed.

The doorbell rang exactly ten minutes later. Colby wiped his hands on a dish towel and went to answer it, his heart doing complicated things in his chest.

Harper stood on his doorstep in jeans and a soft sweater, her auburn hair loose around her shoulders, holding a bottle of wine and looking nervous in a way that made Colby want to kiss her immediately.

"Hi," she said.

"Hi," Colby replied, suddenly feeling as nervous as she looked. This was different from all their other time together. No community around them, no post office work to focus on, no impending town meetings to plan for. Just the two of them, alone in his space, with nothing but honesty and possibility between them.

"Come in," Colby said, stepping back to let her enter.

Harper walked into his house, a small craftsman-style place he'd bought after the Amanda disaster, choosing deliberate smallness over the ambitious future they'd planned together. It was simple but comfortable: hardwood floors, built-in bookshelves, furniture that was more practical than stylish.

"Your place is perfect," Harper said, looking around. "It's so... you."

"Small and slightly awkward?" Colby asked.

"Warm and honest," Harper corrected. She handed him the wine. "I know we said just me, but I couldn't show up empty-handed. Small-town manners are apparently contagious."

"You're learning," Colby said with a smile. "Come on, you can keep me company while I attempt to not burn dinner."

In the kitchen, Harper settled onto a stool at the counter, watching as Colby returned to his pasta preparations. The domesticity of it struck him, this was what he'd wanted with Amanda, what he'd thought he'd lost forever. But this felt different. Better. Like it was happening naturally instead of being forced into some imagined perfect future.

"Can I help?" Harper asked.

"You can talk to me. Tell me about today." Colby started the water boiling. "Did you get the last of the painting done?"

"Quinn and I finished the trim work this afternoon. Dylan declared the building 'presentable' and only mocked my painting skills twice, so I'm calling that a win." Harper paused. "Colby, thank you for organizing all of that. For getting everyone to show up. I know you were behind it."

"I made a few phone calls," Colby admitted. "But everyone showed up because they wanted to. Because they believe in what you're doing."

"What we're doing," Harper corrected. "I couldn't do any of this without you."

Colby looked at her across the counter, this woman who'd walked into his life two weeks ago and somehow made him believe in second chances again. "Harper, I need to tell you something."

"Okay," Harper said, her expression turning serious.

"I'm terrified," Colby admitted. "Of Tuesday, obviously. But also, of this...of us. Of how fast this is happening and how much I already care. Three years ago, I thought I knew what love looked like. I thought it was Amanda and Seattle and building some ambitious future together. And when that fell apart, I convinced myself I was done. That I'd had my chance and blown it."

Harper was quiet, listening.

"But then you showed up," Colby continued, "with your inheritance and your letters and your complete inability to paint trim without getting it on everything except the trim. And suddenly I wasn't done. I was terrified and hopeful and falling in love so fast it made my head spin." He stopped chopping garlic to look at her directly. "What I'm trying to say is, I'm all in, Harper. Tomorrow we face the town council and maybe we win or maybe we lose. But either way, I'm in this with you. For the post office, for Willow Creek, and absolutely for us."

Harper's eyes were bright with tears. "Colby..."

"You don't have to say anything," Colby interrupted gently. "I just needed you to know. Before tomorrow, before whatever happens next, I needed you to know that this, you... are real for me. The most real thing I've felt in years."

Harper stood and came around the counter, stopping right in front of him. "My turn."

"Okay."

"I've spent my entire adult life running from anything that felt real. From Willow Creek, from my grandmother, from any relationship that might require me to stay in one place long enough to fail at it. I became very good at running. At convincing myself that running was the same as succeeding." Harper took a breath. "But then I inherited a post office I didn't want, found letters that didn't belong to me, and met a mail carrier who somehow made staying feel braver than running. And I realized I'd been wrong about everything."

Colby's heart was racing.

"I'm not running anymore," Harper said firmly. "Tomorrow, Tuesday, next month, I'm staying. I'm fighting for the post office, I'm building a life here, and I'm choosing you. Every single day. Because Colby Hayes, you are the best thing that's ever happened to me, and I'm not giving that up just because I'm scared."

Colby closed the distance between them and kissed her, a kiss that felt like a promise, like a celebration, like everything he'd been too afraid to hope for. Harper kissed back with equal intensity, her hands fisting in his shirt, and Colby forgot about dinner, about tomorrow, about everything except the feeling of Harper in his arms, finally, completely his.

When they broke apart, both breathing hard, Harper rested her forehead against his.

"Your water's boiling," she said.

"Let it boil," Colby replied, and kissed her again.

Somehow, they managed to make dinner without burning anything. They ate at Colby's small kitchen table, knees touching underneath, conversation flowing easily between bites. Harper told him about Chicago, not the polished version, but the real version. The loneliness of Sunday mornings with nowhere to go, the work dinners where she'd felt like a performing seal, the studio apartment that never quite felt like home.

Colby told her about the year after Amanda left, the anger and confusion and the slow realization that maybe losing her wasn't the tragedy he'd thought it was. Maybe it was just the end of something that was never quite right to begin with.

"Do you ever regret not going to Seattle?" Harper asked.

"Not anymore," Colby said honestly. "At first, yeah. I felt like I'd chosen small over big, safe over adventurous. Like I'd failed some test of ambition." He reached across the table to take her hand. "But watching you these past two weeks, watching you choose Willow Creek not because you're settling, but because it's actually where you want to be, I've realized that choosing what you love isn't failure. It's courage."

"You told me something similar on our first date," Harper said softly. "About the difference between impressive and real."

"Did it work? The whole 'deep philosophical insight' thing?"

"It worked. You worked. This whole town worked." Harper squeezed his hand. "Colby, I keep waiting for the moment when I wake up and panic. When I realize I've made a huge mistake and need to run back to Chicago. But that moment never comes. Every day I wake up and feel... settled. Like I finally found where I'm supposed to be."

"Good," Colby said. "Because I really like having you here."

After dinner, they moved to the living room couch with fresh wine, sitting close enough that their shoulders touched. Outside, November darkness had fallen early, and through Colby's windows, they could see the lights of Willow Creek, small and peaceful and home.

"Tell me something," Harper said. "Something you've never told anyone else."

Colby thought about it. "When Amanda left, I spent six months sleeping on my mother's couch because I couldn't stand being alone in the house we'd picked out together. My mother never said anything, just let me stay until I was ready to leave. And when I finally bought this place, small and mine and nothing like what Amanda and I had planned—my mother came over with a bottle of champagne and said, 'Now you're home.' Like she'd been waiting for me to stop trying to live someone else's life and start living my own."

"Your mother is the wisest person I've ever met," Harper said.

"She really is." Colby paused. "Your turn. Tell me something you've never told anyone."

Harper was quiet for a long moment. "The day I quit my job in Chicago, the day before I drove here, I sat in my apartment and tried to make myself feel something about leaving. Sadness, fear, regret, anything. But all I felt was relief.

Like I'd been holding my breath for five years and finally got to exhale." She looked at Colby. "That's when I knew I'd been living wrong. When leaving my entire life behind felt like freedom instead of loss."

Colby pulled her closer, and Harper settled against his chest, her head on his shoulder. They sat like that for a while, listening to the quiet house, to each other's breathing, to the sound of a future being built one honest moment at a time.

"I'm nervous about tomorrow," Harper admitted quietly.

"Me too."

"What if we lose?"

"Then we figure out plan B," Colby said. "But Harper, even if we lose the building, we don't lose this. We don't lose us, or the community, or what we've built here. Victor Brennan can't buy that."

Harper tilted her face up to kiss him, slow and deep and full of gratitude. When she pulled back, her hazel eyes were dark with something that made Colby's breath catch.

"Stay tonight?" Colby asked, his voice rough. "Not just for sleep. Stay with me."

"Yes," Harper said simply.

Colby stood and offered his hand. Harper took it, and he led her down the hallway to his bedroom, simple like the rest of the house, but comfortable, his. The curtains were open, showing the stars visible in Willow Creek's dark sky, nothing like the light pollution of Chicago.

"I love you," Colby said, turning to face her. "I know we've said it before, but I need you to hear it again. I love you, Harper. For exactly who you are."

"I love you too," Harper replied, reaching for him. "Show me."

And Colby did.

Morning light filtered through the curtains, painting patterns across the sheets. Colby woke slowly, aware of warmth beside him, of Harper curled against his side, her auburn hair spread across his pillow. For a moment, he just lay there, taking in the reality of it, Harper in his bed, in his house, in his life, choosing to stay.

Harper stirred, her eyes opening slowly. When she saw him watching her, she smiled, a sleepy, satisfied smile that made Colby's heart ache with how much he loved her.

"Morning," she murmured.

"Morning," Colby replied, pressing a kiss to her forehead. "Sleep okay?"

"Better than okay." Harper stretched, then settled back against him. "That was... we should do that again. Soon. Often."

Colby laughed. "I'm amenable to that plan."

They lay in comfortable silence for a while, hands linked, watching the morning light grow stronger. In a few hours, they'd have to get up, get dressed, face Monday and all the final preparations for Tuesday's town council meeting. But for now, they had this, the quiet intimacy of morning, the knowledge that something fundamental had shifted between them.

"Colby?" Harper said eventually.

"Hmm?"

"No matter what happens tomorrow at the meeting, we're okay, right? You and me?"

Colby rolled to face her fully, taking her face in his hands. "Harper, we are more than okay. We are the most okay thing in my life. Win or lose tomorrow, I choose you. Every single time."

Harper's eyes filled with tears. "Good. Because I choose you too. And I'm not going anywhere."

"Promise?" Colby asked, only half-joking.

"Promise," Harper said firmly. "You're stuck with me, Hayes. For the long haul."

"Best news I've heard all week," Colby said, and kissed her.

They made breakfast together, coffee and toast and eggs that Harper insisted on cooking even though Colby protested he was the better cook. She proved him right by slightly burning the eggs, but Colby ate them anyway, and somehow they were the best eggs he'd ever tasted because Harper had made them in his kitchen, in his house, the morning after everything had changed.

"I should probably go home," Harper said reluctantly around nine. "I need to review my notes for tomorrow, make sure I have everything organized."

"I'll come with you," Colby said. "We can prep together."

They drove to the post office in comfortable silence, hands linked across the console. When they pulled into the parking lot, Harper's phone started buzzing with messages, Quinn, Maggie, Dylan, all checking in about tomorrow, offering support, promising to be there.

"The whole town is going to show up," Harper said, reading through the messages. "Colby, what if I mess this up? What if I'm not articulate enough or convincing enough or..."

"Harper." Colby turned off the engine and twisted to face her. "You are the woman who tracked down a stranger to deliver fifty-year-old letters because you thought truth mattered. You are the woman who convinced an entire community to fight for a post office that barely breaks even. You are the woman who made me believe in second chances when I'd given up on first chances." He squeezed her hand. "You're going to walk into that meeting tomorrow and remind everyone why some things matter more than their profit margin. And you're going to be incredible."

Harper took a shaky breath. "You have a lot of faith in me."

"You've earned it," Colby said simply. "Every single day since you got here."

They spent Monday afternoon at the post office, reviewing testimonials, organizing the photo album Quinn had found, making sure they had every piece of evidence ready for the town council. Around three, people started stopping by, not for mail, but to offer encouragement, to promise they'd be at the meeting, to thank Harper for fighting.

Mrs. Patterson brought cookies. Sheriff Mitchell stopped by to say the entire department supported them. Even Mayor Williams, a cautious man who usually avoided conflicts, came by to quietly tell Harper that he thought what she was doing was important, though he couldn't say so publicly until after the meeting.

By evening, Harper was exhausted, emotionally wrung out from a day of gratitude and support and mounting pressure. After everyone left, she and Colby sat in the quiet post office, the weight of tomorrow pressing down on them.

"I'm scared," Harper admitted.

"I know. So am I." Colby pulled her close. "But we're scared together. That makes it better."

"Does it?"

"Yeah. Because whatever happens, we face it together. And on Wednesday morning, whether we won or lost, we'll still have each other. We'll still have this town. We'll still have a life we're building that Victor Brennan can't touch."

Harper was quiet for a moment, then looked up at him. "When did you become such an optimist?"

"About two weeks ago," Colby said. "When a woman showed up with a mess of inherited problems and reminded me that some things are worth fighting for."

Harper kissed him, a kiss that tasted like promise and

possibility and tomorrow's uncertain hope.

"Let's go home," Harper said when they broke apart. "Your place or mine?"

"Yours," Colby said. "I want to wake up with you in Stella's apartment. In your apartment. Where everything started."

They climbed the stairs to the apartment above the post office, the one that was slowly becoming Harper's instead of her grandmother's. They made love again, slower this time, less desperate, more certain. And afterward, lying in Harper's bed with Colby's arms around her, Harper felt something she hadn't felt in years.

Peace. Not the absence of fear, but the presence of something stronger, love, purpose, community, home.

Tomorrow, they'd face the town council. Tomorrow, they'd find out if passion and history could triumph over profit and progress. Tomorrow, everything might change.

But tonight, Harper was exactly where she wanted to be. Where she'd always needed to be, even when she didn't know it.

Home.

CHAPTER NINETEEN

Harper woke Tuesday morning to gray November light filtering through the curtains and the weight of everything pressing down on her chest. For a moment, she lay perfectly still, feeling Colby's arm around her waist, his breath steady against her shoulder, and thought about staying here forever. Not facing the town council, not fighting Victor Brennan, just staying in this bed where everything felt safe and certain.

But that wasn't an option.

Colby stirred beside her, his arm tightening. "You're awake," he murmured against her hair. "I can tell from the way you're breathing."

"How do I breathe when I'm asleep?" Harper asked.

"Peaceful. Right now, you're breathing like you're trying to solve a differential equation." Colby pressed a kiss to her shoulder. "It's going to be okay."

"You don't know that."

"I know that in about six hours, you're going to walk into that meeting and remind everyone why the post office matters. And I know that regardless of what the council decides, you're going to be okay. We're going to be okay."

Harper rolled over to face him. In the morning light, Colby looked rumpled and beautiful and completely certain in a way that made Harper want to believe him. "What if I freeze? What if I get up there and forget everything I planned to say?"

"Then you'll remember why you're fighting in the first place. For Stella, for Nora, for Jamie, for every person who's ever gotten mail in this building and felt connected instead of alone." Colby brushed her hair back from her face. "Harper, you've already done the hard part. You stayed. You fought. You built something worth saving. Today is just about showing the council what you've already proved to everyone else."

Harper kissed him, drawing strength from his certainty. "How are you not nervous?"

"I'm terrified," Colby admitted. "But I'm also absolutely sure that you're going to be incredible. So, I'm choosing to focus on that part."

They got up slowly, neither wanting to start the day but knowing it was inevitable. Harper showered and stood in front of Stella's closet, her closet now, trying to decide what you wore to fight for your grandmother's legacy.

She settled on a navy dress that Stella had given her years

ago, one Harper had never worn because it felt too small-town, too simple. But looking at it now, Harper realized it was perfect. Classic, professional, but unmistakably Willow Creek. She paired it with the locket Stella had left her and low heels that wouldn't make her trip walking into the town hall.

When she emerged from the bedroom, Colby was in the kitchen making coffee, already dressed in dark slacks and a button-down. He looked up when he heard her and stopped mid-pour.

"You look like Stella," he said quietly. "In the best way. Like someone who belongs here completely."

Harper felt tears threaten and blinked them back. "I can't cry yet. I'll ruin my makeup."

"Save it for after we win," Colby said, handing her coffee. "Then you can cry all you want."

Harper's phone buzzed on the counter. Her brother Todd, calling from Seattle. She'd texted him last night about the meeting, and apparently he'd set an alarm to call before it started.

"I should take this," Harper said.

Colby nodded and tactfully moved to give her privacy.

Harper answered. "Hey, Todd."

"Big day," her brother said without preamble. "How are you holding up?"

"I'm terrified I'm going to fail and disappoint everyone who's counting on me," Harper admitted. "Other than that, great."

Todd was quiet for a moment. "You know, I never understood why you ran from Willow Creek so hard. I mean, I left too, but you acted like the town was a prison instead of just a place. Like staying would have killed something in you."

"It felt that way at the time," Harper said. "Like if I stayed, I'd be admitting I wasn't good enough for something bigger."

"And now?"

Harper looked around Stella's apartment, her apartment, at the life she'd built in two weeks. "Now I realize that Willow Creek wasn't the problem. I was. I was so busy trying to become someone impressive that I forgot to figure out who I actually wanted to be."

"And who's that?" Todd asked.

"Someone who shows up," Harper said simply. "Someone who fights for things that matter even when the odds are bad. Someone who delivers truth even when it's fifty years late." She paused. "Someone like Stella."

"She'd be proud of you," Todd said, his voice thick. "I'm proud of you. You quit a job you hated, inherited a mess, and instead of running like both of us expected, you stayed and fought. That takes guts, Harper."

"Or stupidity," Harper said, but she was smiling.

"Sometimes those are the same thing. Look, I can't be there today, but I'm in your corner. And if the council sides with the developer guy..."

"Victor Brennan."

"...if they side with Victor, you're still going to be okay. You've got a whole town that loves you, a boyfriend who's crazy about you, and a brother in Seattle who'll help you figure out plan B if you need it."

Harper felt the tightness in her chest ease slightly. "Thanks, Todd."

"Go save your post office, little sister. And call me after. I want to hear every detail."

After they hung up, Harper found Colby in the living room, looking at the photo album Quinn had found. He glanced up when she entered.

"You okay?" he asked.

"Better. Todd reminded me that even if we lose today, I haven't lost everything I've gained by being here." Harper sat beside him. "But I really want to win."

"We're going to win," Colby said with conviction. "Victor Brennan has money and development plans. We have Nora's story, Clara's history, a century of community connection, and a building that finally looks like something worth saving. We have truth on our side. That has to count for something."

At eleven-thirty, they headed downstairs. The meeting was at one, but people were already gathering outside the post office, ready to walk to town hall together. Harper stepped outside and stopped, overwhelmed by what she saw.

At least fifty people stood in the parking lot and along the sidewalk. Quinn and Dylan at the front. Maggie and Rosie with coffee for everyone. Clara in her walker, flanked by Sheriff Mitchell and two deputies. Mrs. Patterson with a group of elderly residents. The library board. Several business owners. Even some people Harper didn't recognize, community members who'd heard about the fight and shown up to support it.

And at the center, looking elegant and determined, stood Nora Whitfield with Jamie Mitchell beside her, holding hands.

"We're here," Nora announced when she saw Harper. "All of us. Ready to fight for what matters."

Harper couldn't speak past the lump in her throat. Colby squeezed her hand.

"Thank you," Harper finally managed. "All of you. This means everything."

"You reminded us what this place is for," Clara said firmly. "Now we're going to make sure the council remembers too."

They walked to town hall together, a procession of community, determination, and hope. Harper walked between Colby and Quinn, drawing strength from their presence. Behind them, she could hear conversations, laughter, nervous energy. These were people who'd shown up for her, for the post office, for the idea that some things mattered more than profit.

The town hall was a stately brick building that had

probably been impressive in 1920 and now just looked tired. The meeting room was on the second floor, a large space with rows of chairs facing a raised platform where the five council members would sit. Victor's development presentation boards were already set up on an easel to one side.

Harper's stomach dropped when she saw them, glossy, professional, covered in architectural renderings and financial projections. Victor clearly had money behind him, resources Harper couldn't match. His vision of Main Street showed boutique shops, a hotel with modern design, parking structures, tourists. It looked appealing, polished, like progress.

"Don't look at those," Colby murmured. "Look at this."

He gestured to the room filling with people. Every seat was taken, and more people lined the walls. Willow Creek had turned out in force. Harper recognized faces from the renovation weekend, from Nora's speech, from years of half-remembered childhood encounters. This was her community, showing up when it mattered.

Victor Brennan stood near his presentation boards, talking to someone Harper didn't recognize, probably a lawyer or consultant. He looked confident, polished, completely certain he was going to win. When he saw Harper, he smiled, not unkindly, but with the assurance of someone who thought the outcome was already decided.

"Miss Delaney," Victor said, approaching. "Quite a turnout. Though I suspect numbers won't matter much when the council sees the financial projections."

"This isn't about numbers," Harper said, finding her

voice. "It's about what this community values."

"Community values don't pay for infrastructure repairs," Victor replied smoothly. "But I admire your passion. Truly. It's just misplaced." He gestured to his boards. "This is progress, Miss Delaney. Growth, jobs, tax revenue. What you're offering is sentiment and nostalgia. The council will choose wisely."

Before Harper could respond, the council members filed in, five people ranging from middle-aged to elderly, all looking serious and slightly uncomfortable with the packed room. Mayor Williams was among them, carefully not meeting Harper's eyes. The others she recognized vaguely, Mrs. Davidson who ran the real estate office, Mr. Chen from the hardware store (Dylan's father, which hopefully meant an ally), Mrs. Rodriguez who'd been on the council since Harper was a child, and young Councilman Sawyer, probably only thirty, who taught at the high school.

Mayor Williams called the meeting to order, and the room fell silent.

"We're here to discuss the future of the Willow Creek Post Office property," he began. "Miss Harper Delaney, current owner, is opposing a development proposal from Victor Brennan of Brennan Development Group. Both parties have prepared presentations for the council's consideration. Mr. Brennan, as the petitioning party, you'll go first."

Victor stood, confident and polished, and launched into his presentation. He talked about economic opportunity, tax revenue projections, job creation, modern amenities that would attract tourists and young families. His vision was compelling, Willow Creek transformed into a destination, Main Street thriving with boutique shops and a luxury hotel, parking structures that would solve the downtown congestion problem.

Harper watched the council members' faces. Most looked interested, even intrigued. Mrs. Davidson was taking notes. Mr. Chen looked thoughtful but not dismissive. Only Mrs. Rodriguez seemed skeptical, her arms crossed, her expression unchanging.

Victor finished with a flourish, showing a final rendering of his "New Willow Creek", bright, modern, prosperous. "This is what progress looks like," he concluded. "This is what Willow Creek could be if you're brave enough to choose growth over stagnation. Thank you."

There was scattered applause, not from Harper's supporters, but from a few people she didn't recognize. Probably Victor's allies or people swayed by the promise of economic growth.

Mayor Williams nodded. "Thank you, Mr. Brennan. Miss Delaney, you may present your case."

Harper stood on shaking legs. This was it. Everything she'd fought for, everything she'd built, came down to the next few minutes.

She walked to the front of the room, no glossy presentation boards, no financial projections, just her and the truth she'd learned over the past two weeks.

"I'm not going to show you renderings of what Willow Creek could look like," Harper began, her voice steadier than she expected. "I'm going to remind you what it already is."

She pulled out the photo album Quinn had found. "This post office has stood on Main Street for over a century. These photographs show every postal worker who's served there, every customer appreciation day, every moment of community gathered in that space. My grandmother, Stella Delaney, ran that post office for forty years. Not because it made her wealthy, it didn't. Not because it was convenient, it wasn't. She did it because she understood something Mr. Brennan's financial projections can't measure."

Harper looked at the council members, making eye contact with each one. "The post office isn't just about mail. It's about connection. It's about knowing when Mrs. Patterson's getting too many sympathy cards because her husband is sick. It's about holding packages for the Johnson family when they're going through a rough time. It's about making sure birthday cards arrive on time because someone cares enough to remember."

She paused, then gestured to Nora. "Two weeks ago, I found twenty-five letters in my grandmother's desk. Love letters from 1973, written by Jamie Mitchell to Nora Whitfield. Letters that someone had marked 'Return to Sender' and hidden away. Letters that stole fifty years from two people who loved each other."

The room was completely silent now. Harper saw several council members lean forward.

"I could have filed those letters away as interesting historical artifacts. I could have thought 'how sad' and moved on. But I didn't. I tracked Jamie down. I told him the truth. And because of what the post office represents, because of what it's always represented, those two people got their second chance."

Harper looked directly at Nora and Jamie, sitting together, hands clasped. "Nora, would you tell the council your story?"

Nora stood with quiet dignity. In her elegant way, she told the council about falling in love in 1973, about waiting for letters that never came, about fifty years of believing she'd been forgotten. About Harper finding the truth and delivering it fifty years late. About getting a second chance at love because someone believed that connection mattered more than convenience.

By the time Nora finished, several council members were wiping their eyes. Mrs. Rodriguez was crying openly.

Then Clara stood, walker scraping against the floor. "I worked at that post office for forty-three years," she said firmly. "I watched Stella Delaney run it like it was sacred ground. Because to her, it was. Every letter was someone's hope, someone's grief, someone's love delivered into their hands. You can't put that on a financial projection. You can't measure that in tax revenue."

One by one, people stood to speak. Maggie talked about how Stella had been the first to congratulate her on opening The Copper Kettle. Dylan mentioned his grandfather taking him to the post office as a child, teaching him that community meant showing up. Quinn spoke about historical preservation and the importance of maintaining Willow Creek's identity.

And then Colby stood.

"I'm a mail carrier," he said simply. "I deliver mail for a

living. And what I've learned from Stella, and from watching Harper these past two weeks, is that delivery isn't just about getting something from point A to point B. It's about paying attention. It's about noticing when someone's struggling and taking an extra minute to ask if they're okay. It's about understanding that sometimes a letter is just paper, and sometimes it's a lifeline."

He looked at Harper, and she felt tears slide down her cheeks.

"Harper Delaney could have sold that building two weeks ago," Colby continued. "Victor Brennan offered her a hundred and fifty thousand dollars. She could have taken the money and walked away. But she didn't. She stayed. She fought. She delivered truth that was fifty years old because she believed it mattered. That's the kind of person who should own that post office. That's the kind of values this community should be supporting."

The room erupted in applause, genuine, heartfelt, community standing behind one of their own.

Mayor Williams called for order, and the room quieted. He looked at his fellow council members. "I think we need to deliberate. We'll take a fifteen-minute recess and return with our decision."

The council filed out, and Harper felt her legs give way. Colby was there immediately, holding her up, and Quinn grabbed her other arm.

"You were incredible," Quinn said fiercely.

"We don't know if it was enough," Harper said.

"It was enough," Nora said, approaching with Jamie. "Truth is always enough."

But as Harper looked at Victor Brennan across the room, still confident despite the emotional testimonials, she wasn't sure.

In fifteen minutes, she'd know if truth was worth more than profit.

In fifteen minutes, everything would change.

The fifteen minutes felt like fifteen hours. Harper stood outside the council chamber with Colby, Quinn, and the others, her stomach churning with anxiety. She could hear muffled voices through the walls but couldn't make out words.

"Whatever happens..." Colby started.

"Don't," Harper interrupted. "Don't say it doesn't matter, because it does."

"I was going to say, whatever happens, you changed something here. You reminded this town what community means."

The council chamber doors opened. Mayor Williams stood in the doorway, his expression unreadable.

"We've reached a decision," he said. "Please come back in."

Harper's legs felt like water as she returned to her seat. The room was silent except for the sound of papers rustling as the council members took their places.

Mayor Williams cleared his throat. "This was not an easy decision. Victor Brennan made compelling arguments about revenue and development. But..." He paused, looking directly at Harper. "This council was reminded tonight that some things can't be measured in tax dollars. The Willow Creek Post Office will receive historical preservation status, effective immediately."

The room erupted in cheers. Harper felt Colby's arms around her, Quinn screaming with joy, but it all felt distant, dreamlike.

"However," the mayor continued, raising his voice over the celebration, "this building still needs significant repairs. We're requiring a full structural assessment and two hundred thousand dollars in documented improvements within the next year, or the preservation status will be revoked."

Harper's elation faltered. Two hundred thousand dollars. She had seventy-five thousand from Stella's life insurance. That left her one hundred and twenty-five thousand short.

But as she looked around at the faces of her community...Clara beaming, Nora and Jamie holding hands, Rosie giving her a proud nod...Harper realized she'd just been given something more valuable than money.

She'd been given a chance. And a year to figure out how to take it.

CHAPTER TWENTY

The celebration at The Copper Kettle lasted well into the evening. Someone had strung fairy lights across the café's back patio, and Maggie kept bringing out trays of food, comfort dishes that tasted like home, like victory, like the future Harper was finally brave enough to claim.

Harper stood on the patio's edge, watching Willow Creek's Main Street through the twinkling lights. Two weeks ago, she'd stood in the town hall certain she was about to lose everything. Now the post office was officially hers, protected by historical preservation status, and a whole town had shown up to make it happen.

"You're doing that thing again," Colby said, appearing beside her with two glasses of wine.

"What thing?"

"That thing where you look stunned, like you can't quite

believe this is real." He handed her a glass, his fingers brushing hers. "It's real, Harper. You won. The building is safe."

Harper took a sip, letting the wine warm her throat. "The building is safe for now. Did you hear what the council said? Two hundred thousand dollars in repairs. I have seventy-five thousand from Stella's life insurance. That leaves me..." She did the math in her head, her stomach sinking. "A hundred and twenty-five thousand dollars short."

"We'll figure it out," Colby said simply.

"We." Harper tested the word, liking how it sounded. "When did this become 'we'?"

Colby set down his wine glass and turned to face her fully, his expression serious in the soft light. "When I watched you stand up in that council meeting and fight for something you believed in. When I saw you risk everything for a building that represents connection and community. When I realized that somewhere between delivering your mail and watching you deliver those letters, I fell in love with you."

Harper's breath caught. The noise from inside the café faded to nothing.

"You..." She couldn't finish the sentence.

"I love you," Colby said again, clearer this time. "I know it's fast. I know we've only known each other two weeks. But I've spent twelve years delivering mail in this town, and I've never met anyone who understood what it meant the way you do. Every letter matters. Every connection matters. Every person deserves to be seen. That's what Stella taught me, and that's what you're carrying forward."

Harper felt tears slide down her cheeks. "Colby..."

"You don't have to say it back," he interrupted gently. "I'm not trying to pressure you. I just needed you to know. Tonight, after everything you accomplished, I needed you to know that you're not alone in this. Whatever comes next, fundraising, repairs, keeping that building standing, I'm here. If you want me."

"If I want you?" Harper laughed through her tears. "Colby Hayes, I've been trying not to want you for two weeks because wanting you felt terrifying. Wanting you meant staying. Wanting you meant admitting that everything I thought I wanted in Chicago was wrong, and everything I ran from here was actually what I needed."

She stepped closer, closing the distance between them. "But yes. I want you. I love you. I'm terrified and overwhelmed and I have no idea how I'm going to come up with a hundred and twenty-five thousand dollars, but I love you."

Colby pulled her into his arms, and they kissed as the celebration continued inside, as Willow Creek sparkled around them, as the future stretched out uncertain but suddenly, miraculously, possible.

When they finally broke apart, Quinn was standing in the doorway, grinning like she'd won the lottery.

"Finally!" she shouted. "I've been waiting for this since day one! You two are the worst at hiding feelings, by the way. Everyone knew."

Harper laughed, wiping her eyes. "Everyone knew?"

"Everyone," Maggie confirmed, appearing behind Quinn with more wine. "We've been taking bets on when you'd figure it out. Rosie just won fifty dollars."

"My mother was betting on us?" Colby asked, sounding torn between amusement and horror.

"Your mother, my mother, half the town," Maggie said cheerfully. "Welcome to small-town life, Harper. Your business is everyone's business, especially when it's this romantic."

They went back inside to more congratulations, more food, more stories about Stella and the post office and the victory they'd achieved together. But eventually, as midnight approached, people began to drift home, hugging Harper on their way out, promising support, offering hope.

Mrs. Rodriguez was one of the last to leave. She pulled Harper aside near the door.

"About that two hundred thousand dollars," she said quietly. "I have an idea. There's a state grant program for historical preservation, buildings over a century old, still in community use, documented historical significance. The Willow Creek Post Office checks every box."

Harper felt a flicker of hope. "How much?"

"Maximum award is one hundred and fifty thousand. Combined with your seventy-five thousand, that would give you two hundred and twenty-five thousand. More than enough."

"What's the catch?"

"The application is extensive. You'd need detailed renovation plans, community support letters, historical documentation, proof of the building's significance. And the deadline is in two weeks."

Harper's hope dimmed. "Two weeks? That's impossible."

"It's ambitious," Mrs. Rodriguez corrected. "But possible. I've helped with these applications before. I can guide you through it. And you've got something most applicants don't have, a whole town ready to support you. Those letters you delivered? That story about Nora and Jamie? That's exactly the kind of human interest element these committees respond to."

"Two weeks," Harper repeated.

"Two weeks," Mrs. Rodriguez confirmed. "Starting tomorrow, if you're interested. But Harper, you need to understand, there's no guarantee. These grants are competitive. You could do everything right and still not get it."

"And if I don't get it?"

Mrs. Rodriguez's expression turned sympathetic. "Then you'd need to find other funding, or..." She didn't finish, but Harper understood. Or sell to someone like Victor Brennan. Or let the building go.

"I'll do it," Harper said. "I'll apply. We didn't fight this hard to give up now."

After Mrs. Rodriguez left, Harper found Colby helping Maggie clean up.

"We have two weeks to put together a grant application," she told him. "Historical preservation grant. One hundred and fifty thousand dollars if we get it."

"Then we'll get it," Colby said with the same calm certainty he brought to everything. "What do you need?"

"I need..." Harper looked around at the café, at Willow Creek visible through the windows, at this man who'd somehow become essential to her in two weeks. "I need to believe this is possible. I need to believe that fighting for something matters even when the odds are bad."

Colby set down the tray he'd been clearing and came to her. "Harper Delaney, you tracked down a seventy-year-old man from a stack of fifty-year-old letters. You convinced a town council to choose sentiment over profit. You made me believe in love again after I'd given up on it. If anyone can make the impossible happen, it's you."

They walked back to the post office together, hand in hand under the streetlights. The building looked different now, not just because of the renovation work, but because it was officially safe. Protected. Worth fighting for.

Upstairs in Stella's apartment, Harper pulled out her laptop. Sleep could wait. She needed to start researching grant applications, needed to make lists, needed to turn hope into action.

But Colby gently closed the laptop.

"Tomorrow," he said. "Tonight, you rest. You just won an impossible victory. Give yourself one night to celebrate before you start the next battle."

Harper wanted to argue, wanted to dive immediately into planning. But Colby was right. She was exhausted, emotionally wrung out, running on adrenaline and caffeine.

"Okay," she said. "Tomorrow."

They lay down together on Harper's narrow bed, fully clothed, Colby's arms around her, his steady heartbeat against her back. Outside, Willow Creek slept peacefully. Inside, Harper felt something settle in her chest, not peace exactly, but purpose. She knew what she was fighting for now. She knew why it mattered.

"Colby?" she whispered into the darkness.

"Yeah?"

"Thank you for loving me. For seeing something worth fighting for even when I couldn't see it myself."

"Always," Colby murmured. "I'll always see it. Even when you forget."

Harper closed her eyes, Stella's envelope necklace warm against her skin, Colby's warmth solid beside her. Two weeks ago, she'd arrived in Willow Creek planning to sell everything and leave. Now she was planning to stay, to fight, to build a life worth living in the place she'd spent so long running from.

Tomorrow would bring new challenges. Grant applications and renovation plans and the constant worry of funding. But tonight, she had this: a building saved, a community behind her, and a man who loved her for exactly who she was.

Some deliveries took years to arrive. Some showed up exactly when you needed them most, even if you didn't know you were waiting.

Harper was learning to trust the timing, to trust the journey, to trust that love, in all its forms, always found its way home.

CHAPTER TWENTY-ONE

Harper woke to sunlight streaming through the window and the smell of coffee. For a moment, she was disoriented, she hadn't made coffee yet, and then she remembered. Colby had stayed.

She found him in the tiny kitchen, two mugs already poured, looking annoyingly awake for six-thirty in the morning. He was still wearing yesterday's clothes, his hair adorably rumpled, scrolling through something on his laptop.

"Morning," he said, looking up with a smile that made Harper's heart do unnecessary acrobatics. "Hope you don't mind, I borrowed your laptop. I've been researching state historical preservation grants."

Harper accepted the coffee gratefully and peered at the screen. Colby had opened at least fifteen tabs, application requirements, successful proposal examples, historical documentation guidelines, budget templates.

"You've been up for how long?" she asked.

"Hour, maybe. I'm an early riser." He pulled out a chair for her. "I couldn't sleep, and I figured I might as well be productive. Harper, this grant is absolutely achievable. Look at this."

He walked her through what he'd found. The grant program prioritized community-centered buildings with documented historical significance and clear plans for continued public use. The Willow Creek Post Office checked every box.

"The application has four main components," Colby explained. "Historical documentation, community impact statements, detailed renovation plans with cost estimates, and long-term sustainability plans. We can absolutely do this in two weeks."

"We," Harper said, testing the word again. After last night's declarations, it felt both thrilling and terrifying to lean into it. "You really meant it, didn't you? The 'all in' thing?"

"I really meant it," Colby confirmed. "I talked to my supervisor first thing this morning. I'm taking my vacation time, I've got ten days saved up. I'm all yours for the next two weeks."

Harper felt overwhelmed by his support, his confidence, his willingness to invest his limited vacation time in her uncertain future. "Colby, you don't have to…"

"I want to," he interrupted gently, reaching across the table to take her hand. "Harper, I meant what I said last night. This matters to you, which means it matters to me. Besides, I've been delivering mail in this town for twelve years. I know every person who could help with this application. Let me help."

Before Harper could respond, her phone buzzed. A text from Mrs. Rodriguez: *Free at 9am if you want to start on that grant application. Bring coffee...this is a three-cup conversation.*

"She doesn't waste time," Harper said, showing Colby the message.

"Neither should we," Colby replied. "We've got thirteen days until the deadline. Let's make every one count."

They met Mrs. Rodriguez at her real estate office, a small brick building on Main Street with a view of the post office. She'd cleared her conference table and laid out printed copies of previous successful grant applications, budget worksheets, and timeline templates.

"These are from other small-town preservation projects," Mrs. Rodriguez explained, handing them each coffee from the pot she'd clearly made fresh. "They'll give you a sense of what the grant committee responds to. But first, let's talk strategy."

She pulled out a legal pad covered in neat, organized notes.

"The state receives about two hundred applications for these grants annually. They award approximately thirty. Your advantages: documented century-old history, recent demonstrated community support, clear continued public use, photographic evidence, and a compelling human interest story with those letters."

"What are our disadvantages?" Harper asked, needing to hear the worst.

"Limited renovation budget if the grant doesn't come through, you're a new owner with no track record, and the building has been neglected for two years. They're going to want assurance you can complete the project and maintain the building long-term."

"How do we prove that?" Colby asked.

"Three ways," Mrs. Rodriguez said, ticking them off on her fingers. "One, we get written commitments from local contractors willing to do the work at reduced rates, several of them were at the council meeting and will help. Two, we develop a realistic five-year operational budget showing how you'll maintain the building. Three, we demonstrate community investment, people willing to volunteer, donate, support."

Harper felt daunted. "That's a lot to pull together in two weeks."

"Which is why we're starting now," Mrs. Rodriguez said practically. "Harper, I'm going to be blunt. This grant is your best shot at saving the building permanently. If you don't get it, your options are limited. So, we're going to put together the strongest possible application, and we're not going to sleep much for the next two weeks. You up for it?"

Harper thought about Stella, about the letters, about Nora and Jamie's second chance. About the community that had shown up at the council meeting. About Colby sitting beside her, ready to invest his vacation time in something that mattered to her.

"I'm up for it," she said firmly.

"Good. Then let's get to work."

They spent the next four hours breaking down the application into manageable pieces. Mrs. Rodriguez would handle the official documentation and budget sections, she had experience with grant writing and understood the technical requirements. Harper would focus on the historical documentation and narrative sections, the story of the building and why it mattered. Colby volunteered to coordinate with contractors for cost estimates and collect community support letters.

By early afternoon, they had a detailed timeline and task list. It felt overwhelming but achievable.

"I need to talk to Clara," Harper said, studying the historical documentation requirements. "She worked there for forty-three years. Her memories are going to be crucial for this section."

"I'll set it up," Mrs. Rodriguez said, already texting. "Clara will love helping. This is exactly the kind of project she lives for."

Harper's phone rang. Quinn.

"Hey," Harper answered. "How's your head? You had a lot of wine last night."

"Worth it," Quinn replied cheerfully. "I'm calling because I just had an idea. You need historical documentation for that grant, right? What if we created a digital archive of the post office history? Scan all those photos, maybe interview longtime residents, create a whole historical record. It would strengthen your application and be a permanent resource for the town."

"Quinn, that's brilliant," Harper said. "But that's a massive project. Can we do it in two weeks?"

"I've got vacation time too," Quinn said. "And I know half a dozen library science grad students who'd kill for a project like this. Let me make some calls. We can make this happen."

After hanging up, Harper looked at Colby and Mrs. Rodriguez. "I have the best friends."

"You have a community," Mrs. Rodriguez corrected. "That's the real story here, Harper. That's what's going to win you this grant. Not just the building, but what it represents to the people who showed up yesterday."

The next week blurred into intense, focused work. Harper spent hours with Clara, recording stories and sorting through decades of records Clara had meticulously kept. The older woman's memory was sharp, and her stories brought the post office to life, births announced, deaths mourned, celebrations shared, connections maintained across distance and time.

"Every person who came through those doors mattered," Clara told Harper during one interview session. "Stella taught me that. She'd say, 'Clara, we're not just sorting mail. We're handling people's lives.' She meant it. Every birthday card, every love letter, every bill and magazine subscription, they all represented someone's story."

Harper recorded everything, transcribed the interviews, wove Clara's stories into the grant narrative. The building stopped being just wood and brick in her writing. It became a character itself, witness to a century of human connection, repository of community memory, physical manifestation of something intangible but essential.

Colby coordinated with contractors, collecting estimates and negotiating reduced rates. The response was overwhelming. Almost every contractor who'd worked on the renovation weekend volunteered to continue at cost or below. Some offered to donate labor entirely.

"People want to help," Colby told Harper one evening as they worked late in the apartment, papers spread across every surface. "I've talked to twelve different businesses. Every single one wants to contribute. The hardware store is donating supplies. The lumber yard is cutting prices. Even the electrical supply company in the next town over heard about what we're doing and offered a discount."

"Why?" Harper asked, overwhelmed by the generosity.

"Because you reminded them why they're here," Colby said simply. "Most of these people could run bigger businesses in bigger cities. They stay in Willow Creek because they value community over profit. You're fighting for the same thing. They respect that."

Quinn's digital archive project took shape faster than Harper thought possible. She enlisted five grad students who descended on the post office with scanners, cameras, and organizational systems. Within days, they'd digitized hundreds of photographs, documents, and records. Quinn created a website to house everything, designing it to be both functional and beautiful.

"This is incredible," Harper said, scrolling through the archive. Photos from every decade, organized by year and theme. Postal workers through the ages. Community events. Even scanned copies of old letters people had donated, nothing private, but enough to show the variety of connection the post office had facilitated.

"It gets better," Quinn said, opening another section. "We recorded oral histories. Fifteen longtime residents sharing their memories. And look at this, we found newspaper articles dating back to 1923 mentioning the post office. The building has been part of Willow Creek's story from the beginning."

The historical documentation section practically wrote itself with all this material. Harper crafted a narrative that wove together facts and stories, statistics and emotions, making the case that this building wasn't just old, it was essential to understanding Willow Creek's identity.

Halfway through the second week, they hit their first real obstacle. The renovation cost estimates came in higher than expected, two hundred and twenty thousand instead of two hundred. With the maximum grant of one hundred and fifty thousand and Harper's seventy-five thousand, they were still short by twenty thousand dollars.

Harper stared at the numbers, feeling panic rise. "We don't have twenty thousand dollars. I don't have anything else to sell or borrow against."

"Then we fundraise," Colby said calmly. "Community

fundraiser. If everyone who showed up at that council meeting donated even fifty dollars, we'd cover it."

"That's asking a lot," Harper said. "These people already volunteered time and labor."

"So, we ask," Colby replied. "The worst they can say is no. But I'm betting they'll say yes."

He was right. Within twenty-four hours of posting about the funding gap on the community Facebook page and the post office's new website, donations started arriving. Twenty dollars from Mrs. Patterson. Fifty from Maggie and Rosie. A hundred from Dylan's family. Small amounts from dozens of people, adding up faster than Harper expected.

The library board donated five hundred dollars. The historical society matched it. Anonymous donations started appearing, clearly from people with more means who wanted to help but didn't want recognition.

"We're at fifteen thousand," Colby reported three days before the grant deadline. "We're going to make it, Harper."

The night before the application was due, Harper, Colby, Mrs. Rodriguez, and Quinn gathered in the apartment for the final review. Every section complete, every requirement met, every supporting document attached.

"This is the strongest grant application I've ever worked on," Mrs. Rodriguez said, scrolling through the final PDF. "The narrative is compelling, the documentation is thorough, the community support is irrefutable, and the budget is realistic. Harper, you should be proud of this."

"We should be proud," Harper corrected, looking around at the three people who'd invested so much time and energy in her dream. "I couldn't have done this without all of you."

"You could have," Quinn said. "You just wouldn't have done it as well. That's what community means, being better together than we are alone."

They submitted the application at eleven forty-three PM, seventeen minutes before the midnight deadline. Harper hit "submit" and immediately felt both relief and anxiety. It was done. Now they waited.

"How long until we hear back?" Colby asked.

"Six to eight weeks," Mrs. Rodriguez said. "It's going to feel like forever."

Harper looked at the four of them, exhausted, caffeinated, surrounded by empty coffee cups and the remnants of their two-week sprint. They'd done everything possible. The rest was out of their hands.

"Thank you," she said, voice thick with emotion. "All of you. Whatever happens, thank you."

"It's going to be good news," Quinn said confidently. "I can feel it."

After Mrs. Rodriguez and Quinn left, Harper and Colby sat together on the couch, too wired to sleep despite their exhaustion.

"Two weeks ago, I was standing in the town hall waiting for a council decision," Harper said. "Now I'm waiting for a grant decision. This is becoming a pattern."

"At least this time you don't have Victor Brennan working against you," Colby pointed out.

Harper laughed. "True. Small victories." She leaned her head on his shoulder. "I don't know what I'm going to do for the next six weeks while we wait. I'm not good at patience."

"Then we work on that," Colby said. "We run the post office the way it's meant to be run. We keep building connections. We show the grant committee, and ourselves, that this place deserves saving not just because of its history, but because of its future."

"Very philosophical for midnight," Harper teased.

"I'm delirious from lack of sleep," Colby admitted. "But I mean it. This waiting period isn't dead time, Harper. It's opportunity. Let's make the most of it."

Harper thought about that. For two weeks, everything had been focused on the grant application. Now she had space to think about what came next, regardless of the grant outcome.

"I should call my mother," she said suddenly. "Tell her what's happening here. She deserves to know."

Colby looked at her with quiet understanding. "Want me to stay while you call?"

"No, I think I need to do this alone. But thank you."

They went to bed shortly after, falling asleep immediately despite the nervous energy still humming through Harper's veins. Tomorrow would bring new challenges, new uncertainties. But tonight, she had this: a completed application, a community that believed in her, and a man who loved her for exactly who she was.

Harper dreamed of letters, thousands of them, flying through the post office like birds, each one carrying someone's hope to someone else's hands. In the dream, Stella stood behind the counter, smiling, and when Harper asked if she was doing the right thing, Stella simply said, "You're doing the brave thing. That's all I ever asked."

She woke feeling more certain than she had in weeks. The grant might not come through. The building might need other solutions. But she'd done the work. She'd shown up. She'd fought for something that mattered.

And that, Harper was learning, was its own kind of victory.

CHAPTER TWENTY-TWO

The waiting was worse than Harper expected.

The first week after submitting the grant application, she checked her email obsessively, before coffee, during meals, in the middle of conversations, right before bed. By day five, Colby had staged an intervention.

"You're driving yourself crazy," he said gently, physically removing her phone from her hand. "Mrs. Rodriguez said six to eight weeks. It's been five days."

"What if they need more information and I miss the email?" Harper protested.

"Then they'll send a follow-up. Harper, you need to trust the process and actually live your life while you wait."

He was right, of course. Harper forced herself to establish a routine that didn't revolve around refreshing her inbox. She opened the post office every morning at eight, sorting mail alongside Colby, learning the rhythm of delivery routes and postal regulations. It was peaceful work, methodical and satisfying in a way her marketing job had never been.

"You're good at this," Colby observed one morning, watching Harper efficiently sort packages. "You've got Stella's touch, paying attention to the details that matter."

Harper smiled, pleased by the comparison. She'd started noticing things, Mrs. Patterson's daughter sent a care package every Tuesday like clockwork, so Harper made sure to set it aside prominently. The Johnsons were getting more medical bills than usual, so she'd casually mentioned a payment plan program she'd learned about. Small interventions, but they mattered.

The post office felt different now. Not just because of the physical improvements from the renovation weekend, but because Harper understood its purpose. Every transaction was a connection point. Every person who walked through the door had a story. Stella had known this instinctively; Harper was learning it deliberately.

On the tenth day after submitting the grant, Harper finally called her mother.

She'd been putting it off, rehearsing conversations in her head, trying to find the right words. But there were no right words, so one evening after closing the post office, she just dialed.

Her mother answered on the third ring. "Harper? Is everything okay?"

"Everything's fine, Mom. I just wanted to talk."

Silence on the other end, wary and uncertain. Harper's relationship with her mother had always been complicated, not hostile, but distant in a way that left both of them unsatisfied.

"I'm still in Willow Creek," Harper continued when her mother didn't respond. "At Stella's post office."

"I know. Todd told me you quit your job." Her mother's voice was carefully neutral. "That was rash."

"It was necessary," Harper corrected. "Mom, I need to tell you something. About Stella, about the post office, about what I found here."

And then Harper told her everything. The letters. Nora and Jamie's story. The fight against Victor Brennan. The council meeting, the grant application, the community that had shown up to save a building most people thought was beyond saving.

Her mother was quiet throughout, occasionally asking clarifying questions but mostly just listening.

"You delivered fifty-year-old letters?" she finally said when Harper finished.

"Yes."

"That's..." Her mother paused. "That's exactly what Mom would have done. She always said every letter had a mission, even the difficult ones."

Harper heard something in her mother's voice, not quite approval, but something softer than the disappointment she'd expected.

"I know you think I'm being foolish," Harper said. "Walking away from my career, investing in a building that might not survive, staying in a town you couldn't wait to leave."

"I don't think you're being foolish," her mother said quietly. "I think you're being brave. Braver than I was." She took a breath. "Harper, I loved Willow Creek. I loved growing up there, loved working in that post office during summers. But I was terrified of becoming my mother, of getting stuck in one place, of having a small life, of never seeing what else was out there."

"So, you ran," Harper said, understanding dawning.

"So, I ran," her mother confirmed. "And I built a good life in Minneapolis. I don't regret it. But I always wondered if I was running *to* something or just running *away*. You're not running at all. You're staying and fighting and building something. That takes courage I'm not sure I had at your age."

Harper felt tears prick her eyes. "I wish you'd told me this before."

"I wish I'd understood it before," her mother replied. "I was so busy making sure you and Todd had opportunities that I forgot to teach you that staying can be just as brave as leaving. That small towns aren't prisons, they're just different choices."

They talked for another hour, really talked in a way they hadn't since Harper was a child. Her mother shared memories of Stella, stories Harper had never heard. The time Stella stayed up all night helping a young mother whose husband was deployed overseas, waiting for an overdue letter that finally arrived at 2 AM. The way Stella knew everyone's birthdays and made sure birthday cards were hand-delivered with a personal message. The quiet generosity that had defined every day of Stella's forty years at the post office.

"She would be proud of you," Harper's mother said before they hung up. "Not just for saving the building, but for understanding why it matters. I'm proud of you too, sweetheart. I should have said that sooner."

After the call, Harper felt lighter, like she'd been carrying a weight she hadn't fully acknowledged. She found Colby downstairs, closing up for the day.

"How'd it go?" he asked, reading her expression.

"Better than expected. Good, actually." Harper leaned against the counter. "She told me things about Stella I never knew. I think we're going to be okay, my mom and me. Not perfect, but better."

Colby smiled and pulled her into a hug. "Brave conversations deserve celebrating. Want to get dinner at The Copper Kettle?"

"Actually," Harper said, "I want to cook. Here, upstairs, just us. I want one quiet evening in our space."

"Our space?" Colby repeated, eyebrows raised playfully.

Harper blushed. "You've been staying here almost every night. Your toothbrush is in my bathroom. Half your clothes are in my closet. I just thought..." She trailed off, suddenly uncertain.

"I love that it's our space," Colby said firmly. "I was just waiting for you to realize it too."

They cooked together in the tiny kitchen, pasta with vegetables from the farmers market, garlic bread, a cheap bottle of wine. It was domestic and comfortable, and Harper realized this was what she'd been missing in her old life: not excitement or prestige, but connection. Someone to cook dinner with. Someone who knew how she took her coffee. Someone who fit into her daily life so seamlessly she couldn't remember what life had looked like without them.

"What are you thinking?" Colby asked, catching her staring at him.

"That I'm happy," Harper said simply. "Right here, right now, regardless of what happens with the grant. I'm happy."

Colby set down his wine glass and crossed to where she stood. "Good. Because I'm happy too. Happier than I've been in years." He kissed her forehead. "Thank you for letting me be part of this."

"Thank you for choosing to be part of it," Harper replied.

The weeks continued to pass. Harper fell into the rhythm of the post office, learning regulars' names, memorizing delivery routes, understanding the small but essential role this building played in daily community life. Some days were slow, barely a dozen customers. Other days were busy, especially Friday afternoons when people picked up packages before the weekend.

Quinn stopped by regularly, ostensibly to check on the historical archive but really just to hang out and catch up.

They'd developed a routine, Quinn brought lunch from various Main Street restaurants, and they'd eat together while Harper sorted mail.

"So, you and Colby are basically living together now," Quinn said one afternoon, trying to sound casual.

"Basically," Harper confirmed. "Is that crazy? It's been less than three months."

"It's only crazy if it's wrong," Quinn said practically. "Is it wrong?"

Harper thought about it. "No. It feels right. Like the rest of my life was preparation for this, and I just didn't know it."

"Then it's not crazy. It's lucky." Quinn smiled. "Also, I ran into your mom at the grocery store yesterday."

Harper nearly dropped the package she was holding. "My mom? She's in Willow Creek?"

"Apparently she drove down to see the post office. Said she wanted to understand what you were fighting for." Quinn pulled out her phone, showing Harper a photo. "She was crying when she left. Good tears, I think."

The photo showed Harper's mother standing in front of the post office, one hand touching the brick wall, her expression soft with memory. Harper felt her throat tighten.

"She didn't tell me she was coming," Harper said.

"Maybe she wanted to see it without the pressure of a reunion," Quinn suggested. "Give her time. She's processing."

Harper texted her mother that evening: *Quinn told me you visited. Thank you for coming. The door's always open when you're ready to come back.*

Her mother's response came an hour later: *It's beautiful, sweetheart. You're doing something special there. I'll come back soon. Love you.*

Three small words Harper's mother rarely said. Harper read them three times before responding: *Love you too, Mom.*

Three weeks after submitting the grant, Harper received an email from the state preservation committee. Her heart stopped when she saw the subject line: "Application Status Update."

She opened it with shaking hands.

Dear Ms. Delaney,

Thank you for your grant application for the Willow Creek Post Office. We have completed our preliminary review and would like to schedule a site visit to assess the property. Please reply with your availability for the week of November 18-22.

Regards,
Sarah Chen

Director, Historical Preservation Grants Program

A site visit. Harper read the email three times to make sure she understood correctly. They wanted to visit. That meant they were seriously considering the application.

She immediately forwarded the email to Mrs. Rodriguez,

Colby, and Quinn, then called Mrs. Rodriguez.

"A site visit is excellent news," Mrs. Rodriguez confirmed. "It means they're seriously considering your application. They typically visit their top fifteen to twenty candidates. You're in contention, Harper."

"What do I need to do?" Harper asked, already mentally cataloging everything that needed to happen.

"Make the building look its absolute best. Have documentation ready. Be prepared to answer detailed questions about your plans, your budget, your vision. And most importantly, demonstrate community support. If possible, have people there who can speak to the building's importance."

Harper hung up and immediately started making lists. She had two weeks to make the post office shine.

The community rallied again. Dylan organized a deep-cleaning crew. Maggie provided refreshments for the volunteers. Someone donated flowers for window boxes. Clara coordinated a rotation of longtime residents to be available during the site visit, ready to share stories.

Colby took charge of exterior improvements, touching up paint, replacing weathered signage, making sure the building looked cared for and valuable.

"It needs to look like a building worth saving," he explained, standing back to assess their progress. "Not just historically interesting, but actively contributing to the community."

The night before the site visit, Harper couldn't sleep. She

lay in bed next to Colby, staring at the ceiling, running through potential questions and answers.

"Harper," Colby said softly. "I can hear you thinking from here."

"Sorry. I'm just nervous."

"You're going to be amazing tomorrow. Just tell them the truth. Show them what this place means. That's all they need to see."

"What if it's not enough?"

Colby rolled over to face her. "Then we figure out plan B. But Harper, you've done everything right. The application was thorough, the building looks incredible, the community is behind you. Whatever happens tomorrow, you should be proud of how far you've come."

Harper turned to meet his eyes in the darkness. "How are you always so calm?"

"Because I believe in you," Colby said simply. "And because I've learned that the things worth having are worth being patient for. We'll find out what happens when we find out. Worrying won't change the outcome."

Harper kissed him softly. "Thank you for being here."

"Always," Colby promised. "Now try to sleep. Tomorrow's a big day."

The morning of the site visit, Harper woke at five AM, too nervous to sleep any longer. Colby was already up, making coffee and reviewing the documents they'd prepared.

"You're going to be amazing," he said, handing her a mug. "Just tell them the truth. Show them what this place means. That's all they need to see."

The site visit team arrived at ten AM, three people from the state preservation committee, all middle-aged, all carrying clipboards and cameras. Harper met them at the door, trying to project confidence she didn't entirely feel.

"Ms. Delaney? I'm Sarah Chen, director of the preservation grants program. This is Marcus Wilson, our historical architect, and Jennifer Torres, our community impact assessor."

They shook hands, and Harper led them inside. The post office looked beautiful, sunlight streaming through clean windows, fresh flowers on the counter, the historical photo display Quinn had curated prominently featured. Clara, Nora, and Jamie were there, as planned, ready to share their stories.

For the next three hours, Harper answered questions, showed documentation, explained her vision. Marcus examined the building's structure, taking detailed notes. Jennifer interviewed Clara, Nora, and Jamie, documenting their testimonials. Sarah asked probing questions about sustainability, community need, long-term plans.

"What makes this post office essential?" Sarah asked at one point. "We receive applications for many historic buildings. What makes this one worth state investment?"

Harper thought about all the careful answers she'd rehearsed. Then she thought about Stella, about the letters, about everything she'd learned in three months.

"Because it teaches us how to see each other," Harper said finally. "In a world that's increasingly digital and disconnected, this building represents something essential, the idea that we're responsible for each other's stories. That distance doesn't have to mean disconnection. That every person, every message, every moment of reaching out matters enough to handle with care."

She gestured around the room. "These aren't just customers. They're neighbors. Mrs. Patterson gets her daughter's care package every Tuesday, and she waits for it at the counter because it's her connection to family. Mr. Chen picks up his wife's medical supplies here because he trusts us to handle them carefully. This building isn't just about mail, it's about trust, about seeing people, about creating space for connection in a world that makes that harder every day."

Sarah wrote something down, her expression unreadable.

The team thanked Harper, promised a decision within two weeks, and left. Harper watched them drive away, unsure whether she'd said too much or too little, whether her honest answer had helped or hurt.

"You were perfect," Clara said firmly. "You said exactly what Stella would have said."

"She's right," Colby agreed, pulling Harper close. "You didn't just sell them on a building. You showed them what it means. That's what they needed to see."

Now came the hardest part: waiting for the decision that would determine the post office's future.

CHAPTER TWENTY-THREE

The call came on a Wednesday afternoon, two weeks after the site visit. Harper was sorting mail when her phone rang. She almost didn't answer, unknown number, probably spam. But something made her pick up.

"Ms. Delaney? This is Sarah Chen from the Wisconsin Historical Preservation Grants Program."

Harper's heart stopped. She gestured frantically at Colby, who immediately stopped what he was doing.

"We've completed our evaluation process," Sarah continued, her tone professionally neutral. "I'm pleased to inform you that the Willow Creek Post Office has been selected to receive the full grant amount of one hundred and fifty thousand dollars."

Harper couldn't speak. Her hands were shaking so badly she nearly dropped the phone.

"Ms. Delaney? Are you there?"

"Yes," Harper managed. "Yes, I'm here. We got it? We really got it?"

"You really got it," Sarah confirmed, and Harper could hear the smile in her voice now. "Your application was exceptional. The committee was particularly moved by your understanding of the building's community role. You didn't just make a case for historical preservation, you made a case for why connection matters. That's what won them over."

After the call ended, Harper stood frozen, phone in hand, unable to process what had just happened.

"Harper?" Colby said gently. "What did they say?"

"We got it," she whispered. Then louder: "We got the grant! Colby, we got the full amount!"

Colby whooped and grabbed her, spinning her around the post office. Through the window, Mrs. Patterson looked up from the sidewalk, saw them celebrating, and started clapping.

Within an hour, word had spread through Willow Creek. By evening, The Copper Kettle was packed with people celebrating. Maggie had declared it a spontaneous party, closing to outside customers and bringing out champagne someone had been saving for a special occasion.

"Speech!" someone called, and the crowd took up the chant.

Harper stood, overwhelmed and grateful and so full of joy she thought she might burst.

"Three months ago, I stood in a town hall meeting and told you that the post office mattered," she began, her voice shaking with emotion. "That it represented something we couldn't measure in tax revenue or development plans. That connection, community, and continuity were worth fighting for."

She looked around the room, meeting eyes, seeing the people who'd shown up when it mattered.

"You believed me. You showed up. You volunteered and donated and fought alongside me for something bigger than any of us individually. And today, that fight paid off. The state of Wisconsin has awarded us the full grant amount. The Willow Creek Post Office is saved."

The café erupted in applause and cheers. Harper felt Colby's arm around her waist, anchoring her through the emotion.

"This is just the beginning," Harper continued when the noise subsided. "Now comes the real work, the renovations, the improvements, the building of something that will serve this community for another hundred years. But if the past three months have taught me anything, it's that this community shows up. And together, we can build something remarkable."

Clara raised her glass, hand shaking slightly but voice firm. "To Harper Delaney. To Stella's legacy. To the next hundred years of connection."

"To the next hundred years!" the room echoed.

The celebration continued into the evening. Stories were shared, memories recounted, plans made for the renovation work that would begin after the holidays.

Late in the evening, Harper found herself outside the café, needing air and a moment to process everything. Colby found her there, leaning against the building, looking up at the stars.

"Hey," he said softly. "You okay?"

"I'm perfect," Harper said. "I'm just... processing. Three months ago, I thought I was going to lose everything. The building, the dream, the fight. And now..."

"Now you've won," Colby finished. "You saved what mattered. You delivered on a promise fifty years overdue and saved a building that represents a century of connection. Harper, you're remarkable."

"We're remarkable," Harper corrected, pulling him close. "I couldn't have done this alone."

"Maybe not. But you were brave enough to try. That's what changed everything." Colby kissed her forehead. "What happens now?"

Harper thought about that. The grant was secured, the post office saved, the immediate crisis resolved. But the future still stretched ahead, uncertain and full of possibility.

"Now we build," she said simply. "We renovate the building. We expand the services. We make the post office not just a place that survived, but a place that thrives. We prove that choosing community over profit was the right decision."

"And us?" Colby asked quietly. "What happens with us?"

Harper looked up at him, this man who'd shown up every

day, who'd believed in her dream, who'd loved her through uncertainty and fear and impossible odds.

"Us, I keep," she said firmly. "If you'll have me. All of me, the anxious parts and the stubborn parts and the parts that are still figuring out who they want to be."

"I'll have all of you," Colby replied. "Today, tomorrow, for as long as you'll let me stick around."

"That might be a while," Harper warned.

"Good," Colby said, and kissed her under the stars on Main Street in Willow Creek, Wisconsin, where everything had changed because someone found letters that were fifty years late and decided that some deliveries were worth making no matter how long they took.

Inside the café, their community celebrated. Tomorrow would bring new challenges, new work, new questions to answer. But tonight, they had this: victory hard-won, love freely given, and the promise of a future built on connection rather than convenience.

The reality of the grant approval set in over the following week.

Mrs. Rodriguez called a meeting at The Copper Kettle to discuss next steps. Harper, Colby, Quinn, and Dylan gathered around the largest table, which Mrs. Rodriguez had covered with paperwork.

"The money won't arrive until mid-January," she explained, deflating Harper's hopes for immediate action. "State disbursements move at their own pace. Which actually works in our favor, it gives us time to plan properly and let the building settle through winter before we start major work."

"So, we wait again," Harper said, trying not to sound disappointed.

"We plan," Mrs. Rodriguez corrected firmly. "There's a difference. Waiting is passive. Planning is how we make sure we don't waste a dollar of that grant money."

Over the next two weeks, their casual operation transformed into something more professional. Mrs. Rodriguez recruited a project manager, her cousin Diego, who'd overseen historic renovations in Madison and agreed to consult at a reduced rate. Diego arrived with blueprints, building codes, and a healthy respect for century-old structures.

"You can't rush these buildings," he told Harper during his first site inspection, running his hand along the exposed brick in the back room. "They've been standing for a hundred years because they were built right. Our job is to honor that while bringing them up to modern standards. It's a conversation, not a conquest."

Harper liked him immediately.

They spent December in careful preparation. Diego created detailed renovation plans, prioritizing structural work first, the foundation reinforcement that would keep the building standing for another century, the roof replacement that would prevent water damage, the electrical and plumbing upgrades that would bring everything up to code.

"The cosmetic stuff comes last," Diego explained at one planning meeting. "No point painting walls if they might need to be opened for wiring. We work from the bones out."

The post office stayed open through December, though Harper reduced hours slightly to accommodate planning meetings and contractor consultations. She'd worried customers would mind, but most seemed excited about the coming renovations.

"About time this place got some love," Mrs. Patterson said one afternoon, picking up her daughter's weekly package. "Stella would have done it herself if she'd had the money. She always said this building deserved better than she could give it."

"She gave it everything she had," Harper replied, emotion tightening her throat.

"And now you're finishing what she started," Mrs. Patterson said gently. "That's what family does, dear. We pick up where the ones before us left off."

Winter settled over Willow Creek with unusual gentleness. No dramatic storms, no power outages, just a slow accumulation of gray days and early darkness that made the post office's warm interior feel even more welcoming.

The week before Christmas, Harper's mother called.

"I'm coming for the holidays," she announced without preamble. "Your brother's spending Christmas with his girlfriend's family in Vancouver, and I'd rather be in Willow Creek than Minneapolis alone. If that's okay."

Harper felt tears prick her eyes. Since their phone call months ago, they'd talked weekly, slowly rebuilding a relationship that had been more about obligation than connection. But this was different. This was her mother choosing Willow Creek, choosing Harper.

"It's more than okay," Harper said. "When?"

"Christmas Eve. I'm driving down." A pause. "I want to see the post office. Really see it. Understand what you're building."

"I'd like that, Mom."

After hanging up, Harper found Colby in the sorting room, organizing mail for the next day's delivery.

"My mom's coming for Christmas," she said, still processing.

Colby looked up, reading her expression. "That's good?"

"That's really good." Harper leaned against the doorframe. "I think we're actually going to be okay. Better than okay."

"Your mom's smart," Colby said. "She raised someone worth knowing. Of course she's going to come around."

Christmas Eve arrived with light snow, enough to make everything look magical without making the roads dangerous. Harper spent the morning cleaning the apartment and the afternoon preparing dinner. Colby helped, his presence steady and calming even as Harper's anxiety built.

Her mother arrived at four, pulling up in front of the post office in her practical sedan. Harper watched from the window as her mother sat in the car for a moment, looking at the building, before finally getting out.

They hugged on the sidewalk, awkward at first, then genuine.

"It's beautiful," her mother said, looking up at the post office. "I forgot how beautiful it was."

"Want the tour?" Harper asked.

"I want the tour."

Harper led her mother through the building, explaining the renovation plans, showing her the historical photo display, introducing her to the space that had become Harper's life. Her mother listened, asked questions, ran her hands along the old wooden counter with something like reverence.

"I used to stand right here," her mother said, touching a worn spot on the counter. "During summer breaks, I'd help Mom sort mail. She'd let me handle the easy deliveries, magazines, catalogs, things that weren't urgent. I thought it was the most boring job in the world."

"And now?" Harper asked.

"Now I understand what she was teaching me." Her mother's eyes were bright with unshed tears. "Every person mattered. Every piece of mail was someone's story. She knew every customer by name, knew their lives, cared about their troubles. I thought it was small. I didn't understand it was everything."

They went upstairs to the apartment, where Colby had dinner ready. The evening was surprisingly easy, conversation flowed, laughter came naturally, and Harper's mother seemed genuinely interested in their plans, their lives, their future.

"You remind me of her," Harper's mother said after dinner, sitting on the couch with wine. "Not just in the work you're doing, but in how you see people. That was Mom's gift, making everyone feel seen. You have that."

"I'm still learning," Harper said.

"We're all still learning," her mother replied. "But you're learning the right lessons. That's what matters."

They stayed up late, talking about Stella, about the past, about the future. When her mother finally went to bed in the apartment's small guest room, Harper curled up next to Colby on the couch.

"That went well," Colby observed.

"That went really well," Harper agreed. "I think we're going to be okay."

"I know you are," Colby said, kissing the top of her head. "You're both brave enough to try."

Christmas Day was quiet and perfect. They opened presents in the morning, small, thoughtful gifts that showed how well they knew each other. Harper's mother gave her a framed photo of Stella standing in front of the post office in 1985, wearing her postal uniform and smiling at the camera.

"I found it in a box of Mom's things," her mother said. "I thought you should have it."

Harper hung it on the wall behind the post office counter,

where Stella could watch over everything she'd built.

The renovation planning continued through the rest of December. By New Year's Eve, they had detailed blueprints, contractor commitments, a realistic timeline, and a comprehensive budget that accounted for every dollar of the grant money plus the community contributions.

"We start work on January fifteenth," Diego announced at their final planning meeting. "The grant money should be disbursed by then, and we'll have time to order materials. Weather permitting, we should be done by the end of March."

"Three months," Harper said, trying to imagine it.

"Three intense months," Diego corrected. "The post office will need to close for at least six weeks while we do the major structural work. Can you handle that?"

Harper looked at Colby, who nodded. "We'll handle it," she said. "Whatever it takes."

On New Year's Eve, the community gathered at The Copper Kettle for a celebration. Harper stood with Colby, watching people laugh and toast and make plans for the year ahead.

"Last year at this time, I was in Chicago," Harper said. "Miserable at my job, thinking I had everything figured out. Now look at me."

"Now look at you," Colby agreed. "You saved a building, found your calling, built a community. Not a bad year."

"I also fell in love," Harper added, smiling up at him.

"That was a pretty good part."

"The best part," Colby corrected, and kissed her as the countdown to midnight began around them.

At midnight, surrounded by people who'd become family, Harper made a silent resolution: to show up every day, to honor Stella's legacy, to build something worth preserving. Not just a building, but a life, one filled with connection, purpose, and love that arrived exactly when it was meant to.

The post office on Main Street had survived another year. In the year ahead, it would be transformed, renovated, brought back to its full glory.

But the real transformation had already happened, not to the building, but to the woman who'd inherited it and learned to see what her grandmother had always known: that every letter matters, every person deserves to be seen, and showing up is the bravest thing we can do.

CHAPTER TWENTY-FOUR

Spring arrived in Willow Creek with an enthusiasm that felt personal. Daffodils pushed through the last patches of snow, cherry blossoms exploded into pink clouds along Main Street, and the morning air carried the scent of possibility and new beginnings.

Harper stood in the doorway of the post office two weeks before the grand reopening, watching the town wake up. The building behind her was finished, perfect and waiting. Four months of renovation had transformed the century-old structure from worn and weary to vibrant and vital. Diego and his team had worked miracles.

"You're doing that thing again," Colby said, appearing beside her with two cups of coffee.

"What thing?"

"That thing where you stare at the town like you're trying

to memorize it. Like you still can't quite believe you're staying."

Harper accepted the coffee, considering his observation. He was right. Seven months ago, she'd driven into Willow Creek certain she'd be gone in three weeks. Now, standing in front of her grandmother's post office, her post office, she was trying to reconcile the person she'd been with the person she'd become.

"I'm not memorizing it," she said finally. "I'm just...appreciating it. All of it. The second chance this town gave me."

"The town didn't give you anything," Colby corrected gently. "You earned it. You showed up, you fought, you stayed. That's not a gift, Harper. That's courage."

She leaned into his warmth, breathing in the familiar scent of him, soap and coffee and something distinctly Colby. They'd been living together for months now, their routines intertwined so completely that Harper couldn't remember what mornings had felt like before him.

"We need to finalize the reopening plans," Harper said. "Quinn's been texting me daily asking about the program."

"Quinn's been texting you daily about everything," Colby pointed out. "She's excited. Everyone is."

Harper pulled out her phone, scrolling through the planning document she and Quinn had been building for weeks. The grand reopening would be more than just unlocking doors. It would be a celebration of community, a tribute to Stella, and a declaration that some things were worth fighting for.

"Let's go through it," Harper said, settling at one of the new café tables they'd added near the window. Colby sat across from her, pulling out his own notes.

The plan had evolved organically. Mayor Williams would give opening remarks, acknowledging the town's role in saving the building. Clara would speak about Stella's legacy. Harper would say a few words, though she was still terrified about that part. Then they'd officially reopen with a ribbon cutting, followed by an open house where people could tour the renovated space.

"Maggie's handling the refreshments," Harper said, checking off items. "The historical society is setting up a display. Quinn's got the photo timeline ready. Diego's team will be there to answer questions about the renovation."

"Music?" Colby asked.

"Dylan's band. They're doing an acoustic set, covers, nothing too loud. Background ambiance."

"Sounds perfect." Colby paused, pen hovering over his list. "What about Nora and Jamie? Are they coming?"

"I called Nora yesterday. They'll both be there." Harper smiled, remembering the conversation. "She said they wouldn't miss it for anything. That this building gave them their second chance, and they want to celebrate it finding its own second chance."

"That's beautiful," Colby said softly.

They worked through the rest of the logistics, parking arrangements, accessibility considerations for Clara and others with mobility issues, a backup plan in case of rain. The attention to detail was exhausting but necessary.

As they finalized the timeline, Harper noticed Colby seemed distracted, checking his watch, fidgeting with his pen, small tells that he had something on his mind.

"What is it?" she asked.

"What's what?"

"You're nervous about something. I can tell."

Colby smiled ruefully. "Can't hide anything from you anymore, can I?"

"Not really. So, what's going on?"

He took a breath. "I want to do something at the reopening. Something for Stella. I've been thinking about it since the renovation finished, and I want to make sure you're okay with it."

Harper felt curiosity replace concern. "Tell me."

"I want to read one of Jamie's letters," Colby said. "Not a private one, Nora said there's one where Jamie talks about the post office, about Stella, about what this place meant to their courtship. I thought...I don't know, I thought it might be meaningful. To honor both Stella and the love story that brought you here in the first place."

Harper felt tears prick her eyes. "Colby, that's perfect. Yes. Absolutely yes."

Relief flooded his face. "You're sure? I don't want to

overstep..."

"You're not overstepping. You're honoring something that matters. That's exactly what this celebration should be about."

They returned to planning with renewed energy, adding Colby's reading to the program. By mid-morning, they had a solid plan, a backup plan, and color-coded spreadsheets that Quinn would appreciate.

"Two weeks," Harper said, staring at the calendar. "I can't believe it's only two weeks away."

"Nervous?"

"Terrified. What if nobody comes? What if they come and it's disappointing? What if I mess up my speech?"

Colby reached across the table, taking her hand. "Harper. This town fought alongside you to save this building. They donated money, time, labor. They testified at the council meeting and showed up for the grant site visit. They're not going to skip the celebration. And even if you stumble through your speech, they'll love you anyway. Because you're theirs now. You belong here."

Harper squeezed his hand, drawing strength from his certainty. "When did I get so lucky?"

"The day you found those letters," Colby said simply. "The day you decided to deliver them instead of filing them away."

The next two weeks blurred into focused preparation.

Harper cleaned the post office obsessively, rearranged displays three times, second-guessed every decision. Quinn acted as project manager, keeping everyone on task and gently redirecting Harper's anxious energy into productive channels.

"You're going to wear grooves in that floor if you keep pacing," Quinn said one afternoon, watching Harper make her sixth lap around the main room.

"I just want everything to be perfect."

"It already is perfect. The building is beautiful. The program is solid. The community is excited. Harper, you need to trust that you've done enough."

"What if Stella would have done it differently?"

Quinn stopped what she was doing and turned to face Harper fully. "Stella would be proud of exactly what you've done. You saved her building, honored her legacy, and created something that will serve this town for generations. Stop second-guessing yourself."

Harper took a breath, letting Quinn's words settle in. "You're right. I know you're right. I'm just..."

"Scared," Quinn finished. "Because this is real now. This is your life, your business, your community. It's not temporary anymore. You're all in, and that's terrifying."

"When did you get so wise?"

"I've always been this wise. You just finally started listening." Quinn grinned. "Now come help me hang these photos. I can't reach the high spots."

Three days before the reopening, Harper's mother called.

"I'm coming," she announced. "I know you didn't invite me because you thought I'd be too busy, but Harper, this is important. I'm coming."

Harper felt emotion clog her throat. "Really?"

"Really. I'm leaving Friday morning, should be there by afternoon. I want to help with last-minute preparations. I want to be part of this."

After hanging up, Harper found Colby reorganizing the mail sorting room, a task he'd claimed as stress relief when his own anxiety about the reopening needed an outlet.

"My mom's coming," Harper said, still processing.

"That's wonderful."

"She wants to help with preparations. She wants to be part of it." Harper leaned against the doorframe. "Seven months ago, she thought I was throwing my life away by staying here. Now she's driving six hours to celebrate what I've built."

"People can change their minds when they see what matters," Colby said. "Your mom saw you were happy. She understood Stella's choice. Now she's supporting yours."

"I love her," Harper said simply. "I don't think I realized how much I'd missed having her in my life until we started building it back."

"Family's worth fighting for," Colby said. "All kinds of family."

Friday arrived with unseasonably warm weather and a town buzzing with excitement. Harper's mother pulled up at two o'clock, and this time there was no hesitation, no uncertainty—just a mother and daughter who'd found their way back to each other.

"Show me what needs doing," her mother said after hugging Harper tightly. "Put me to work."

They spent the afternoon in productive chaos—Harper's mother helping Quinn arrange chairs, Maggie bringing over sample refreshments for approval, Dylan's band setting up for a sound check. The post office became a hub of activity, everyone invested in making the celebration perfect.

That evening, after everyone had left, Harper gave her mother a private tour of the completed building.

"This was always beautiful," her mother said, running her hand along the restored counter. "But Mom didn't have the resources to maintain it properly. You gave it back its dignity."

"We gave it back its dignity," Harper corrected. "The community made this happen."

Her mother looked at her with an expression Harper couldn't quite read, pride mixed with something deeper, more bittersweet. "You found what I was looking for when I left. I spent thirty years in Minneapolis searching for something important to do, some way to matter. And you found it in the place I ran from."

"You mattered too, Mom. You built a life, raised two kids, had a career. That's not nothing."

"No, it's not nothing. But it's not this, either." She gestured around the post office. "This is legacy. This is roots. This is home in the deepest sense. I chose differently, and that's okay. But I'm glad you chose this."

They stood together in the quiet post office, three generations of women connected by a building that had witnessed a century of human connection.

"She'd be proud of you," Harper's mother said softly. "More proud than I can express."

"I hope so," Harper whispered.

The night before the reopening, Harper couldn't sleep. She lay in bed in Stella's apartment, her apartment, staring at the ceiling and running through everything that could go wrong. Beside her, Colby slept peacefully, his presence grounding but not quite enough to quiet her spiraling thoughts.

Finally, she gave up and went to the window, looking out at Main Street bathed in streetlight. This view. She knew every brick of every building, every crack in the sidewalk, every tree that would bloom in spring. This was home.

"Can't sleep?" Colby's voice came from the bed, rough with interrupted dreams.

"Sorry. Didn't mean to wake you."

"You didn't. Come here."

Harper returned to bed, and Colby pulled her close, his warmth immediately soothing.

"Talk to me," he said. "What's going on in that brilliant,

anxious brain?"

"I'm scared," Harper admitted. "Not about tomorrow going wrong. I'm scared it'll go right. That this is really my life now. That I get to keep this, the town, the post office, you. What if I mess it up?"

"You won't."

"You don't know that."

"I know you," Colby countered. "I know that you show up every day. That you care about people. That you fight for what matters. That's not going to change tomorrow or next year or ten years from now. You're not going to mess this up, Harper. You're going to build something beautiful. You already have."

Harper turned to face him in the darkness. "How are you always so sure about everything?"

"I'm not sure about everything. But I'm sure about you. I'm sure about us. And I'm sure that tomorrow is going to be wonderful, because you made it happen."

She kissed him then, pouring her gratitude and love and lingering fear into the contact. Colby kissed her back, steady and certain, anchoring her to this moment, this life, this choice.

"Try to sleep," he murmured. "Tomorrow's your day. You need to be rested for it."

Harper closed her eyes, Colby's heartbeat steady beneath her ear, and finally let herself believe that yes, she got to keep this. All of it.

The morning of the grand reopening arrived with perfect spring weather, sunny, warm, with a gentle breeze that carried the scent of cherry blossoms. Harper woke early, nerves and excitement tangled together in her chest.

Colby was already up, setting out her favorite breakfast and a note: *You've got this. I love you. - C*

The next few hours passed in a blur of final preparations. Quinn arrived at eight to help with last-minute details. Harper's mother showed up with fresh flowers for all the displays. Clara came early to practice her speech one more time, her hands shaking slightly with emotion.

By ten-thirty, people started arriving. By eleven, Main Street was crowded with residents, business owners, former customers, everyone who'd played a role in saving the post office. Harper watched from the window, overwhelmed by the turnout.

"Told you they'd come," Colby said, appearing beside her.

"There's so many," Harper whispered.

"Because you matter to them. This place matters. Come on. It's time."

They walked outside together to where a podium and ribbon had been set up. Mayor Williams called for attention, and the crowd quieted.

"Seven months ago," the mayor began, "we almost lost this building. We almost chose development over history, profit over preservation. But one young woman refused to accept that choice. Harper Delaney stood in front of this council and reminded us what we were supposed to value. She fought for this building, and in doing so, reminded us why it was worth fighting for."

Applause rippled through the crowd. Harper felt her face flush.

Clara spoke next, her voice wavering but strong. "Stella Delaney ran this post office for forty years. She treated every letter like it mattered, because to her, they all did. She knew that mail wasn't just paper and ink, it was connection. It was people reaching across distance to say 'you matter to me.' Harper has honored that legacy and built on it. This post office will serve Willow Creek for another hundred years because of her courage."

More applause. Harper's mother squeezed her hand.

Then it was Harper's turn. She stepped to the podium, looking out at all these faces, friends now, family, community. She'd written a speech, practiced it a dozen times. But standing here, she set aside her notes.

"I came to Willow Creek to settle my grandmother's estate and leave," Harper said, her voice carrying across the quiet crowd. "I had my life planned out, career in Chicago, success that looked impressive to strangers, a life that felt important. Instead, I found all of that here. In this building. In this town. With all of you."

She paused, emotion thick in her throat. "Stella taught me something through the letters she never got to deliver. She taught me that every connection matters. That showing up for people, even when it's hard, even when the outcome is uncertain—is the bravest thing we can do. You all showed up for this building. You showed up for me. You proved that choosing community over profit, connection over convenience, isn't naive or impractical, it's essential."

Harper looked at the post office behind her. "This building stands because of all of you. It will serve this town because you believed it was worth saving. Thank you for fighting alongside me. Thank you for teaching me what home really means. Thank you for letting me be part of your story."

The applause was thunderous. Harper stepped back, and Colby appeared at her side, offering silent support.

The ribbon cutting was ceremonial and sweet. Clara and Harper held the scissors together, cutting the red ribbon as everyone cheered. Then the doors opened, and people flooded in to tour the renovated space.

The transformation was stunning. The original character preserved, exposed brick, vintage fixtures, the sense of history, but updated with modern efficiency and accessibility. Quinn's photo timeline adorned one wall, showing the building's century of service. The sorting room gleamed with new equipment. The café area offered seating for those who wanted to linger.

For hours, Harper answered questions, gave tours, accepted congratulations. Her mother stayed close, beaming with pride. Quinn documented everything with her camera. Diego explained renovation techniques to anyone who'd listen.

As afternoon edged toward evening, the crowd began to thin. But a core group remained, the people who'd been there from the beginning. Maggie, Mrs. Rodriguez, Dylan, Clara, Nora and Jamie, Quinn, Harper's mother. And Colby, always Colby.

"There's one more thing," Colby said, drawing everyone's attention. "Harper gave me permission to share something. With Nora's blessing, I'd like to read from one of Jamie's letters."

He pulled out a carefully preserved letter, its edges yellowed with age. As he began to read, Harper felt tears slide down her cheeks.

The letter was beautiful, Jamie writing about meeting Nora at the post office, about Stella's kindness in letting them linger at the counter, about how this building had become sacred to him because it was where he'd first understood what love could be.

When Colby finished, there wasn't a dry eye in the room. Nora and Jamie held each other, fifty years of separation and reunion written on their faces.

"Thank you," Nora said quietly. "For delivering our letters. For giving us our second chance. For making sure this place survives to give other people theirs."

As the sun set, casting golden light through the windows, people began to leave. Harper's mother hugged her tightly, promising to visit again soon. Clara pressed a kiss to Harper's cheek. Quinn declared it "the most beautiful event she'd ever documented."

Finally, it was just Harper and Colby, standing in the quiet post office as the last light faded from the sky.

"You did it," Colby said softly.

"We did it," Harper corrected.

"No." Colby turned her to face him, his expression serious. "You need to own this, Harper. You changed your life. You saved this building. You built a community. You did that."

"I couldn't have done it without you."

"Maybe not. But the courage to try? That was all you." He took her hand. "Come with me. I want to show you something."

He led her outside to the back patio, the small garden space behind the building that had been part of the renovation. Someone had strung lights overhead, and in their glow, Harper saw a bench had been placed there, with a brass plaque: *In Memory of Stella Delaney, who knew that every letter matters.*

Harper pressed her hand to her mouth, overwhelmed.

"I wanted you to have a place to remember her," Colby said. "To sit and think about all she gave you."

"It's perfect," Harper whispered.

They sat together on the bench, the spring evening warm around them, the post office glowing behind them. Harper leaned her head on Colby's shoulder, feeling completely, perfectly content.

"Harper," Colby said after a moment. "I need to tell you something."

She looked up at him, suddenly alert to the nervousness in

his voice.

"These past seven months have been the best of my life," Colby continued. "Watching you fight for this building, watching you become part of this community, watching you become yourself, it's been an honor. You're brave and stubborn and kind and brilliant, and every day I wake up grateful that you found those letters, grateful that you decided to stay, grateful that you let me be part of your story."

He stood, pulling her up with him, then took both her hands.

"I know it's fast. I know we've only been together seven months. But Harper, I also know with absolute certainty that I want to spend the rest of my life with you. I want to wake up next to you every morning. I want to sort mail with you every afternoon. I want to build a life that honors connection, that shows up for people, that matters in the ways that really count."

Harper's heart was pounding so hard she could barely breathe.

"I want to be the person you trust with your fears and your dreams. I want to be your partner in every sense, in business, in life, in the everyday work of choosing love over and over again. I want to deliver that love to you every single day, for as long as you'll let me."

Colby dropped to one knee, pulling out a small velvet box.

"Harper Delaney, will you marry me?"

Harper was crying, laughing, nodding before he even

finished the question. "Yes. Yes, of course yes."

He opened the box, revealing a simple, beautiful ring, vintage style, with a small diamond that caught the string lights. "It was my grandmother's," he said. "She and my grandfather were married for sixty-two years. She used to say that commitment wasn't about grand gestures, it was about showing up every day and choosing love. I thought...I thought you'd understand that."

"I do," Harper said, voice breaking. "I understand completely."

Colby slipped the ring on her finger, then stood and pulled her into a kiss that tasted like tears and joy and promises. Around them, Willow Creek settled into evening, the post office standing solid behind them, bearing witness to another love story beginning in its shadow.

"I love you," Harper whispered against his lips.

"I love you too," Colby replied. "Today, tomorrow, for every delivery that matters."

They stood there in the garden, under the lights, the future stretching ahead, uncertain in its details but certain in its foundation. They had each other. They had this town. They had work that mattered and a community that cared and a building that would stand for another century, facilitating connections, honoring stories, proving that some things were always worth delivering.

Harper looked at her ring, at Colby, at the post office glowing in the twilight. Seven months ago, she'd driven into Willow Creek to settle an estate. Instead, she'd found a home, a purpose, a love worth building a life around.

Some letters took fifty years to arrive.

Some took seven months and changed everything.

Both were worth delivering.

CHAPTER TWENTY-FIVE
ONE YEAR LATER

The morning of Harper and Colby's wedding dawned clear and perfect, as if Willow Creek itself had conspired to make everything beautiful. Harper stood at the window of Stella's apartment, her apartment, though she still thought of it as Stella's sometimes, watching Main Street come alive with preparations.

A year. It had been a full year since Colby had proposed on the back patio, since the post office had reopened, since Harper had fully stepped into the life she'd been building. Twelve months of running the post office, serving the community, loving Colby, and finally, finally feeling like she'd found where she belonged.

"You're not supposed to see the venue before the ceremony," Quinn said from the doorway, carrying a garment bag and two cups of coffee. "Isn't that some kind of bad luck?"

"That's the groom," Harper corrected, accepting the coffee. "And besides, this is my post office. I see it every day. A little late to worry about luck now."

Because that's what they'd decided, to get married right here, in the building where everything had changed. The post office would close for the day, transforming from federal building to wedding venue, honoring both Stella's legacy and the love story that had bloomed within its walls.

Quinn set down the garment bag containing Harper's dress, simple, elegant, vintage-inspired to match Colby's ring. "Your mom's downstairs directing traffic like a general. Diego's team is setting up chairs. Maggie's been in the back room for an hour arranging flowers. It's controlled chaos."

"The best kind of chaos," Harper said, smiling.

The past year had been full of the best kind of chaos. The post office had thrived beyond Harper's hopes. Word had spread about the historic building's salvation, and people came from neighboring towns just to see it, to send mail from a place that had become a small symbol of what communities could accomplish when they chose connection over convenience.

Harper had hired an assistant, a recent college graduate named Emma who reminded Harper of herself at that age, eager and anxious and trying to figure out where she fit. Together they'd expanded services, adding community programs, historical tours, even a small letter-writing station where people could sit and compose messages on vintage stationery.

The wedding preparations had taken six months of

planning, but not because Harper and Colby wanted anything elaborate. They'd simply wanted to include everyone who mattered, and in Willow Creek, that meant most of the town.

"How are you feeling?" Quinn asked, studying Harper with the particular intensity of a best friend looking for cracks in the facade.

"Happy," Harper said honestly. "Nervous, but happy. Is that normal?"

"Completely normal. You're about to marry the love of your life in front of everyone you know. Nervous is appropriate." Quinn grinned. "But you're going to be beautiful, the ceremony is going to be perfect, and Colby's going to cry when he sees you. I've got money on it."

"He will not."

"Harper. The man cries at sentimental commercials. He's absolutely going to cry at his own wedding."

Harper laughed, the sound releasing some of the nervous energy coiled in her chest. "Okay, fine. He'll probably cry. But so will I."

"Everyone will cry," Quinn confirmed. "That's what makes it good."

Harper's mother arrived moments later, along with Rosie Hayes, Colby's mother, who'd become Harper's second mom over the past year. The two women had formed an unexpected friendship, bonding over their children's happiness and shared love of orchestrating family gatherings.

"The flowers are perfect," Rosie announced, pulling Harper into a hug. "Maggie outdid herself. And Dylan's band is set up and sound-checked. Everything's ready, sweetheart."

"Colby?" Harper asked, trying not to sound as anxious as she felt.

"Is at our place with his father, probably wearing a hole in our carpet from pacing," Rosie said fondly. "He's as nervous as you are. It's adorable."

Harper's mother brushed hair from Harper's face, a gesture so familiar and comforting that Harper felt tears threaten. Their relationship over the past year had deepened into something Harper had never expected, genuine friendship, not just familial obligation. Her mother visited once a month, sometimes more, and they talked weekly, sharing lives in a way they never had before.

"You look beautiful already," her mother said softly. "But we should probably get you into that dress. It's almost time."

The next hour passed in a blur of activity. Quinn helped Harper into her dress, a simple ivory gown with lace sleeves and a vintage silhouette that Stella would have loved. Harper's mother did her hair, pinning it up with small flowers. Rosie fussed over details, making sure everything was perfect.

When Harper finally looked in the mirror, she barely recognized herself. Not because she looked different, but because she looked happy. Completely, radiantly happy in a way she'd never imagined possible eighteen months ago.

"Oh, honey," her mother said, tears already streaming. "You're stunning."

"Don't cry yet," Harper protested, her own eyes stinging. "We haven't even started."

"Too late," Quinn said, dabbing at her eyes. "We're all going to be a mess. Might as well embrace it."

There was a soft knock at the door. Harper's brother Todd poked his head in, stopping short when he saw her.

"Wow," he said simply. "Harper, you look...wow."

Todd had flown in from Vancouver the day before with his girlfriend Sarah, whom Harper had immediately loved. Seeing her brother, who'd supported her decision to stay in Willow Creek even when he didn't fully understand it, made the day feel complete.

"Ready to walk me down?" Harper asked.

"More than ready," Todd replied, offering his arm. "Though I should warn you, I'm going to cry. Sarah made me watch the video of your engagement three times, and I cried every time."

"Told you it runs in the family," Rosie said to Quinn, who laughed.

Downstairs, the post office had been completely transformed. White chairs filled the main floor, separated by an aisle scattered with flower petals. Spring flowers adorned every surface, cherry blossoms and daffodils and tulips, making the whole space feel like a garden. Dylan's band played soft acoustic music. And filling every seat were the people who'd become Harper's family, the community that had saved this building and, in doing so, saved her.

Harper waited behind the closed door with Todd, her heart pounding. Through the wood, she could hear the music shift, signaling the ceremony was about to begin.

"You okay?" Todd asked quietly.

"I'm perfect," Harper said, and meant it.

The doors opened, and Harper saw Colby waiting at the end of the aisle. He was wearing a simple gray suit with a vest that matched her ring, his hair slightly messy in that way she loved, and when he saw her, his face broke into the biggest smile she'd ever seen.

Quinn had been right. He was crying. Beautiful, unashamed tears that made Harper's own eyes well up immediately.

Harper and Todd walked down the aisle slowly, Harper taking in every detail, Clara sitting in the front row, beaming. Nora and Jamie holding hands, their own second-chance love story witnessing another beginning. Mrs. Rodriguez looking proud. Maggie and Dylan smiling. Emma, her assistant, recording everything on her phone. Her mother and Rosie already reaching for tissues.

And Colby, always Colby, watching her walk toward him like she was the only person in the room.

When they reached the front, Todd kissed Harper's cheek, whispered "Be happy," and placed her hand in Colby's before taking his seat.

Colby squeezed her hand, tears still streaming down his face. "You're beautiful," he whispered.

"You're crying," Harper whispered back, smiling.

"Yeah," Colby admitted, not even trying to wipe them away. "I am."

Sheriff Mitchell, who'd agreed to officiate, cleared his throat and smiled at the assembled crowd. "We are gathered here today to witness the marriage of Harper Delaney and Colby Hayes, two people who found love in the most unexpected way, through fifty-year-old letters and a building that refused to die."

Gentle laughter rippled through the crowd.

"I've known Colby his whole life," Sheriff Mitchell continued. "Watched him grow up, watched him become one of the finest mail carriers this town has ever had. He understands something essential, that every delivery matters. Every person matters. Every connection is worth the care it takes to maintain it."

He turned to Harper. "And Harper, you came to us eighteen months ago as a stranger. But you taught us that strangers are just family we haven't met yet. You fought for this building, for this community, for the idea that some things are worth preserving even when the world says they're not profitable. You reminded us what we value, and in doing so, became part of what we value most, our community, our family, our home."

Harper felt tears sliding down her cheeks. Colby gently wiped them away with his thumb, his own tears still falling.

"Marriage," Sheriff Mitchell said, "is a lot like mail delivery. It's about showing up every day, even when it's hard.

It's about caring for what you carry, even when it's heavy. It's about understanding that the everyday work of love, the sorting, the organizing, the attention to detail, is what makes the grand gestures possible. It's about delivering your best self to the person you love, over and over, for the rest of your lives."

He nodded to Colby. "Your vows."

Colby took a shaky breath, pulling out a folded piece of paper but not looking at it. Instead, he looked directly at Harper, his hands finding hers.

"Harper, eighteen months ago, I knocked on the door of this post office to deliver mail to someone I'd never met. I thought it would be a routine delivery. Instead, it changed my entire life."

His voice broke, and he paused to compose himself.

"You taught me that love isn't about finding someone perfect. It's about finding someone worth showing up for, even when it's scary. Even when the outcome is uncertain. You showed me that being brave enough to stay, to fight, to build something beautiful, that's the greatest adventure anyone can have."

Colby squeezed her hands tighter. "I promise to show up for you every day, in sunshine and in rain, in easy moments and hard ones. I promise to deliver love, truth, and partnership for the rest of our lives. You're my favorite delivery, Harper. You always will be."

Harper was crying so hard now she could barely see, but she managed to pull out her own vows, written and rewritten a dozen times over the past months.

"Colby, eighteen months ago, I thought I knew what I wanted. I thought success looked like a corner office and a title and a career that impressed strangers. I thought home was something to escape from, not something to build."

She looked around at the post office, at the community filling it. "You showed me I was wrong about everything. You showed me that the most important work is caring for people. That home isn't a place that traps you, it's people who see you, know you, and love you anyway. You showed me what it means to build a life that matters."

Harper's voice broke, but she pushed through. "I promise to show up for you. To be your partner in every delivery, the easy ones and the hard ones, the joyful ones and the heartbreaking ones. I promise to build a life with you that honors connection over convenience, that chooses love every single day."

She looked around at their community again, at the faces that had become family. "And I promise to keep delivering truth, even when it's difficult. Because you taught me that's what love is, delivering what's real, what's needed, what matters most."

Sheriff Mitchell smiled through his own tears. "The rings?"

Quinn stepped forward with Colby's ring, a simple gold band that matched Harper's engagement ring. Todd produced Harper's band, designed to sit perfectly with the vintage engagement ring Colby had given her.

"Harper, do you take Colby to be your husband, to have

and to hold from this day forward, for better or worse, for richer or poorer, in sickness and in health, to love and to cherish, until death do you part?"

"I do," Harper said clearly, her voice strong despite the tears.

"Colby, do you take Harper to be your wife, to have and to hold from this day forward, for better or worse, for richer or poorer, in sickness and in health, to love and to cherish, until death do you part?"

"I do," Colby said, voice thick with emotion.

"By the power vested in me by the state of Wisconsin and this wonderful community, I now pronounce you husband and wife. Colby, you may kiss your bride."

Colby pulled Harper close, and they kissed while the room erupted in applause and cheers. This was it. They were married. Partners officially, finally, completely.

The reception that followed was pure Willow Creek joy. Someone had strung lights throughout the post office, transforming it into a magical space. Maggie had provided an incredible spread, her famous dishes plus contributions from half the town. Dylan's band played while people danced, laughed, celebrated.

Harper and Colby cut their cake, a simple two-tier creation decorated with postal stamps and tiny envelope details that Maggie had hand-crafted. They danced their first dance to an acoustic cover of a song Dylan had learned specifically for them.

Clara made a toast, her voice wavering but fierce. "Stella would be so proud. Not just of this beautiful wedding, but of what you've both built here. You've proven that some things are worth saving. That community matters. That love, in all its forms, is the most important delivery we'll ever make. To Harper and Colby!"

"To Harper and Colby!" the room echoed.

Harper's mother gave a toast that made everyone cry, talking about watching her daughter find home in the place she'd run from, about healing old wounds, about the courage it takes to choose differently than your parents did. Todd made everyone laugh with stories from their childhood, then turned serious as he talked about how proud he was of his sister's bravery.

Nora and Jamie approached during a quiet moment, both of them glowing with happiness.

"Thank you," Nora said simply, taking Harper's hands. "For delivering those letters. For giving us our second chance. For showing us that some love stories don't end, they just wait for the right time to continue."

"Thank you for trusting me with them," Harper replied. "Your story changed everything for me. It showed me what was possible when you're brave enough to deliver what matters."

Later, as the sun set and the celebration continued, Harper found a quiet moment on the back patio, the place where Colby had proposed a year ago. The spring flowers were in full bloom again, cherry blossoms drifting on the evening breeze.

Colby found her there, as he always did.

"Hi, wife," he said softly.

"Hi, husband," Harper replied, still getting used to the words.

They stood together, looking out at Willow Creek bathed in golden light. A year ago, Harper had been terrified about the grand reopening, about the future, about whether she'd made the right choice. Now, she knew with absolute certainty that she had.

"What are you thinking?" Colby asked.

Harper leaned into him, feeling the solid warmth of her husband, her husband, beside her. "I'm thinking about Stella. About how she spent forty years delivering mail, connecting people, showing up every day even when it was hard. I'm thinking about those letters I found, and how delivering them changed everything."

"Best delivery you ever made," Colby agreed.

"Second best," Harper corrected. She turned to face him, rising on her toes to kiss him softly. "The best delivery is this. Us. Every day, for the rest of our lives."

They stayed on the patio as the celebration continued inside, the lights twinkling, music drifting through the open windows. Tomorrow would bring new challenges, new deliveries, new opportunities to show up and care and connect. But tonight, they had this moment, a mail carrier and a post office owner, a husband and wife, two people who'd found each other in the most unlikely way and built something beautiful from letters that should have arrived fifty years earlier.

Harper thought about Stella, about Nora and Jamie, about all the love stories that had passed through this building over the years. Some arrived on time. Some arrived late. But all of them mattered. All of them were worth delivering.

And this one, hers and Colby's, was still being written, one day at a time, one delivery at a time, one act of love at a time.

The post office on Main Street would stand for another hundred years. Harper and Colby would make sure of it. They'd deliver mail, facilitate connections, show up for their community, and prove every single day that some things were worth preserving.

Not because they were profitable. Not because they were convenient. But because they were true.

And truth, like love, was always worth delivering, no matter how long it took to arrive.

ABOUT THE AUTHOR

Wren Calloway writes contemporary romance novels about small towns, second chances, and the unexpected ways people find home. A former city dweller who discovered the magic of rural communities, Wren brings authenticity and heart to stories about connection, community, and love that refuses to be forgotten.

When not writing, Wren can be found exploring small-town main streets, collecting vintage postcards, and believing in the power of handwritten letters.

UNDELIVERED is Book One of Wren's debut novel which is part of *The Willow Creek Series.*

For all author inquiries, please contact: MK Storyworks

Website: www.mkstoryworks.com

Email: contact@mkstoryworks.com

A NOTE FROM
THE AUTHOR

Dear Readers,

Thank you for reading UNDELIVERED! If Harper and Colby's story touched your heart, I'd be so grateful if you'd consider:

- *Leaving a review on your favorite book retailer or Amazon, Barnes & Noble or MK Storyworks*
- *Sharing with a friend who loves small-town romance*
- *Following MK Storyworks on social media for updates on upcoming releases @mkstoryworks*

Your support means the world to indie authors. Every review, share, and recommendation helps other readers discover these stories.

With gratitude,

Wren Calloway

DISCUSSION QUESTIONS FOR BOOK CLUBS

1. Harper initially plans to sell the post office and return to Chicago. What specific moments or interactions change her mind? At what point do you think she truly commits to staying?

2. The 50-year-old letters between Jamie and Nora parallel Harper and Colby's developing relationship. How do the two love stories inform each other? What themes connect them?

3. Harper's relationship with her mother is complicated and distant at the start. How does Harper's journey in Willow Creek affect this relationship? What does the novel suggest about generational patterns and breaking them?

4. The post office itself is almost a character in the story. What does it symbolize for different characters (Stella, Harper, the community, Victor Brennan)?

5. Victor Brennan isn't portrayed as a villain, but as someone with a different vision for Willow Creek's future. Did you find his perspective understandable? How does the novel handle the tension between progress and preservation?

6. Quinn is Harper's best friend despite living far away. How does their friendship sustain Harper through her transformation? What role do different types of friendship play in the novel?

7. The novel explores the theme of "showing up" as an act of bravery and love. Where do you see this theme demonstrated? How do different characters embody it?

8. Harper leaves a successful marketing career to run a small-town post office. Do you think she made the right choice? How does the novel define "success"?

9. Colby is described as steady and patient, in contrast to Harper's anxiety and impulsiveness. How do their different temperaments complement each other? What does each learn from the other?

10. The title "UNDELIVERED" has multiple meanings in the story. What are the different things that go "undelivered," and what does it mean when they finally arrive?

11. How does the community of Willow Creek function as a whole? What role do supporting characters like Clara,

Maggie, Mrs. Rodriguez, and Dylan play in Harper's journey?

12. The novel ends with a wedding eighteen months after Harper first arrives. Do you feel this timeline is realistic for Harper's transformation and the romance? Why or why not?

13. What part of the story did you feel was most emotional and soul searching? What is it Harper and Colby's relationship or the long lost relationship that didn't come to fruition between Nora and Jamie?

ACKNOWLEDGMENTS

This book wouldn't exist without the support of countless people who believed in Harper and Colby's story.

To my early readers who encouraged me to keep writing even when I doubted: thank you for seeing what this story could become.

To the small-town communities that inspired Willow Creek: thank you for showing me what it means to choose connection over convenience, and for demonstrating that preservation and progress aren't opposites.

To every postal worker who delivers mail with care and treats every letter like it matters: you inspired Colby's character and reminded me of the everyday heroes in our communities.

To the independent bookstores, book bloggers, and BookTokers who champion romance novels and indie authors: your passion creates space for stories like this one.

To MK Storyworks for believing in this debut novel and bringing it into the world: thank you for your vision and support.

And to you, dear reader, for choosing to spend your time in Willow Creek: thank you for believing that love stories, all kinds of love stories, are worth reading. I hope you found something here that felt like home.

Don't forget to subscribe to newsletters, new releases and updates on all the other books in **The Willow Creek Series.** Simply subscribe on www.mkstoryworks.com

With gratitude and love,

Wren Calloway

COMING SOON FROM WREN CALLOWAY

OVERDUE

A Library Romance

Book Two of The Willow Creek Series

Quinn Mitchell has spent years building her career at a prestigious Chicago library, but when budget cuts threaten everything she's worked for, she returns home to Willow Creek. The town's century-old library is on the verge of closing, and Quinn is asked to catalog its rare book collection, possibly for sale.

Dylan Chen has been quietly running the library's music and literacy programs while teaching at the local school. He's also been quietly in love with Quinn since high school, long before she left town and never looked back.

When Quinn discovers a collection of first editions hidden in the library's basement, books that could save the library or make her career in Chicago, she and Dylan must decide what's worth preserving: buildings, books, or the love story that's been overdue for a decade.

A second-chance romance about coming home, the books that change us, and learning that some stories are worth the wait.

REROUTED

A Flower Shop Romance

Book Three of The Willow Creek Series

Maggie Torres has run The Copper Kettle café for twenty years, watching everyone else's love stories bloom while her own life stayed carefully controlled. She's perfected her routine, her recipes, and her reasons for keeping people at arm's length.

Wilfred Santos just escaped a controlling relationship and moved to Willow Creek to start fresh with his mobile flower truck business. He's done with plans, done with expectations, and definitely done with falling for complicated women who don't know what they want.

But when Wilfred parks his flower truck outside Maggie's café every morning, their collision course becomes inevitable.

Between wedding orders and coffee deliveries, Maggie and Wilfred discover that sometimes love doesn't follow the route you planned, and sometimes that's exactly the point.

A slow-burn romance about second chances, learning to bloom after trauma, and finding the courage to be rerouted toward happiness.

TODD'S STORY

A Holiday Romance

Book Four of The Willow Creek Series

Todd Delaney has spent three years building a comfortable life in Vancouver with his girlfriend Sarah. They have a nice apartment, stable careers, and a relationship that works, mostly. When Sarah's job relocates them to Chicago, just blocks from where his sister Harper used to work, Todd can't shake the feeling that he's being given a second chance at something.

But a second chance at what? The proposal he's been putting off? The creative career he abandoned? The relationship with his mother that he's kept at arm's length? Or maybe just the chance to figure out what he actually wants instead of what's comfortable?

When a snowstorm strands him at O'Hare on Christmas Eve with only a mysterious woman, a delayed flight, and a collection of letters from his sister, Todd must decide what he's ready to deliver to the people he loves, and to himself.

A holiday romance about brothers, belonging, and the courage it takes to write your own happy ending.

THE LAST LETTER

*A Library Romance about Adoption, Secrets, Forgiveness, and
the letters that finally bring families together.*

Book Five of The Willow Creek Series

Clara Whitmore has lived in Willow Creek for ninety-two years. She's been Stella's best friend, the post office's longest employee, and the keeper of more town secrets than anyone realizes. Now, as her health fails, she has one final task: delivering the letters she never sent.

For forty years, Clara wrote letters to the daughter she gave up for adoption in 1953, letters she never mailed because she'd signed away her right to contact. Now, with time running out, she asks Harper to find her daughter and deliver what was never delivered.

The search leads Harper to Grace Sullivan, a sixty-nine-year-old woman who never knew she was adopted, and to Ryan

Whitmore, Clara's great-nephew who comes to Willow Creek to help his aunt through her final days. As past and present collide, Ryan and Grace must navigate their unexpected connection while Harper learns that some deliveries change everyone involved.

A multi-generational romance about adoption, secrets, forgiveness, and the letters that finally bring families home.

THE KEEPER'S LIGHT

A Standalone Romance

Also by Wren Calloway

Adelaide "Addie" Winters never expected to inherit anything from the grandmother she barely knew. But when a lawyer calls with news of a lighthouse keeper position on a remote Maine island, Addie sees it as the escape she desperately needs from her imploding engagement and suffocating corporate job.

The island has one other year-round resident: Finn MacLeod, a gruff marine biologist who's been studying the island's seal population for five years and has perfected the art of solitude. He's not thrilled about a new neighbor, especially one who clearly has no idea what island winters are actually like.

But when Addie discovers a cache of unsent letters hidden in the lighthouse, letters that reveal a decades-old mystery involving Finn's grandfather and a woman who disappeared from the island in 1952, they're forced to work together. As storms isolate them and secrets emerge, Addie and Finn must decide if they're brave enough to let each other's light in.

A grumpy/sunshine romance about isolation and connection, inherited mysteries, and learning that sometimes the way forward is to finally stop running.

THE RECIPE BOX

A Standalone Romance

Also by Wren Calloway

Seventy-six-year-old Barbara Clarke decides it's time to stop grieving and start living. Her lifelong dream was to open a bakery, and if not now, then when?

Her practical daughter thinks she's lost her mind. The bank thinks she's a bad investment. The town thinks she should enjoy retirement, not start a business.

But Sam Foster, the sixty-nine-year-old contractor renovating her space, thinks she's the bravest person he's met since his wife died five years ago. He also thinks she makes the best apple pie in Wisconsin, and that her smile still makes his heart do things he thought it forgot how to do.

As the bakery takes shape, so does their unexpected connection. Together, Barbara and Sam prove that some recipes are worth perfecting at any age, and that love doesn't come with an expiration date.

An older romance about it never being too late to start over, the sweetness of second chances, and discovering that the best years might still be ahead.

MORE FROM
MK STORYWORKS

Love small-town romance? Community-focused stories? Second chances and heartfelt happily-ever-afters?

Visit www.mkstoryworks.com for:

- New release announcements
- Exclusive bonus content
- Behind-the-scenes author insights
- Special reader giveaways
- Updates on The Willow Creek Series

Follow MK Storyworks:

- Instagram: @mkstoryworks

- TikTok: @mkstoryworks
- Facebook: @mkstoryworks
- X: @mkstoryworks
- Pinterest: @mkstoryworks

Contact:

- Email: contact@mkstoryworks.com
- Website: www.mkstoryworks.com

ONE LAST THING...

Thank you for reading UNDELIVERED.

If this story touched your heart, please consider leaving a review on your favorite book retailer or Amazon, Barnes & Noble, Kobo and MK Storyworks. Reviews help other readers discover Harper and Colby's story, and they make a tremendous difference for indie authors and publishers like MK Storyworks.

Every review matters. Every reader counts.

With gratitude,

Wren Calloway & All The Team at MK Storyworks

SNEAK PEEK
OVERDUE
CHAPTER ONE

Quinn Mitchell stood in the Chicago Public Library's rare books vault, surrounded by first editions worth more than her annual salary, and tried not to cry.

"I'm sorry, Quinn." Her supervisor's voice was professionally sympathetic in that way that meant the decision was already made. "The entire Special Collections department is being restructured. It's not about your work, you know you're one of our best."

"Then why..."

"Budget cuts. City-wide. They're keeping two positions in Special Collections. Yours isn't one of them."

Quinn had worked at this library for five years. She'd

cataloged collections, secured grants, built programs. She'd made this place matter.

And now she was being restructured out of existence.

"You have two months," her supervisor continued. "We'll provide excellent references, of course. And there's a severance package..."

But Quinn had stopped listening. Through the vault's small window, she could see the reading room where she'd spent countless hours helping patrons discover rare books, where she'd fallen in love with this work, where she'd built a life that had just been dismantled in five minutes.

Her phone buzzed. A text from her mother: *The Willow Creek Library Board voted tonight. They're closing the library unless someone can prove it's worth saving. I know you're busy, but thought you should know.*

Quinn stared at the message. Willow Creek. The town she'd left at eighteen and visited only for obligatory holidays. The town that had felt too small for her dreams. The town where Dylan Chen probably still taught music and organized the summer reading program and definitely still had no idea that Quinn had been in love with him since sophomore year.

Willow Creek, with its tiny library that had been her refuge as a teenager, was closing.

And Chicago, with its grand library and her dream job, was letting her go.

Quinn looked around the vault one last time, then made a decision that would change everything.

"I need to make a call."

Want to read more?

OVERDUE - Coming Soon from MK Storyworks

Visit www.mkstoryworks.com for updates.

ABOUT THE PUBLISHER

MK Storyworks is a truly global book publisher, dedicated to the timeless mission of connecting compelling authors with enthusiastic readers across the world.

We pride ourselves on curating a diverse and dynamic list that spans the full spectrum of literary interests. Whether you are looking for an immersive escape into a bestselling fiction novel, seeking wisdom and knowledge from groundbreaking non-fiction titles, perfecting a dish with our acclaimed cookbooks, or introducing the magic of reading to the next generation with our enchanting children's books, MK Storyworks delivers stories that inform, entertain, and inspire.

Our commitment to quality, creativity, and global reach ensures that every book we publish finds its place in the hands and hearts of readers, no matter where they are.

Connect with MK Storyworks

Stay up-to-date with our latest releases, author news, and

behind-the-scenes glimpses by connecting with us online:

Website: www.mkstoryworks.com

Social Media:

- YouTube: @mkstoryworks
- Instagram: @mkstoryworks
- Facebook: @mkstoryworks
- X: @mkstoryworks
- Pinterest: @mkstoryworks
- TikTok: @mkstoryworks